Slade sl... behind her neck.

Celina reached up to grip his wrists, making one last attempt to slow down the inevitable.

His thumbs brushed her jaw. "You want to know why I haven't called, don't you?"

She tried to ignore the feel of him against her. "No."

"Why I haven't tried to explain?"

Her eyes drifted closed. "No."

He whispered into the silence, his thumbs against her lips, "Liar."

"Damn you," she murmured, and wished she'd said nothing. His thumb touched her tongue, and she coaxed it into her mouth.

She heard his intake of breath. In a husky voice, he murmured, "And what if I told you that right now, this moment, you don't care about anything but what we're about to do?"

She wanted to tell him to stop talking, to stop making her think and rationalize and face where they were going.

She brushed her mouth across his and whispered, "Don't go."

Dear Reader,

In a world of constant dizzying change, some things, fortunately, remain the same. One of those things is the Silhouette **Special Edition** commitment to our readers—a commitment, renewed each month, to bring you six stimulating, sensitive, substantial novels of living and loving in today's world, novels blending deep, vivid emotions with high romance.

This month, six fabulous authors step up to fulfill that commitment: Terese Ramin brings you the uproarious, unforgettable and decidedly adult *Accompanying Alice;* Jo Ann Algermissen lends her unique voice—and heart—to fond family feuding in *Would You Marry Me Anyway?;* Judi Edwards stirs our deepest hunger for love and healing in *Step from a Dream;* Christine Flynn enchants the senses with a tale of legendary love in *Out of the Mist;* Pat Warren deftly balances both the fears and the courage intimacy generates in *Till I Loved You;* and Dee Holmes delivers a mature, perceptive novel of the true nature of loving and heroism in *The Return of Slade Garner*. All six novels are sterling examples of the Silhouette **Special Edition** experience: romance you can believe in.

Next month also features a sensational array of talent, including two tantalizing volumes many of you have been clamoring for, by bestselling authors Ginna Gray and Debbie Macomber.

So don't miss a moment of the Silhouette **Special Edition** experience!

From all the authors and editors
of Silhouette **Special Edition**—warmest wishes.

DEE HOLMES
The Return of Slade Garner

Silhouette Special Edition

Published by Silhouette Books New York

America's Publisher of Contemporary Romance

To David and Suzanne,
thanks for the hockey memories.
And to Reinier . . .

SILHOUETTE BOOKS
300 East 42nd St., New York, N.Y. 10017

THE RETURN OF SLADE GARNER

ISBN: 0-373-09660-7

First Silhouette Books printing March 1991

All the characters in this book are fictitious. Any
resemblance to actual persons, living or dead, is
purely coincidental.

®: Trademark used under license and
registered in the United States Patent and
Trademark Office and in other countries.

Printed in the U.S.A.

Books by Dee Holmes

Silhouette Intimate Moments

Black Horse Island #327

Silhouette Special Edition

The Return of Slade Garner #660

DEE HOLMES

would love to tell her readers about exciting trips to Europe or that she has mastered a dozen languages. But the truth is that traveling isn't her thing, and she flunked French twice. Perhaps because of a military background where she got uprooted so much, she married a permanent civilian.

Dee is an obsessive reader who started writing casually, only to discover that "writing is hard! Writing a publishable book is even harder." She has since become involved in her local RWA chapter and says that she loves to write about "relationships between two people who are about to fall in love, but they don't know how exciting it is going to be for them."

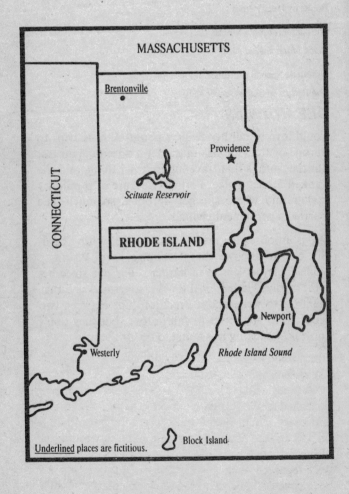

MASSACHUSETTS

Brentonville

Providence

CONNECTICUT

Scituate Reservoir

RHODE ISLAND

Newport

Westerly

Rhode Island Sound

Underlined places are fictitious.

Block Island

Chapter One

Score!

A slick, impressive goal, Slade thought, even though the St. Luke players and not the Brentonville team raised their sticks in victory. St. Luke fans came to their feet, shouting and clapping. Hoots and whistles filled the arena. And incredibly, from under the din, Slade swore he could hear the sighs and groans from Brentonville. At his left, the coach slammed his fist against the Plexiglas wall.

"Ya see what I mean? Ya see?" Nick Murphy screeched in Slade's ear so loudly, he winced. Broad and beefy, Nick looked more like a bouncer than a hockey coach. His logic when it came to winning or losing any game was simple: wins were expected; losses were regarded as an insult. "More 'n twenty years I been coachin', and this kind of sloppy playin' is what I get for my last season."

Dressed in an off-white cable-knit sweater, a pair of jeans and worn black boots, Slade kept his smile to a slight twitch. Nick's "last season" wail was familiar. He'd said the same thing more than fifteen years ago when Slade played for Brentonville.

With his shoulder propped against one of the support beams, Slade watched the teams prepare for a face-off. He'd stopped at Nick's house only long enough to drop off his hockey equipment and duffel bags, then walked over to the rink. After his mother died when he was six, the Brentonville Arena became like a second home to him, and it had never lost its ability to draw him. The raw bone-deep coldness, the slick glide of sharp blades slicing across the ice, the smell of coffee, the shout of *score* and, of course, Nick—all were reminders of where his love for hockey had begun.

He reached down and rubbed his hand around the ball of his left knee, at the same time testing and flexing the hard muscle in his thigh. He winced slightly at a particularly tender spot. His knee had given him minor problems all season, and then a particularly brutal game against a Canadian team had sent him to the hospital. There had been tests, long thoughtful looks exchanged between doctors, and more tests until Slade was sure the next step was leg amputation. Instead he was told no more hockey games for the rest of the season, and maybe no more seasons, period. He didn't want to think about that possibility. Retirement at thirty-three held zero appeal, but more than that, it scared him.

Nick peered at him, his frown ragged and old, looking as if no smile could ever soften the wrinkles. Slade knew he was expected to reveal some professional secret or a new strategy that would pull a win for Brentonville out of what was shaping up to be a loss. He considered advising Nick not to push the kids so hard, to let them enjoy the sport instead of turning every game into a do-or-die situation. But Slade knew if he was the coach he'd push, too. The sentiment that it wasn't winning but how the game was played was inspiring in a sports column or on a banner in the locker room, but the reality of hockey had little to do with how it was played. It had everything to do with winning.

"They're not working as a team, for one thing," Slade said with a husky tightness in his voice. The dull throb in his knee bore down on him with such familiarity he'd forgotten what normal felt like. "Too many of them trying to be stars."

"Tell me about it," Nick growled, his bushy eyebrows pinching into a sharp vee. "Hey, St. Luke is tough. You know that. They've gone to the finals in past seasons like they were the only team in the league. But this year..." He sighed. "This year with Hearn in there playin' center for us, I knew we could beat them." He dragged a hand down his face in a gesture of weariness. He then lowered his gaze to where Slade was massaging his knee. "Hey, kid, that knee is really botherin' you, huh?"

Slade straightened up, letting out a long breath as he flexed his leg. "It'll pass."

Doc Pierce had given him a prescription for pain pills, but Slade hadn't filled it. Call it stubbornness or just a revulsion to pills beyond a common aspirin, but the prescription was still in his wallet. The pain was considerably less now. He lifted his foot and bent his leg, easing the sore area. Maybe after the rink cleared out, he'd lace up his skates and see if he could work out the tenderness. Nothing strenuous, but it had been weeks since he'd skated, and like a long-formed habit, he'd been feeling the pangs of withdrawal.

He shoved the sleeves of his sweater up. "Isn't Jeremy Hearn the kid you bragged about?"

"Yeah. He's got a near-perfect wrist shot. Reminds me a lot of you. Fact is, coachin' Jeremy was like coachin' you in the old days."

"The old days. Come on, Nick. It was only fifteen years ago." *Only,* he thought, recalling his I'm-gonna-do-this-forever attitude that he'd had at eighteen.

"At my age, fifteen years is like yesterday," Nick said with a sageness that Slade had heard before. "And Hearn would be out there scorin' goals against St. Luke if it weren't for her." He folded his arms and glared at the exit door on the opposite side of the arena. His chin did the gesturing while his face tightened with dark fury. "It's a good thing my poor saintly mother ain't alive to know what I'm thinking."

Slade glanced at the door. He expected to see Jeremy's girlfriend, but the only "her" Slade could see was a woman wearing a red coat belted around a slender waist. She definitely was not Jeremy's girlfriend, and she looked too young to be his mother. Her hair was whiskey brown, and she'd confined it in one of those doughnut buns that he instantly associated with his fourth-grade teacher.

Slade grimly recalled the image of Miss Agnes Potter standing over him, her fists on her hips and the closet smell of mothballs coming from somewhere within the bag-like folds of her dark wool dress. His desire to play hockey instead of read, according to her, was unacceptable.

The resemblance of this woman to his old teacher, however, ended with the bun. A shoulder bag deep enough to hold his hockey skates rode along her right hip as she walked to the refreshment stand. She'll order tea, Slade thought automatically, and realized he was slotting her. Unfair and sexist, he knew, but for most of his teammates figuring out a woman's slot was a continuing pastime. Figure, body language, how she dressed—or undressed—and, of course, the big question: how good would she be in the sack?

That question remained in his mind, and he reminded himself that this was Brentonville. Taking a woman to bed in his hometown wouldn't simply be a few hours of pleasure as it was when he was on the road with the team. In Brentonville, he'd likely see her in the drugstore, pass her on the street and run into her here at the rink.

Scowling now, he decided his interest came from her red coat in contrast to the staid bun, or else plain old male curiosity about the opposite sex that had been around since the days of clubs and caves.

Nick was still glaring, as if she were the pariah of the hockey arena. Slade commented, "Come on, Nick. You've never had a bad thought about a woman in your life."

"In her case, I made an exception."

Despite the hockey game Slade was supposed to be watching, he continued to follow her movements as she walked over to speak to someone and then returned to the refreshment stand.

A sense of familiarity stirred inside him. Her back was straight, not rigid but with a sureness, as though she rarely had doubts about what she wanted and what was important. Slade had a feeling she had a strong stubborn streak. His gaze wandered down the backs of her calves. Nicely shaped, he decided, but when he saw her shoes he grinned. He'd expected sensible pumps. Sling-back red high heels didn't fit with the severe hairstyle, but, then, neither did the red coat.

Folding his arms across his chest, he found himself contemplating the length of her hair, how the soft texture would feel tangled around his fingers....

Suddenly his painful knee, the hockey game and Nick were forgotten. He'd expected to see her while he was home, but not this soon, and dammit, not with hot awareness driving through his gut.

Nick called the first line off the ice and sent out the second, all the while grumbling about the missing Jeremy Hearn. He glanced at Slade. "Come on, you know her."

"Yeah, I know her."

"I was beginnin' to wonder if that knee had affected your memory." Nick scowled. "I don't care if she is Brian's widow—God rest his soul—she's been a real pain in the butt."

"Celina," Slade murmured, not hearing Nick, only sounds from the past. Sounds and thoughts and memories he should have forgotten, or at the very least have left safely behind him. The red coat and sling-back heels brought together fragments of yesteryears as if they were the missing pieces of a puzzle. The Celina he'd known had a sense of daring and sureness, as well as a surprising sensuality that Slade recalled in intimate detail.

They'd started dating after their high-school senior prom, and continued into that summer. From the first time they'd made love, Slade knew that if he'd allowed himself to, he could easily have fallen in love with her. And falling in love with Celina or any other woman hadn't been in his plans. Playing hockey in the National Hockey League was what he wanted, and when the Providence Sabers offered him a contract, he'd left Brentonville.

Celina wanted to be a teacher. She planned to go to college and then return to Brentonville to live and teach. They'd lost touch, and Slade had focused all his time and energy on hockey. Then his old man had called him one snowy night in January, when the Sabers were in Detroit, to tell him Celina had married his best friend, Brian Dennett.

Slade told himself he didn't care. Celina had been only a summer girlfriend. Sure they'd been serious for a while, but intense feelings at eighteen weren't unusual.

Even when he'd called Brian to congratulate him, he'd pretended indifference, but long after he'd hung up he couldn't shake the image of Celina making love with Brian. Regret, jealousy and a deep possessiveness stayed with him for days.

Then three years ago, Brian, a Marine stationed in the Middle East, had been killed when his helicopter crashed. Slade came home for his funeral. Celina had worn a black dress that made her skin look like delicate porcelain. When the Marine honor guard had presented her with the flag from Brian's coffin, she'd dropped the folded triangle. Five people had stooped to pick it up. Celina hadn't moved, swaying slightly as though any movement would shatter her the way a high-pitched sound can shatter glass.

He'd spoken to her briefly, fighting the sudden urge to draw her into his arms and comfort her. The depth of feeling had been a scary twist on his urges when it came to women. Usually comfort wasn't his first thought, yet Celina that day had reminded him of himself. Of how it felt to be frightened and doggedly determined to not allow anyone to stir and poke and discover those things that remained private. Brian's funeral was the last time he'd seen her.

Still with his gaze on Celina, Slade said to Nick, "I know I'm gonna regret this question, but what does Celina have to do with Jeremy not playing?"

She stepped away from the refreshment booth, a paper cup in her hand. Watching her sip, he found himself looking for the dangling tea-bag string.

"She's his English teacher. That's bad enough, but when the department head retired last fall, she got his job." Nick said it as if it was the worst appointment the school committee could have made.

The head of the English department. Slade wasn't surprised. A member of the National Honor Society, she'd won a full scholarship to college given by the Rhode Island Education Foundation to one student of exceptional merit. No student at Brentonville High, before or since, had won the award.

"Sounds like the kind of job she'd be good at," Slade said, ignoring Nick's scowl.

"Yeah, too good. So now she teaches and runs the English department, like studyin' is all a kid should be thinkin' about."

The referee blew the whistle to stop the play when two players got into a fight in one corner. Nick folded his arms and watched the ref break up the melee, sending the St. Luke player to the penalty box.

After setting up some new strategy with his extra-player advantage, Nick went back to the subject of Celina. "She has Jeremy in her class, and she's decided that a few failin' marks are more important than hockey. I told her he can pass English anytime. Do I refuse to let the kid go to English class because he messes up on the ice? No way."

Slade's mouth moved into an amused grin. "I bet she loved hearing that."

"She didn't say one word. Just studied me with those eyes of hers. I ain't never known a woman with violet eyes. Maybe it's the way she looks at you so directly, you're sure she can read your mind."

Virgin violet, he remembered thinking that first night they'd made love. Intensity had poured from her, and he found his thoughts rushing from the past to the present. Would she be...?

Again Nick gestured with his chin. "She won't let him play. She calls it priorities. I call it interference and stubbornness and a one-way ticket to a losing season."

Get a grip on yourself, Garner. You don't need this kind of hassle. To Nick, he said, "I think you're being a little rough on her."

"I'm being rough! Look what she's done. We're talkin' major problems when we hit those finals. The rock-bottom truth is that without Jeremy, we can't win."

Slade watched her ease closer to the Plexiglas that topped the wooden boards around the rink. Was she at the rink because she still loved hockey, or to see how the team was managing without Jeremy?

"Wait a minute!" Nick hit his palm on one of the support beams. "Dammit, I'm so steamed about Hearn, I didn't think. You could talk to her."

Slade felt his earlier interest drain away. He'd come home to rest his knee, attend his high-school class's fifteen-year reunion and give Nick some help with the team. Recalling his past with Celina was one thing, but she wasn't in his future. Hell, right now he didn't even know what kind of future he had. "Forget it."

Nick waved his hand in a gesture of dismissal. "Sure, you could. You used to date her. You and Brian were buddies. And you guys all went to high school together. You're a prime example of how far a high-school hockey star can go. Charm her. Take her out to dinner. Kiss her a few times."

Slade arched an eyebrow, a gut-deep sureness in his words. "Kiss her a few times? You make her sound like some brainless groupie. Trust me on this one, Nick. When it comes to education over hockey, a full-blown seduction wouldn't change her mind about Jeremy."

"How will you know if you don't try? Hey, I got eyes. I saw the way the women looked at you when you came in. They sure weren't interested in what you got in English."

Slade dropped the foot he'd braced on the bench to the wooden floor. His body tightened, as if he were a lone defenseman guarding the net against the oncoming team. Years of discipline kept his body language neutral and controlled. His face muscles pounded. Only when he was sure he wouldn't burn Nick with language hot enough to melt the ice, did he look at him.

The ruddiness had drained out of Nick's face, leaving his cheeks a pasty gray. He lowered his voice to a whisper. "I didn't mean that the way it sounded. You know me, Slade, poppin' off at the mouth without thinkin'."

"Yeah," Slade said, not yet trusting himself to say any more.

"You ain't mad at me, are ya? I need your help for the weeks you're here. I just figured maybe Celina might listen to you. You two being friends, and all."

"Friends, and all" sounded so innocent as though they'd only shared ice-cream bars and laughter. She'd been out of his league when it came to smarts in school, but beyond that he wanted to play pro hockey. That was his future, and he'd known it the summer after graduation when, for a few months, he'd allowed his world to spin around Celina McKinley. "Forget the high-school-friends ploy. That was too long ago."

"But you could at least try."

Slade turned his full attention on Celina, making no pretense of looking anywhere else. *You could at least try.* Weak words that almost begged rather than demanded, but then Nick wouldn't demand—and Slade supposed he owed him. The thought of talking to Celina and spending some time with her intrigued him, although he had no intention of letting interest become involvement.

He could hardly avoid her while he was here, and he knew one safe subject. Talking hockey, and especially about a team star like Jeremy, was what Brentonville did all year round.

No, avoiding her would be stupid. What they'd felt for each other had been intense and hot, but it had also ended a long time ago. Keep it light, keep the conversation on hockey and Jeremy, and add a dash of charm.

He frowned. *You got charm, Garner. You've got that down as natural as breathing. You got charm you can dole out by the poundful. You been doing it for years and it's gotten you out of a helluva lot of tight corners.*

Celina glanced up, as though she sensed him watching her.

Slade narrowed his eyes and let his mind wander into territory he knew he shouldn't be in. *Sweetheart, I wonder if you know how much I want to take your hair down.*

"All right. I'll talk to her."

Nick grinned for the first time since the game had begun. "Atta boy, Slade. I knew I could count on you."

Brentonville lost by four goals. While Nick chewed out the kids in the locker room, Slade made his way through the disgruntled parents and fans. Losing, Slade noted, still had all the grimness of a disaster recovery. He was slightly annoyed at the crowd's one-dimensional thinking, but at the same time he agreed with them. Hockey was his life, too. It had been since his father told him that someday he wanted to see him play for the Boston Bruins.

While he'd never played for Boston, his father had been obsessively proud, showing it by attending every one of Slade's games. He'd followed the team until his death the year the Providence Sabers lost the Stanley Cup.

Now, between the handshakes, the welcome-home comments and the autographs he stopped to sign, getting out to the rink parking lot took him fifteen minutes.

March in Brentonville, Rhode Island was wet, chilly and uncertain. A few piles of dirty snow turned to slush bordered the asphalt, as cars made their way toward the exits. He saw a flash of red as Celina slid into a white compact.

Slade pulled on his black leather bomber jacket and jammed his hands into its side pockets. His dark hair was ruffled by the wind. Terrific, he thought with dismay, as he watched her drive out of her parking place. He'd just decided to go back into the rink and wait for another time to talk to her when he saw her brake lights flash on, then a few seconds later her backup lights. Beyond her, two cars loaded with teenagers blocked her way. She backed into the space she'd just left, swung the car around and headed toward Slade and the other exit. To his surprise, his pulse picked up speed.

If she hadn't looked up and seen him. If she'd waited until the kids moved their cars. If he'd gone with his earlier inclination to avoid her. And beyond all those ifs lay the biggest one.

If he'd listened to the warning bell in his head. Despite years and distance, despite her marrying Brian, he'd never forgotten that the first time he'd kissed her she'd worn pink roses in her hair. The warning bell clanged louder. Who was he kidding? Kissing her, taking her hair down, feeling their bodies move next to each other... Need rushed through him with an urgency that had nothing to do with the past and too much to do with right now.

He stepped out in front the car. She hit the brakes, and he planted his hands on the hood.

Through the windshield he could see her widened eyes and her frightened expression. Then, with a sag of relief, she leaned forward and rested her forehead on the steering wheel. Finally she lowered the window and leaned out. "I could have hit you."

He brushed off his hands and came around to her side. "Nah, you weren't going fast enough. Hi. It's been a long time."

She took a breath. "Hi, yourself. I heard you were home."

Years had added depth and maturity to her face, and suddenly he wished he'd been around to watch her change and grow. A long strand of hair had come loose from her bun and Slade resisted the sudden urge to wind it around his finger. She gave him a tentative smile.

Three years, he thought. No wonder they were both struggling for words. Finally he asked. "How about a ride?"

"A ride? Oh, uh, sure. I'm sorry." Licking her lips, she quickly put the car in park, then leaned across the seat and unlocked the passenger door. She put a brown leather briefcase in the back and anchored her handbag between the two bucket seats. "Are you going to have enough room? The seat goes back."

He slid into the seat and maneuvered his long legs under the dash, careful to keep his knee from getting jammed or bumped. "As long as you're not planning a trip to Boston, I'll make it."

Nick was right about her eyes. The deep violet was enticing, and the dazzling sweep of black spiky lashes didn't even come close to schoolteacher prim. Her cheeks were flushed either from the wind or his sudden appearance. He studied the bun, wondering what she would do if he pulled the pins out. He let the dangerous moment pass. "I meant to get back in touch with you after Brian's funeral."

She sucked in her cheeks, the hollows highlighting the fine bones in her face. "I'm glad you were able to be there."

He turned in the seat, gingerly pulling up his left leg. "Has it been hard for you? I mean since the funeral?" He raked back his hair. "I'm sorry. Those were dumb questions. It's just . . ."

She made a gesture with her hand as if to touch his arm, but then withdrew it, as if contact with him might be misunderstood. Softly she said, "It's okay. It's difficult to know what to say. And Brian was your friend." She paused for a moment. He wondered if she thought he'd resented Brian for marrying her.

Not wanting Brian to be an issue, he said, "He was my best friend. Always. From the day we learned to skate together."

She let out a breath. Relief? he wondered. "Actually," she continued, "the hardest time was right after the funeral. His death was so unexpected that all I felt was numbness and disbelief. Not until days later, when I was alone, did it hit me that he was really gone."

Slade felt a twist of disturbing annoyance. "No one stayed with you? Not your parents? Or Lauren and Russ?"

She shook her head. "There was nothing they could do, and I needed the time alone. I was really concerned about the Dennetts. Brian's mother was hysterical, and his dad . . ." She lowered her head and fussed with the folds of her coat. "I'd never seen him so withdrawn and pale."

Slade didn't know what to say. He admired her courage and concern over the Dennetts, but he couldn't help but wonder who'd been there for her.

Finally he said, "They'd always been proud of Brian. I remember back in our senior year when he told his dad he wanted to be a Marine. Like father, like son, I guess." He paused, watching a big truck maneuver around a tight corner.

She, too, stared through the windshield, and Slade wondered if Brian had ever tapped the intensity so evident in her face. Then she slumped back in the seat as if she'd suddenly run out of things to say. "This isn't exactly a lighthearted subject for two friends who haven't seen each other in three years."

Slade didn't disagree.

She sighed and put the car back in gear. "Where can I drop you?"

"Where are you going?"

"Unfortunately, back to the high school. It's been a rough week. I've got a briefcase full of test papers to correct, plus a student I need to check on in one of the study halls." She shivered. "And my feet are freezing."

He glanced down at the impractical high heels. "Boots would help."

She flipped the heater gauge to high. "I meant to go home and change, but I wanted to get to the rink before the game ended."

Slade tried to stretch his legs straight out, and gave up. "You wouldn't have missed much. Nick was ready to string them up after the first period."

"I'm sure. I dread telling Jeremy. He had to take a makeup test." She pulled her coat sleeve aside and glanced at her watch. Slade studied the delicate size of her wrist.

The same small wrist that had lain against the back of his neck at their senior prom.

You know what, Slade Garner?

What, Celina McKinley?

This is the first time I ever danced with you.

Yeah, well, dancing isn't what I do best.

Oh? And what do you do best? Besides playing hockey, I mean.

Uh, well, that's what I meant. Hockey. That's what I do best.

And he'd proved it with the Sabers. And he would again. He stared at his knee, daring it to destroy his future.

Celina drove out of the parking lot. "As a matter of fact, as long as you're here, you can do me a favor." She gave him a quick glance. "That is, if you don't mind."

"I don't mind. What's the favor?"

"You'd be the perfect person to get through to Jeremy."

"Jeremy Hearn seems to be the hot topic."

"You know him?"

"Nick mentioned him."

She stiffened slightly as she drove into the parking lot at Brentonville High School.

Slade glanced at the four-story granite building that had been built in the mid-thirties. Imposing and stern, the structure loomed above him like a judge passing sentence.

She parked close to the entrance, shut off the engine and turned to Slade. "I'm sure it was more than a mention. Nick isn't too fond of me these days."

"Nick sees everything through a win/lose perspective. Taking his star player off the team isn't exactly the kind of thing that brings buckets of roses from the coach."

She closed her eyes briefly, then glanced over at him. "He told you about my decision. From his point of view, his anger is understandable. From my point of view, he needs to realize that I'm concerned about Jeremy's education and his ability to function in some area of life besides a hockey rink."

He twisted in the seat, recalling his first impression of her—stubborn, with no doubts about what was important. "You're making the issue too cut-and-dried, Celina. It's more than a point of view to Nick. All he sees is a guaranteed championship slipping through his fingers."

She shook her head and a few more wisps of hair escaped. "You're not listening to what I'm saying, Slade.. It isn't just some hockey games. It's the perception that if you're good in sports, then you don't need anything else. Look at all the problems some of the colleges have gotten into by admitting students who can play basketball or football or hockey but can't write a simple sentence. It's appalling. Do you know I have a senior who doesn't know how to properly address an envelope?"

Slade blinked. "An envelope? You're not serious."

"I'm very serious."

"Who cares?"

"What?"

"Who cares if someone doesn't address an envelope right? I'd hardly put that in the top-ten list of important things to know in life." He should have been prepared for the snap and passion in her eyes.

"Are you telling me, Slade Garner, that knowing how to put a hockey puck into a net is in the top ten?"

How had they gotten on this subject? He sighed. "I hate to sound like a hockey player, but for me, scoring goals isn't even in the same league with the other nine."

She chewed on her lip as though she couldn't decide if she wanted to continue the argument. "I didn't mean to insult you."

"You didn't."

"But you can't expect me to feel the same way about the game as you do."

"As I recall, you cheered the loudest at all my games."

"That was because I . . ." She turned away.

Slade rolled down the window and let in some cold air. He felt a different kind of tension behind the argument. That, in itself, was a tip-off. Two people who had seen each other only once in the last three years shouldn't be arguing.

"What do you want me to tell Jeremy?" he asked, wanting to change the subject.

To his surprise, he saw the beginnings of a smile. "That graduation is more important than a hockey game."

He wanted to agree with her, to encourage the smile to widen, to tell her not to worry, he'd convince Jeremy. A picture of an angry Nick appeared in his mind, but Nick wasn't really what made him hesitate. After seeing the way Brentonville had played this afternoon, Slade was curious about the ability of Jeremy Hearn. Nick's instincts about hockey players were rarely wrong. If this Jeremy was as good as Nick said . . .

His knee began to ache, and momentarily he wished he'd simply waved and let her drive by. He had enough complications in his life without adding a woman he should have forgotten years ago.

"Celina, I can save us both a lot of time. Jeremy won't buy my agreeing with you. He won't believe it, and coming from me, it's going to sound like a farce."

"On the contrary. You at least graduated." When he scowled, she said, "I didn't mean that as a put-down. I'm aware that most of the hockey players take skate courses." She paused, grinning. "Was that a pun? Anyway, Jeremy is failing. I'm not asking you to trash hockey, but you could explain to him what happens to the kids who don't walk into a six-figure hockey contract the first day out of high school."

"In the first place you're exaggerating. In the second place, I don't know what happens to those kids. The guys I played with here in Brentonville went on to college or other jobs. They seemed to do okay."

"Jeremy doesn't want to do okay. He wants to be like you." Then he heard resentment slip into her voice. "He wants to go on to the NHL. To be a star. Brentonville's pride and joy. Charm and gloss."

Slade studied her for a long moment. He didn't want to argue with her, but the jibe annoyed him. "Why the sudden anger?"

With a coolness he doubted she felt, she said, "I'm not angry, but I'm not going to be taken in by your legendary charm. If you don't want to talk to Jeremy—"

"Hold it!" He pulled the zipper down on his jacket, suddenly feeling uncomfortably warm and trapped. He didn't like her accusing him of something he hadn't tried to do. "I wasn't trying to charm you."

"Try?" She laughed. "You don't have to try. All you have to do is appear. All the women at the rink were talking about you. Even way back in high school, Slade Garner was the guy every girl wanted."

"Including you," he shot back, and immediately regretted it, especially in a hot car with their tempers flaring.

Her violet eyes darkened defensively. "It was a crush."

Let it go, he told himself. Back off. That'll end it right here. "It was no crush, sweetheart, and you know it."

She flushed and looked away. For the first time since that summer, he touched her, cupping her chin gently but persuasively and drew her around so that she faced him. She kept her eyes lowered.

"Celina, look at me."

"I can't."

He moved his thumb along her chin. "Please?"

Finally she lifted her lashes. Slade's eyes met hers. "Don't deny what we had or what it meant. True, it didn't have a chance of survival and both of us knew it, but don't reduce it to a lousy teenage crush."

She pressed her lips together, and he rubbed his thumb lightly across them. Their eyes held for one long instant of silent awareness. Slade slowly withdrew his hand.

Celina let out a long breath, then as though the few fraught moments had never taken place, she said, "Jeremy will not play hockey until I see improvement in his grades."

With those parting words, she snatched the keys from the ignition, shouldered her handbag and got out of the car. She retrieved her briefcase and closed the door. Then with her back in that same stubborn line, she walked resolutely toward the granite building.

Slade swore and pressed his fist into his thigh. So much for being friends. So much for just talking.

He got out of the car and slammed the door behind him.

Walk back over to the rink, he told himself. Put on the skates and work out the kinks. Leave her alone. Don't think about how good it felt to touch her, or how badly you want to see her really smile.

He stood in the raw, cold wind and thought about her red coat and the red heels and pulling the pins out of her hair. He thought about the flush in her cheeks and her denial of what they'd shared. Why couldn't she just be Brian's widow? Why had what happened between them fifteen years ago suddenly turned into an argument today?

He kicked a small stone across the pavement and zipped up his jacket. He'd made sure the women in his life were uncomplicated. No hassles. No arguments. Just seductive bodies and forgettable faces.

He glanced at the high school. He couldn't remember any time since he'd gone to the NHL when he'd thought about a woman before hockey. And Celina was not just any woman, but the head of the Brentonville High School English department. The irony in that blew his mind.

He leaned against the car and folded his arms to stop the sudden shiver. Shame, but most of all regret, tugged and coiled inside him. One thing was clear.

Slade didn't want Celina to know he could barely read.

Chapter Two

Inside the high school, Celina went to the teachers' lounge to privately rein in her feelings and her memories. Now that she was away from him, she pressed two fingers against her mouth where he'd rubbed his thumb. Her lips still tingled with awareness.

If she'd had to give herself a grade on coolness and unflappability, in all honesty, a *C* would have been generous. She drew a long, steadying breath, and admitted to herself that she'd felt as moonstruck about Slade as the other women at the rink.

How had a simple "Hi, yourself. I heard you were home" become so complicated?

She'd seen him the moment she walked into the rink but, then, she'd expected he'd be there. What she didn't expect was to find herself so aware of him.

He'd been leaning against the support beam, concentrating on the action on the ice. She'd wondered if he was remembering the games he'd played and won, or the losses that he'd always used to make himself a better player.

When he'd played for Brentonville he'd been cocky and sure of himself, but it wasn't ego as much as natural ability. *Grace and precision when he scores* had been beneath his picture in their yearbook. Someone, either deliberately or unknowingly, had omitted the word goals, and Slade's reputation as a jock had been greatly enhanced.

For Celina, he'd been breath-stopping and an obsession, yes. Never to be forgotten, definitely. One summer out of her thirty-two summers, and yet those few months remained exquisitely detailed in her thoughts.

Watching him today, she found herself recalling bits of potent memories. His long, muscular legs clad in those snug jeans that molded his thighs as if they'd been worn for years. Jeans that had reminded her of the night on the bus when they were on their way back to Brentonville after a summer-league game.

She'd asked him: *"How come you look so sexy in jeans?"*

He'd leaned close and whispered: *"How come you look just plain sexy?"*

Seeing him in the leather jacket reminded her of when she'd worn his hockey jacket and she'd been the envy of all the girls who wanted Slade Garner.

"I don't care if it's summer, Slade, I'll wear the jacket in the rink."

"Just make sure you wear something under it."

His mouth, which had kissed her first with sweet gentleness and then with a raw passion unmatched in her experience.

"Who taught you how to kiss like that?"

"You taught me, Celina. Wanting you taught me."

His deep, dark and dangerous green eyes when he watched her for too long, like the afternoon at the beach when they'd hurried into one of the tiny bathhouses.

"You make me all tingly when you look at me like that."

"I want to make you wild for me, Celina. Come here...."

She shivered now at the compelling memories, pressing her hands against her hot cheeks. For her, she realized, there was no simple "welcome home" when it came to Slade.

In the small bathroom off the teachers' lounge, she patted her face with a cold, wet paper towel.

Avoiding him was unrealistic, especially with their fifteenth-year reunion only days away, but seeing him didn't mean she had to make a fool out of herself. Considering their disagreement about Jeremy, plus her own strong feelings about sports and education, she had enough to handle without getting into a personal relationship.

She didn't want to give in to the nudge of curiosity she felt about him. He's simply an old boyfriend, she told herself. Just because he's Slade Garner... Just because she'd welcomed his lovemaking and given him her virginity when she was seventeen... Just because he still made her stomach flutter...

She scowled at her reflection. "Thoughts like those," she muttered aloud, "are a good start to making a fool out of yourself." Impatiently she snapped off the bathroom light.

* * *

"Any problems?" Celina asked Lauren Kelsey, who laid down the mystery novel she was reading when Celina walked into the study hall. Lauren was a substitute teacher and a good friend. Like Celina, she had returned to Brentonville after college and married.

"Everything is fine," Lauren said.

Celina had left her coat in the teachers' lounge. She wore a soft charcoal-gray wool suit, a cranberry red blouse and a string of pearls Brian had given her on their fifth wedding anniversary. She put her briefcase on the floor next to the desk.

The large study hall was quiet except for the distant sound of the school furnace. A half dozen students were there for discipline reasons or makeup work. In the third seat in the row by the windows slouched Jeremy Hearn.

"So how was the game?" Lauren whispered.

"They lost." Jeremy didn't look up, and Celina knew he must have seen her. "Is Jeremy still working on that test?"

Lauren tapped a red fingernail on four stapled sheets of paper. "This is it. Instead of leaving, he went back over there and slouched down in the seat. You didn't say anything about him staying, but I thought you might have forgotten to mention it to me." Lauren pushed her chair back. She motioned Celina over near the door where they wouldn't be overheard but could still monitor the room.

Whispering, Lauren asked. "Well?"

Celina sighed and unbuttoned her suit jacket. "I saw him."

"Just saw him or *really* saw him?"

"He rode over here with me."

Lauren's blue eyes filled with expectation. "Do I have to drag it out of you? What happened?"

"Nothing happened. We talked about Jeremy."

Her face fell in disappointment. "Jeremy! Oh, Celina, you didn't go into that long crusading speech about education versus sports? Not with Slade."

"It isn't a speech," she said in defense of herself. "It's the way I feel. Slade has a blind spot when it comes to hockey."

"No kidding. Probably the same one he had when you two broke up because he wanted to leave Brentonville and play for the pros."

"And I had a fully paid scholarship to college. It was a mutual decision."

"That was then. This is now."

"Lauren, there is no now. He's home for the reunion, and he's helping Nick with the team."

Lauren sighed deeply. "So what did you talk about?"

Celina thought of the conversation they'd had regarding Brian, but she didn't want to share that and she wasn't sure why. Maybe because she'd been so unsure of Slade's feelings about her marrying his best friend, or maybe because his feelings mattered. She slipped her hands into her skirt pockets. "We had a disagreement."

"It must have been a humdinger. You look unraveled." Lauren grinned, her eyes mischievous. "So how much time are you going to waste before you go to bed with him?"

Celina felt a small woosh of something she refused to call eagerness or excitement or yearning. She counted to five. "You, my friend, have a one-track mind when it comes to Slade and me."

"This is me you're talking to, Celina. I was the one who watched you cry enough tears, after Slade left town, to fill the fountain in the park."

"You've mentioned that three times in the last week. I was seventeen and emotional," Celina countered, remembering also how miserably unhappy she'd been. The right decision had been a painful one.

Lauren said, "Ever since we heard he was coming home for the reunion, you've had a sort of eager anticipation in your eyes." Denial rushed to Celina's lips, but Lauren held up her hand. "I know you don't want to admit it—"

This time she interrupted Lauren. "All right, I admit it. I'll even admit I enjoyed seeing him and talking to him. Wait. Before you get off on a tangent, listen to me. I also know we're on opposite sides on this hockey issue. Plus, I doubt he's going to be here longer than a couple of weeks."

"So have a fling with him. Sleep with him. Take what you can get. The worst thing that could happen is that you'll miss him when he leaves. But at least you'll have something to remember."

Celina pressed her fingers to her temples, trying to think and reason. "Or something to regret." She buttoned her jacket. "I better find out why Jeremy is hanging around. Probably hiding from his father. I saw Eddie Hearn at the game and he wasn't happy when he didn't see his son on the ice." She glanced at her watch. "Why don't you go on home? I'll dismiss the kids."

"Yeah, I should run. The Sachuest Chorale is practicing in the auditorium today. I've got just enough time to grab a cup of coffee. We're doing a medley of songs from old Broadway musicals."

Celina sighed. Old Broadway musicals were her fa-
vorites. Unfortunately, her ability to sing them was
best suited to a non-audience. She gave Lauren a
pained look which Lauren returned with a sympa-
thetic smile.

Lauren got her purse out of the desk drawer, said
goodbye and left the room. Celina began to leaf
through Jeremy's test.

Slade stopped after he'd walked a few steps down
the high-school corridor. The big double doors
slammed behind him, making him suddenly feel
locked in a cell. He wasn't quite sure what he had in
mind. Talking to Jeremy or seeing Celina.

If he were smart, he'd be at the rink instead of in the
one place he'd gladly left behind years ago. Since the
fourth grade, when he'd been told that playing hockey
was an unacceptable substitute for learning to read,
Slade had set out to prove hockey was more than
enough. Who wanted to read, when he could play
hockey better than any other kid his age? His father
didn't care what kind of grades he got in school, only
how many goals he scored. He'd finessed and charmed
his way through school on the barest of reading skills.
He'd managed and he'd been successful, despite some
moments of regret.

One of those moments had come a few years before when he'd gathered his courage and gone to sign
up for an adult reading course. Before Slade had said
anything, a chinless man with a Providence Sabers
button on his jacket recognized him. He promptly
announced to the entire room who Slade was. Slade
appreciated his fans and never minded signing autographs or answering questions, but that night, all that

went through his mind was how would they react if they knew why he was there? Would they laugh? Would they call him stupid? Would he see banners at rival rinks with comments like: *Can you read this, Garner? See Garner skate. See Garner score. Hey Garner, ya know what score means?*

Panic had seized him, and his pride wouldn't let him register for the course, so he'd signed autographs, murmured an excuse about looking for a buddy, and gotten out of there as quickly as he could.

Apart from Nick and his agent, Izzy Bozwell, who went apoplectic when Slade told him what he'd almost done, no one else knew.

Celina was aware he'd never been a hotshot when it came to grades, but she didn't know he could barely read. At eighteen he would have died rather than admit that to one of the smartest girls in school. His pride and ego over the past fifteen years hadn't changed, they'd only hardened. That being true, he had to ask himself why he was in Brentonville High School? Why was he taking chances?

Frowning with annoyance, he decided his interest in Celina was pure insanity. Perhaps it was the challenge of pursuit, the vividness of her violet eyes, or that awful bun he wanted to take apart so he could tangle his hands in her hair.

Okay, he admitted to those, but he wanted more than the kick of arousal with Celina. What he wanted was—what? He wasn't even sure. Something deeper, something he was missing. Something like those few minutes he'd just spent with her. They'd talked about Brian and even argued about Jeremy, but he'd felt as if he'd crawled out of the boredom that had plagued him in the past couple of months.

The high school was her territory, and yet here he stood. His grin was filled with amazement more than amusement. What did he really want with Celina? Sex? Yeah, that was an easy one to answer. Friendship? Yeah, he'd like to be friends with her. A relationship? That scared him. Just the word sounded complicated and intimate, with too many possibilities she'd find out he could barely read. Dammit, why did he keep thinking about it? Why did it bother him so much, now?

He shrugged out of his leather jacket and looked at the open door leading into the main study hall. His last memories of that room had nothing to do with reading.

With Jeremy's test in her hand, Celina walked over to where the teenager sat slouched low in his seat with a glum look on his face. The dirty blond hair needed to be cut. His shirt, with the words Brentonville Hockey across the front, was untucked over faded jeans with holes in the knees. He'd pushed the sleeves up above the elbows and crossed his arms over his chest. He gave her no more than a flicker of a glance when she pulled one of the chairs close to him and sat down.

"Brentonville lost," she said without preliminaries.

"Yeah, I saw some of the guys come outta the team bus." He nodded toward the windows. "I figured we got smeared."

There was nothing she could add to that. "I've gone through your test," she said, laying the sheaf of papers down.

He shrugged.

"If you were finished, then why did you stay?"

Again he shrugged. "Ain't nothing to leave for. The old man is probably lookin' for me. I didn't tell him I wasn't playin' today. He'll be pissed." He sunk deeper into the chair. "And the way things are goin' I might as well chain myself to this desk for the next fifty years."

"Jeremy, I'm not doing this to make your life miserable."

He gave her a defeated look. "Yeah? Then how come it feels like it?"

Celina took a few seconds before answering. It would be so easy to dismiss him, to tell him that since hockey was what he loved, then that was all that was important, but she couldn't do it. She'd seen too many teachers allow kids to slide by with the reasoning that keeping them back a grade would do them more harm than passing them. Or in some cases allowing kids to move on because there simply wasn't enough time to give them the extra attention. Or worst of all, allowing sports to become too important. For Jeremy, she knew hockey was ninety percent of the problem.

Celina said, "I know book reports and tests on sentence construction aren't as interesting as playing hockey, but they're necessary for you to graduate."

"Graduate to what? I ain't plannin' on being some scientist or brain surgeon. I wanna play hockey. Since I was four, that's what I've wanted. Who needs to know about dangling particles or whatever you call 'em." It wasn't a question but a pronouncement.

"Participles," Celina corrected, and felt a discouraging weariness slide down her body.

Not caring if he graduated was an old argument. She'd faced it with other students and held her ground without much fanfare. Unfortunately for her, Jeremy Hearn wasn't just any student. Refusing to allow the best player since Slade Garner to play was tantamount to treason.

"I'm sorry, Jeremy. If I allow you to play, then I'm setting a different standard for hockey players than for the other students—and that isn't fair. I told you I would help you, but you must help yourself. Now—" she picked up the sheaf of papers "—this test doesn't look very complete. A lot of questions aren't answered."

Nothing she said had any effect on the set look on his face. "I didn't know the answers," he muttered.

"Why? I told you what the test was on and you had all weekend to study."

He stared at her as though she'd suggested he fly around the room. "You gotta be kiddin'. Who wants to spend the weekend studying for some dumb test?" Suddenly he straightened up. "Aw, jeez, it's him. It's really him."

Celina twisted around in the chair. "Him" was exactly who she expected it to be. The only person who could put that look of intensity in Jeremy's eyes was Slade Garner.

He'd taken off his leather jacket and laid it across one of the desks. The off-white sweater made his skin seem darker, his hair a richer brown, and his eyes a deeper green. He hadn't come too far into the room, and she wondered for a moment if he felt awkward. He seemed cautious, as though he'd invaded foreign territory and was about to face some kind of stern judgment. Celina had seen parents act the same way at conferences, when they weren't sure if they were going to hear good news or bad news about their child's progress.

Slade allowed his gaze to settle only on Celina, and for one long moment the connection sizzled ten degrees hotter than it had in her car.

Celina knew she should look away, lower her head, fiddle with Jeremy's papers. Do something. Anything. Slade didn't look away, either. Time suspended and swayed and seized them with a sensual sweep into the past.

As if in mutual response they both glanced at the wall beside the door and then back at each other.

"Slade, we can't. Someone might come in."

"Just one kiss, Celina. Call it a graduation kiss."

"I thought you weren't good at anything but hockey."

"I lied. Ah, Celina, you weren't supposed to taste so good."

Celina shivered at the vivid, deeply arousing memory.

Slade, too, wondered at the wisdom of coming into this room. It was only a study hall that he'd rarely been in while in high school, and yet it was in this room where he'd found a passion that still had the power to grip him. He could feel a growing heaviness begin in his loins, and deliberately killed his thoughts.

Celina realized only about seven seconds had lapsed, but she felt stripped and weak as though she'd survived an hour of grueling testing.

The students rushed over to Slade, pushing desks aside and knocking someone's books on the floor. Jeremy, too, was on his feet, zigzagging between desks. Celina let him go, glad for the opportunity to get her thoughts and feelings in check.

A hometown hero, she thought as she watched them clamor and circle around Slade. She wondered if Slade was aware of how much influence he could have on their lives. She shook away the idea, telling herself she was beginning to sound like some boring moralist.

Slade signed some notebooks, and in the case of a senior girl who told him his signature on her shoulder would be really cool, he compromised and signed the back of her hand. Then with an okay nod from Celina, the kids left except for Jeremy.

He stood with his hands deep in his pockets and tried for a nonchalant, no-hurry pose that Celina knew was as phony as his admiration for Slade was real.

When he turned to Jeremy with a genuine eagerness to meet him, Celina found herself with a mammoth lump in her throat. She picked up Jeremy's test and crossed to where they stood.

Slade, she noted, looked directly into Jeremy's eyes, not with the need to see admiration of himself, but with a kind of studied intensity. She wondered if he was trying to gauge if Jeremy had the same gut love for hockey he had.

"I've heard a lot about you, Jeremy," Slade said easily. "And I sure would be interested in seeing that famous wrist shot of yours."

He means it, Celina thought, not sure how she knew it. But there was no mistaking the sincerity.

Jeremy's mouth opened and closed. "Uh, jeez... you, uh... you heard about me?" His voice climbed to a high squeak, and Celina saw the red stain of embarrassment on the back of his neck. Then came a long, gulping swallow. "You heard about me?" he asked again, as if he wanted to make sure he'd heard right.

Slade laughed and offered his hand. "It's a pleasure to meet you."

Speechless now, Jeremy shook his hand, smiling broadly.

Slade asked, "How are you for some free time?"

"Free time? Like you mean with nothin' to do?"

"Like I mean with nothin' to do."

"I got a ton of that." He glanced at Celina and the test she held. "Especially now. She won't let me play."

"Maybe we can work that out," Slade said. Celina gave him a warning look, but he wasn't paying any attention to her. "Anyway, what do you say to skating with me? Doing some stop-and-goes. Some slap shots. Maybe we can get a bunch of the guys together."

Awestruck, Jeremy stared, his eyes round. "You mean it? You'd skate with me and some of the guys?"

"What about Saturday afternoon? Say about four?"

The teenager blinked and Slade repeated what he'd said. Then as if he were afraid Slade might change his mind, he said, "We'll be there."

"I'm looking forward to it."

Jeremy started for the door, then turned back, a worried look on his face. "You won't forget, will ya?"

Slade shook his head. "Not a chance. See you then."

Celina listened to Jeremy's steps clamor down the hall. The outside doors opened and slammed closed with vigor. Slade sat down at her desk and leaned back.

"He'll be in the clouds for the rest of the week," she said, trying to combine both pleasure at Jeremy's excitement and admiration for Slade's approachability. He was a real hometown hero.

"Come over here and tell me what is going through your head," he said matter-of-factly, pulling open a drawer and bracing his booted foot on the edge.

"I'd be more interested in why you came in here. Did you change your mind?"

"I guess. I'm curious to see if this kid is as good on the ice as I've heard he is, but since you won't allow him to play, then I thought by setting up some time with him I'd get a chance to see for myself."

Celina tossed Jeremy's test on the desk, feeling her defensive shield come up. She was getting tired of taking all the heat for a decision that she knew was in Jeremy's best interests. "In other words, it's my fault."

"I didn't say that, but I know the passion Jeremy feels for hockey. And it's not likely some English test is going to replace it."

"And what am I supposed to do? Say, fine, play hockey, and it doesn't matter if he ever learns anything?"

"Take it easy," he said quietly, obviously trying to calm her down. "You're trying to force learning on him like a dose of bad medicine. Taking away the one thing he loves isn't going to make him love you or English."

She bristled, and she didn't want to. She didn't want anything he said to have any effect on her one way or the other. "Loving English isn't the issue. Learning it is."

Slade tipped the chair back on its hind legs, and Celina found her eyes drawn to the way his sweater lay over his flat stomach, and the far too mesmerizing way his jeans molded his hips. Terrific, she thought, when she realized her own body was poised to respond at only the slightest urging.

"...loving it." Her eyes flew to his face only to find him watching her, his eyes steady and direct. "You aren't listening to me," he said in the same way she spoke to a student who didn't have the slightest interest in studying. "I said 'The issue is loving it.' English, I mean. Look at you. You love to teach, and I bet you still love to learn. Jeremy loves hockey, and his eagerness a few minutes ago tells me he wants to learn to play better. That's not wrong. Some kids just aren't big on the school scene."

While they talked she eased closer and perched on the edge of the desk. Slade watched her, and when she realized how close their legs were to touching, she started to move away. He lightly touched her ankle.

"Stay," he said so softly she almost didn't hear him. She did, only because she was afraid the weakness in her knees would betray her if she stood up.

Slade drew her foot forward. "Red high heels," he murmured, tracing the heel strap and slipping it down the back of her foot. "I bet you're the only English-department head in Brentonville's history to wear red high heels. By the way, congratulations."

"Thank you." She tried to pull her foot away, at the same time wondering if some subliminal desire had made her move closer to him. "I almost didn't accept it. Arthur Flinch, my predecessor, spent most of his time on administration details. I didn't want to quit teaching. Although with my decision on Jeremy, a lot of people wish I had."

He placed his thumb and forefinger around her ankle, rubbing either side, pressing lightly before he slipped the red heel strap back into place. He didn't say anything, and Celina wondered if he agreed with the town's opinion.

She stood, her knees a little wobbly, then lifted the briefcase and laid it on the desk. He leaned back once more, watching her. Her fingers felt cold and shaky as she snapped open the latches.

She started to put Jeremy's test inside, but instead took out the papers of one of her other students.

"I want you to see something," she said to Slade. He gave the two tests a strange look, as though touching them might burn his fingers.

Reluctantly he took them.

"Jeremy," Celina said briskly, "is far ahead of this other student when it comes to intelligence and ability and yet, well, you can see by looking at the answers what I mean."

He glanced at one set and then the other. "Interesting," he said with what she thought was disinterest.

Celina scowled. "Interesting isn't what I want you to say. The word is appalling."

He tossed them on top of her desk. "I'm not a teacher."

Celina felt momentarily confused but then dismissed it. Maybe he really didn't see the big difference between the two tests, but he had to have noticed the poorly constructed sentences, the missing answers, plus all the misspellings on Jeremy's paper. "You have to admit Jeremy's test isn't anywhere near as complete as the other student's."

He shrugged and came up out of the chair. Her scowl deepened, and she told herself not to get into another argument with him. "You really think I'm making an issue out of nothing, don't you? If Jeremy was a slow learner, or if he had serious problems such as reading or comprehension, then that would be one thing. But he scores consistently high in national testing scores. His problem is laziness. And there is no excuse for that."

His eyes, so warm before, suddenly turned an icy green. With his hands propped low on his hips, he snapped, "How the hell do you know there isn't an excuse?"

Celina stepped back and blinked, feeling as if she'd opened a door and found a dragon. He walked away from her, rubbing his hand across the back of his neck. She took a deep breath and remained silent.

Swearing softly, he turned to face her. "Look, I didn't mean to jump all over you. It's just that maybe there *is* an excuse. Maybe it isn't good or acceptable or even right, but each kid deals with things in different ways."

Celina leaned against the edge of her desk, feeling a little overwhelmed. Had she missed something with Jeremy that Slade had seen? She knew Jeremy's parents were divorced. His mother and two younger sisters had moved to Connecticut, and Jeremy lived with his father. Eddie Hearn bragged all over town about his kid, the hockey star. One-track thinking, but then this was Brentonville, she reminded herself. "Tell me what kind of excuses you mean."

He leveled a long look at her. "Like pressure. Like wanting one thing so bad everything else is pushed aside, including learning. Like knowing that if the team needed you, that was what mattered. Like trying, but—" He stopped suddenly, and Celina waited. Abruptly he said, "We oughta get out of here."

Celina picked up her briefcase and adjusted her purse strap on her shoulder. At the door she asked, "What were you going to say?"

"Nothing. It's not important."

She touched his arm. "Maybe it is."

Slade glanced at the wall by the door, then back at her. "No. Now, this is the only thing that's important."

She knew what he meant without his saying the words. She knew she should leave, but he was too tempting, the memories too special to allow the moment to pass.

She took a step back, the chair rail along the wall hitting her in a different place than when she was seventeen, but the low churn in her womb was the same—deep and expectant. Her briefcase slipped from her hand, and Slade eased her purse down so that it dropped to the floor forgotten. His hand moved up her arm to cup her neck. Their breathing seemed to stop and start as if each was trying to gauge when to speak, when to move, how intimately to touch.

He flattened his hands against the wall on either side of her head. His muscular arms were dusted with dark hair where the sleeves of the sweater had been pushed up his forearms. His body made no contact with hers, yet she felt the long, raw heat of him. Dangerous lights glittered in his green eyes.

"I remember that you wore pink roses in your hair," he whispered, his mouth a breath away from hers. A silken trap, she thought, as escape-proof as the desire she saw in his eyes.

"And you complained you found two thorns when you pulled them out."

Lightly he brushed her mouth, nipped her bottom lip with only the slightest pressure, and then drew back. "That was at the park. Right here, I only kissed you, tasted you and worried that you wouldn't kiss me back."

Celina felt winded, as if she'd run too long. Her body burned with heat. She laid her hands on his sweater, feeling the muscles in his chest through the wool. "I kissed you back. French-kissed you back."

Again he touched her mouth, this time allowing the very tip of his tongue to sweep over her lips. "With us there was never any other kind, was there?"

She shook her head, feeling almost shy about admitting how he'd made her feel. "I was afraid I'd disappoint you."

He leaned into her, his thighs bracketing her hips, caging her with warmth and hardness and lush adult sensations.

"You made me want to take you right here against the wall," he murmured, nuzzling her neck below her ear.

Celina closed her eyes, the heady feel of him making her ache to wiggle closer. She wanted to lose herself in his kiss, but at the same time she heard the warning that said: Don't start this. Don't get involved.

Slade touched the first button of her blouse. "Sweetheart, you're freezing up on me."

She didn't want to. She didn't want to say no. Every nerve screamed to simply go along with the delicious sensations he created when he touched her. But then what? She nudged his finger away from the button. "We have no place to go with this, Slade."

He grinned at her, watching her mouth. "I can think of a few places."

"I can't," she said, deliberately ignoring what she knew he meant. She didn't want to hear "your bed or mine." "We're not kids any longer. Making love isn't enough."

"Making love with you was always more than enough. Besides," he murmured kissing her lightly, "who says it has to last forever?"

His matter-of-fact attitude hurt, but then what did she expect? A confession of love? Hardly. Closing her eyes when he once again kissed her, she allowed herself a moment of indulgence before pulling away. "That's what we said that summer. You left to play hockey. I went to college. A lot has happened in between." Then a bit desperately she added, "We're practically strangers."

He tucked one finger into her bun and tried to loosen it. "Why question it, like some damn test with right-and-wrong answers? It's called being turned on. Why complicate it?"

And then as though they'd already complicated it with words, he pressed her against the wall and stopped any further talk with his mouth. Celina's stiffness lasted all of three seconds, and then she melted. His mouth moved first with a demand that said he wanted to absorb any denial, and then softened, reacquainting her with the kind of kiss he'd taught her to give. Openmouthed, deep and wet.

Her hands slid up around his neck, and she allowed herself to drift off to some exquisite place where their disagreement over Jeremy, the fifteen years that separated them, their own starkly different lives didn't matter; a place where pleasure was a temptation to be enjoyed and explored.

Finally he drew back. Celina opened her eyes, trying to focus through the haze of thick, honeyed passion.

She could feel the sudden change in him, and she wondered what caused it. She hadn't played coy and fought the kiss.

He slipped her purse back on her shoulder, then stepped back, his hands raking his hair back. She heard him swear and swear again. She knew she should walk out without asking any questions. He'd asked, why complicate it? Why indeed? But was the passion and desire that sizzled between them enough?

Still reeling from the taste of him, she pushed away from the wall and reached down for her briefcase.

"Wait." He cupped the back of her neck, his hand sliding up into her hair, his fingers tunneling beneath her bun. With the thumb on his other hand he rubbed her still wet and warm mouth. "You're probably right. Getting involved is a bad idea, sweetheart. When the time comes to say goodbye..."

He didn't finish, but then he didn't have to. She made herself look at him and ignore the sudden crush of disappointment. She certainly couldn't accuse him of meaningless promises.

And he had answered her question. The passion that sizzled between them wasn't enough anymore.

Chapter Three

For days, news of Slade's return dominated Brentonville conversations. Celina decided that if she heard one more anecdote about Slade Garner, one more telling of "when he played hockey no opposing team could touch us," or one more gushy woman giggle out his name...

Outside the principal's office, she paused to get her thoughts organized about Jeremy and off Slade. She was convinced she'd made the best decision in both situations, despite some twinges of regret over Slade.

"Well, I think the town should vote to name a street after him," Grace Twitchell was saying, when Celina opened the door. She hid her groan at yet another accolade for Slade. Grace went on breezily. "They do it for rock 'n' roll singers, and we did it for Brentonville's longest-serving town clerk. And Slade is certainly— oh, good afternoon, Celina."

With her white hair, frilly dresses—pink today—and
yard-sale jewelry, Grace, the secretary at Brentonville
High for twenty years, preened happily. Celina had
never seen her so exuberant, and decided that Slade,
himself, stirred up more enthusiasm than hockey. She
returned the greeting with a smile.

Also present were Bill Knight, the president of the
Brentonville Booster Club, Nick Murphy, the hockey
coach, and the principal, Glen Harvey, who sat at his
desk. Bill and Nick were looking through a pile of
eight-by-ten pictures of the hockey team. Grace sat
beside the window, glancing out as though expecting
someone.

"I apologize for being late. I had to do a last-minute
proofreading of the *Gray and Gold*," Celina said, referring to the school newspaper, which needed her final approval before going to press.

"I guess we can get started," the principal said, adjusting his bifocals. "The issue of Jeremy not playing
has caused more angry phone calls to the school committee members and to myself than I've had since I
became principal. That said, one point should be
made clear." He glanced around the room and specif-
ically at Nick. "Celina is within her right as head of
the English department to keep him from playing."

Celina had been thinking about this meeting since
this morning, when she found the memo in her box.
Was it going to be a subtle pressure tactic or was she
simply going to be ordered to allow Jeremy to play?
The unpopularity of her decision didn't concern her as
much as Jeremy did. She'd been pleased with his attitude in class the past few days. He hadn't shown
boundless enthusiasm for conjugating verbs, but he
hadn't exhibited the bored passiveness she'd seen since

hockey season began. As much as she wanted to believe the teenager had taken a sudden interest in
school, she knew she was reaping the benefits of his
reaction to Slade and his "let's play some hockey"
invitation. However, Jeremy's attitude change was an
opening, and she didn't intend to let the door close.

Glen Harvey continued, "... and since, according
to Nick, the boy not playing is having a detrimental
effect on the team, we thought this meeting might help
us work toward a solution that would please all of us."

Celina glanced at Nick, refusing to allow the hostil-
ity in his eyes to make her back down. "I don't want
to prevent Jeremy from playing, but I can't give passing grades to a failing student."

"Maybe it ain't all Jeremy's fault," Nick said,
scowling. He slouched in the chair and folded his arms
across his chest. "Maybe you ain't doin' your job."

"I am doing my job. That's what bothers you."
Celina didn't feel as calm as she hoped she sounded.

The principal held up his hand in a conciliatory
gesture. "Now wait a minute. No one is questioning
Celina's teaching capabilities."

"Celina is a wonderful teacher," Grace added, her
attention on the window. "Here he comes. Oh, my, he
certainly has grown into a devilishly attractive hunk."
Her cheeks flushed red, and she giggled. "That's what
the girls at my beauty parlor call him. Too bad his
mother isn't alive to see him. She'd be so proud. Slade
Garner Drive or just Garner Drive? What does everyone think?"

Nick and Bill glanced at each other and chuckled.

"Grace, please," Glen Harvey said. "We're not
here to rename the town's streets."

Celina's annoyance over Brentonville's obsession with Slade suddenly turned to anger. Maybe he was a terrific hockey player, but he knew nothing about school policy. He didn't even live in Brentonville.

"Why is Slade invited, Glen?"

He cleared his throat. "Nick requested it, since Slade is helping him with the coaching. He's giving a lot of extra time to the kids, and well . . . I agreed that he might have some valuable input for all of us."

Celina lowered her head and took a deep breath. She had the ominous feeling that whatever she said now wouldn't make any difference.

"The booster club has gone all out this year," Bill Knight exclaimed with the enthusiasm of a carnival barker. "We're way over budget. We're doing T-shirts, hats, and the play-off games will be pushed on the local talk shows. When the TV stations heard Slade will be here to assist Nick, they said they'd be here to cover it. If Hearn isn't playing, we stand to lose a lot of money." He peered at Celina. "Your husband was one of our biggest supporters. If Brian were here . . ."

Celina felt the muscles in her jaw tighten, and the beginnings of a nasty headache build. She let the comment about Brian pass. "I hope the issue isn't the booster club's success." She looked at each face. "Or is it?"

"Of course not." Glen Harvey smiled and gestured toward the door. "Slade, glad you could come. And let me tell you, we appreciate your time and your expertise."

Slade stood just inside the door, his hair disheveled from the wind. His leather jacket hung open to reveal a gray Providence Sabers sweatshirt. His jeans were black and snug. Celina hadn't seen him since they'd kissed, and she felt her pulse speed up when his eyes lingered on her. She wasn't a mind reader, but his closed expression and the tightness of his body gave an impression of restlessness.

He slipped his hands into his jacket pockets, still watching her. "It's my pleasure. And Bill," he said softly—too softly, Celina thought—"if Brian were here he would have backed up Celina's decision. You owe her an apology." She felt a sudden rush of warmth toward him for taking her side. Bill Knight nodded and mumbled he was sorry.

Then Slade spoke to the room in general. He frankly and truthfully told them what he'd seen at the game earlier in the week and at the subsequent practices. "As for Jeremy, I'd rather wait to give an opinion after I've seen him skate."

Glen Harvey looked positively enraptured by Slade. "You really know what you're talking about, and I agree, although I'm no expert." He looked at Celina. "What about giving Jeremy some extra help?"

Celina rolled her eyes. "Jeremy and I are trying to work something out."

Nick tapped the pictures into a neat pile and put them back into a manila envelope. "Yeah, well, while you're tryin', I got a team that's dyin'. See what happens when you give a woman a little authority? She thinks she's in charge. All I'm asking for is a few lousy weeks. Then she can strap Hearn to a desk until graduation."

"Oh, that sounds wonderful, Nick," Celina said, not bothering to hide her disgust at his suggestion. "Use Jeremy while you need him, and then you don't care what happens."

He pointed the envelope at her. "I care about bringin' home a state championship."

"And I care about his future," she shot back. "There is life after hockey."

"Yeah? Well, lookin' at Slade here tells me it can be a good life. What's he missin', huh? He's got money and success and a future that's only gonna get better. And Jeremy is as good as Slade was. You're holdin' the kid back, Celina. You're messin' up that future you say you care about."

Disgusted, she snapped, "I don't believe I'm hearing this. This is a school, not a sports program. And to compare Jeremy with Slade as though Jeremy's future in hockey is in jeopardy is ridiculous." She glared at Slade. "Tell us what you think."

"After I see him on the ice," he said quietly.

She met his eyes, refusing to let him sidestep her question, while at the same time wanting him to agree with her, but knowing . . . Why did it even matter, she asked herself.

"I'd like to know," she said as though she were speaking only to him.

Slade looked at her as if to say, You don't want to hear this. Glen Harvey leaned forward. Bill Knight put a piece of spearmint gum into his mouth. Grace beamed. Nick scowled. Celina wished she hadn't pressed him.

Finally he said, "Keeping Jeremy from playing won't solve his school problems. In fact, it will probably make them worse."

She immediately thought of what he'd said in the study hall about excuses. But how could he know so much about Jeremy? He barely knew him. She rubbed her temples, wishing she was home where she could think. Even she was beginning to consider Slade's opinion as important.

Nick and Bill happily slapped each other on the back. "I knew, when I asked him to give the kids pointers, he'd be on my side." Nick grinned broadly.

Celina spoke to all of them. "I can't believe you expect academic decisions to be made based on the biased opinion of a hockey player."

Nick's smile died. "Come on, Celina. Slade ain't hardly just any hockey player."

"That's enough, Nick," Slade said, giving the coach a warning look.

"Yes, Nick. Slade is quite right." Glen Harvey pushed his chair back from the desk.

Celina sighed wearily. "Are you going to order me to let Jeremy play?"

The principal thought for a moment, then stood. "Despite Slade's opinion, I want to be fair and consider all the facts."

"And in the meantime?" Celina asked.

"I suggest you continue working with Jeremy. And, Nick, you'd better impress on the team that they depend too much on one player. I'll have a final decision soon."

Celina slung her purse onto her shoulder and lifted her briefcase. Without looking at anyone, she stalked to the door. The only problem was that Slade blocked her way.

"Excuse me," she said coldly.

He slipped his fingers around her upper arm. "We need to talk." His voice was low and soft.

She glanced at where he touched her, not wanting to remember how his hands had felt against her skin, how their gentleness had slid into her hair. She shook away the memory, hating that she could feel desire for him, despite her anger. "Talk about what? Your opinion? All the facts? Or is there a difference? Don't worry, the whole town will agree with you. What's really sad is that Jeremy will be the real loser long after hockey season is over."

Slade let her go, watching her walk down the long corridor. *Jeremy will be the real loser.* Familiar words from his own past that no teacher since fourth grade had ever said to him. But at eighteen, would he have listened? Not likely.

Nick slapped him on the back. "We ain't dead yet, thanks to you, kid. She can't argue with success."

Slade continued to look down the now-empty corridor. Success suddenly had everything to do with Celina and very little to do with a winning hockey season. So much for keeping his opinion to himself. He had to credit her for gutsiness. She hadn't backed down, and he liked that. What really puzzled him was that he didn't like disagreeing with her.

"Celina is right, you know," he said to Nick as they walked out of the high school and over to the rink.

"Huh? Right about what?"

"The opinion of a biased hockey player shouldn't carry any weight."

"Come on, kid! You're Slade Garner."

He looked at the banner that someone had hung over the arena's doors. WELCOME HOME, SLADE. He knew the words because Nick had repeated them a dozen times. He knew the welcome came from Brentonville's heart. But for a reason he didn't like and had thought too much about, he wanted the words to come from Celina.

* * *

Celina fixed herself a cup of herbal tea while the music from the old Broadway musical *Oklahoma* played in the background. It was Saturday, and because it was a chilly day she had decided to make some soup. While the vegetables and meat simmered into a slow boil, she read through the new issue of *Gray and Gold*.

She'd allowed the opinion piece titled, "Let Jeremy Play," go through unedited. She didn't agree with it, and she knew she could have ordered it rewritten or even killed, but she hadn't. Freedom of speech in action, she thought, with a sigh.

When the soup boiled she added salt but no pepper, barley and some herbs, then turned the heat to low.

She walked into the spacious living room she'd decorated in cool blues with splashes of red for contrast, and set her teacup down on the coffee table. The newspaper carried a picture of Slade on the front page. Grace was right. The man was a devilishly attractive hunk.

She wasn't angry at Slade any longer, though her concern about Jeremy hadn't changed. What really bothered her was that she wanted Slade to agree with her. She told herself it had nothing to do with her personal feelings for him, but only with Jeremy. If Slade had agreed with her, she knew the whole question of Jeremy playing would be moot.

She glanced at the stack of book reports she had to correct, turned off *Oklahoma* and decided to get started.

Two hours later when her doorbell rang, she'd taken a break to watch a local TV sports commentator talk about the knee injuries that plagued hockey players—Slade Garner, in particular.

"You didn't tell me you had knee problems," she said to Slade when she opened her front door. Dressed in soft, worn jeans, a tan brushed-suede shirt and his leather jacket, she thought he looked casual and sexy. He carried three videocassette tapes in one hand, and in the other, a six-pack of beer.

He handed her the beer, which she took as automatically as if he brought her a six-pack about three times a week. Their fingers brushed for a second during the exchange.

"I didn't think my knees would be a subject you'd want to explore," he said with an arch of one eyebrow, and just enough mischief to make her wonder if he was serious or teasing. His eyes absorbed her in her black cotton sweats and red sweater with a slow, detailed thoroughness as if he'd waited a lifetime to see her. "You look great in red. I'm not messing up a hot date, am I?"

"Actually," she said, wishing she could say yes, "I canceled all my hot dates. Too many papers to correct."

She could feel the warmth coming off his body, even though he hadn't touched her. Behind him, the sky darkened with the threat of rain.

In a low voice, he asked, "Don't you know what they say about all work and no play?"

Feeling reckless, and despite her annoyance at their previous meeting, she was pleased that he'd sought her out. She switched the six-pack from one hand to the other. "And is that what you're here for? To play?"

He grinned at her comeback, which Celina found delighted her about ten times more than it should have. "If I say what I'm thinking, I'll probably get the door slammed in my face." He glanced at the heavy oak door. "And I don't deal real well with pain."

She thought again of his knees and shivered in the cold wind, wondering why they were standing there in the doorway. She opened the door wider, inviting him inside. She found herself thinking more about the kiss in the study hall than their confrontation in the principal's office, which wasn't a good sign.

As he crossed the blue carpet, she noted there was nothing particularly different about the way he walked. He had that same sure-of-himself stride that he managed to transfer onto the ice with subtle grace.

He looked around the living room, his gaze stopping on the flagstone fireplace. "The last time I was here—it must have been eight years ago—Brian wanted to show off the fireplace he'd built." He studied the layers of stone, then glanced at her. "I heard the Dennetts are in California?"

She nodded. "Actually, they're with my parents. The four of them usually take some time in the spring to do some traveling. The Dennetts bought a new camper, so they decided to head west this year." She paused. "Spring is difficult for them, so getting away helps."

He ran his hand along the edge of the mantel. "I've thought a lot about Brian since the funeral, about how damn lousy it was he had to die. He had so much going for him, so much to live for." He picked up a figurine and put it back down. "What has the town done for him?"

Celina blinked. "What do you mean, done?"

"Done, as in a memorial or naming something after him. A park or a playground. He was a hero,

Celina. He died for his country. There should be some recognition of him somewhere. I haven't seen even a plaque."

Touched by his caring, she hated to disappoint him, but she shook her head.

"Nothing?" His anger was genuine, and Celina was taken aback by its depth. She suddenly realized she'd thought of Slade as being a hometown hero, but she'd never thought of Brian in that way.

She said, "Brian was always just Brian. He did his job without any fanfare, and I doubt anyone thought about him being a hero."

"Amazing," he said in disbelief. "I always envied him. He was smart and dedicated." He hesitated a few moments, then in a neutral voice, he added, "And he was married to you."

She tightened her grip on the six-pack, not able to meet his eyes. Slade envied Brian? His words puzzled her, and she wondered if he knew how much Brian had envied Slade and how much his friendship meant. Wanting to know more, she said, "Brian was scared to talk to you when you called after we were married. He told me, 'Slade will hate me. You were his girl.' He was so relieved that you didn't. Hate him, I mean."

"I could never have hated Brian," he said finally. When he didn't add anything else, she realized his words confirmed what he really felt about her. Her feminine pride wanted him to be jealous or angry or at least a little resentful of Brian.

The rain started, thumping on the roof and crowding in on the long silence.

Slade began to stack the book reports. One table lamp was on where Celina had been working, and another light in the kitchen. After standing there for a full ten seconds and telling herself she didn't feel hurt and empty, she decided to find out exactly why he was here with tapes and beer. She put the six-pack on the coffee table.

"I don't recall inviting you," she said briskly.

"You didn't."

"Then what are you doing here?"

"I thought you were concerned about Jeremy."

"I hardly think a six-pack and videos have anything to do with Jeremy."

"How about if the videos are of Jeremy?" He picked up the six-pack, took it to the kitchen and returned with a handful of cookies. "I couldn't resist. Oatmeal-raisin is my favorite." He slid one of the tapes into the slot. "Nick gave me the tapes of this season's games. I wanted to watch some of the earlier ones, to see if Jeremy is the glue that holds the team together."

She scowled, planted both hands on her hips, and said, "Slade, what is this? Some attempt to convince me to let him play?"

"Did you bake these? They're great." He bit down on a second cookie.

"I bought them at the bakery. And you're not answering my question."

He looked at the last cookie as though it had betrayed him, and Celina felt a little thump of pleasure that he'd thought she'd baked them.

He picked up the remote and settled down on her couch, as if that was where he spent most of his spare time. His long legs were stretched out in front of him, his ankles crossed, his feet shod in old, expensive sneakers. He'd propped his feet on her coffee table smack down on top of the newspaper. He patted the space beside him. Celina ignored it and sat in a chair. She picked up one of the book reports.

Slade stopped the tape. He said nothing until she looked up at him. His eyes were a deep green. She was probably revealing her uncertainty, but for a fleeting moment she wanted to kiss him and to indulge herself in those sweet sensations he'd tapped into at the high school.

Slade kept looking at her. "When did you last see Jeremy play?"

She crossed her legs to try to kill the sudden warmth. "I went to the opening game."

"One game? One lousy game? Then that explains it."

"Explains what?"

"Why you don't see how Nick needs him."

In disgust, she tossed the report on the table. "What Nick needs isn't going to change my mind."

"Celina," he said in a low voice that sounded entirely too patient, as if he were indulging her. "Would you come over here?" She stared at him, and he stared back. "Just to watch the tapes with me." When she didn't move, he extended his hand. "Are you afraid I'm gonna come on to you?"

"I wasn't worried about that."

He didn't smile or let the comment pass. "Yes, you were. Your eyes tell me a lot when you're not on guard."

Still she hesitated, and then asked herself why. It wasn't as though he were a stranger, nor had she been cold and detached when he'd kissed her. And in truth he hadn't come swaggering in like some super jock and tried to come on to her. She got up and moved over to the couch.

"You must think I'm being silly." She arranged herself and then rearranged herself when she realized she was too close to him.

"Cautious," he muttered, then swore when she wiggled against him in an attempt to get comfortable but not be draped around him. Her usually firm cushions billowed and dipped until Slade finally clamped a hand on her thigh.

"Stay right there, dammit!"

"Stop yelling. This wasn't my idea."

"I am not yelling," he said in a precise tone.

"Yes, you are. I might as well be sitting on your lap."

Then in a move so quick that she didn't have a chance to make any protest, she found herself straddling him, their bodies meshed, their eyes meeting.

His combative. Hers confrontational.

"Now, you're sitting on my lap," he snapped.

Her knees pressed into the cushions on either side of his thighs. His chest rose and fell, his hands cupped her hips. Celina's hands were pressed into his shoulders. With only the slightest motion from her and a matching rhythm from him, they'd be perfectly positioned to...

He wasn't heavily aroused, and she turned her face away as the thought scurried through her mind.

"Look at me."

She wouldn't. "This is the second time, Slade. I mean we've been alone twice since you got home and both times..." She couldn't finish the obvious, but she lifted her lashes.

He moved his hands to her waist. "Both times we've been turned on."

Her throat felt dry, and to her horror she flushed.

"Sweetheart, you've been in Brentonville too long. Turned on is tame, compared to what I could have said." He shifted her back just slightly. "Now, are we gonna to watch Jeremy burn the ice or are we gonna kiss each other?"

Her eyes widened, and a battle raged quickly between what she wanted to do and what she should do.

"You waited too long to answer," he murmured as his mouth glided down onto hers. His tongue swept deep; his hands held her solid against him. Perhaps his fingers making no attempt to skim into intimate places gave her confidence or fed her recklessness. For whatever reason, she returned the kiss, indulging her mouth with the taste of him.

The kiss lasted long enough to make her senses spin, yet short enough to tell her he really had come to watch Jeremy burn the ice.

When he moved her back onto the couch to sit beside him, she stayed perfectly still with her hands in her lap and made herself stare at the television. She wasn't disappointed that he preferred videos of old hockey games to her. She wasn't. Dammit, she wasn't.

He pushed the play button. Celina stared at the opening face-off of the game and tried to ignore his proximity to her. Thigh to thigh. Hip to hip. If she leaned a little, she could rest her head on his shoulder.

About three quarters through the video, Jeremy came down the ice, his stick moving the puck toward the net. Slade stopped the tape in the freeze position with Jeremy poised to shoot. "Look at that."

Celina tried to see whatever it was that had generated the intensity in Slade's voice. The shot wasn't particularly unusual, not did Jeremy look as if he'd done anything differently from the previous five shots he'd made at the net. Slade had stopped the tape each of those times, too, but had studied the position without making a comment.

"What am I looking for?" she asked, scooting closer to him so that her cheek was almost touching his. His skin smelled clean, uncluttered of cologne or shaving lotion. She'd kicked her shoes off and tucked her knees under her, a position that brought her contentedly against him. The rain splattered down the windows. In the past half hour his arm had brushed her knee numerous times as he rewound the tape to watch a particular play.

"Not the shot, sweetheart. His face. Look at Jeremy's face."

She stared at the freeze-frame for something he obviously had no trouble seeing. "He looks...uh...I don't know. Maybe determined?"

Slade leaned back and put one arm around her to draw her into his line of vision. He laid his hands on either side of her face. Celina felt her stomach go into a free-fall.

"He's not looking at the puck. Look at his eyes. He's searching for or watching someone in the crowd."

"Oh." The significance of that was lost on her, and when he removed his hands to restart the tape, she tried to keep her attention on the plays that involved Jeremy. Though not an avid hockey fan since high school, even she had to admit watching Jeremy was like watching Slade. They were both fast and precise and exceptionally gifted when it came to handling a stick.

They finished the first tape. Slade went to the kitchen, got two of the beers and returned. "What kind of soup is that? It smells good." He stood beside the couch, popped the top on one and handed it to her.

"Vegetable beef." She took the can. As she sipped, she debated asking him to stay for dinner. Then she remembered this was the day he was supposed to play hockey with Jeremy. "Slade?"

He put his can down on the table. "Hmm?" He slid in the second tape, then sat beside her. This time his feet were on the floor and he leaned slightly forward, his legs apart and his forearms resting on his knees. She almost missed the slight wince he made.

"Weren't you and Jeremy going to meet this afternoon?"

"Yeah, but I changed it to Monday night."

"Because your knees are bothering you?"

"Only my left knee. His old man had to work. Jeremy wanted him there to watch."

"Eddie Hearn is—" She wanted to tell Slade what she thought of Jeremy's father without sounding as though she didn't like him. "He pushes Jeremy."

"Probably." Slade didn't elaborate on whether or not he approved, and she let the subject drop.

They watched the second tape and when Slade slid the third one in, Celina grabbed the remote and turned the VCR off. "No more. You've freeze-framed every shot he's made."

He didn't object, and settling back, he stared at the blank screen. "I'll bet he's watching his old man."

"Watching his father for what?"

"Approval. The 'I won't disappoint you' pressure."

"Jeremy did say his father would be upset."

"Hearn hasn't tried to see you?"

"Eddie Hearn doesn't keep appointments, never mind making them."

Scowling, Slade leaned back. "He sure has Nick's ear."

"Nick must be thrilled with his enthusiasm."

"Sometimes. A father on a kid's back about how to play can be a real pain if the coach says something else."

"Does Nick get a lot of that?"

"Yeah. The kid wants his old man to be proud. Then there's the coach, the fans and maybe a girl-friend." Slade paused, his eyes distant. "Pride in himself on the ice. Damning himself for missed plays and rethinking the plays to improve them."

A new realization of Slade's deep commitment to hockey rushed through her, giving her some insight into Jeremy. "You really know how the players think, don't you? That's how you are when you play. Not just skating and scoring goals for the fans and the team, but for your own self-approval."

He rubbed his palm around his left knee, an action Celina had noticed he now did frequently. Without thinking about it, she rested her hand over his. "What's wrong with your knee?"

"What's right with it?" he said, as if the joint had betrayed him. "Bone chips, swelling, pressure, torn ligaments. This one has bothered me off and on for the past two seasons."

"Then why did you play?"

He gave her a blank look as if the answer should be obvious. "Because hockey is what I do. Like teaching is what you do. Not playing..." He paused. "If I'd sat out games, word would have gotten around. Messed-up knees to a hockey player is like a deathwatch. Other teams will try to take you down at your weakest point."

Celina couldn't help her gasp of outrage. "So much for sportsmanship and fair play."

Slade shrugged. "And the time you spend off the ice is usually spent trying to get your injuries healed for the next game."

"Are you seeing a doctor?"

"Doc Pierce is the team doc. After the last game, when I wound up in the hospital, Doc called in the experts." He told her about the probing and the X rays. "I had more X rays done before I came home."

He reached into his pocket and pulled out a long envelope that had been folded in thirds. He handed it to Celina, and when she unfolded it, she saw not only the return address of a respected medical complex in Boston but that the letter hadn't been opened.

"Yeah, I got it a couple of days ago, but I couldn't bring myself to look." He rubbed his knee, his head down.

Celina brushed her fingers over his hair. "Maybe it's good news."

"You read it."

She ran her finger under the flap. "I don't see how you could have carried this around and not read it."

"An old habit. I try to avoid bad news as long as possible."

Celina scanned it. "They've used a lot of medical terminology that I don't understand, but, oh . . ."

Slade got to his feet, a groan escaping despite his attempt to quell it. He took a few seconds to allow his knee to adjust to his weight. Slowly he walked to the window. He stood with his legs slightly apart and his hands in his pockets, gearing himself for the words. "What does it say?"

Celina stood up, the letter in her hand. "I think you should read it."

He rubbed his hand across the back of his neck. "Just tell me what it says," he growled, and she chided herself for acting as if he were a child incapable of handling disappointment.

"It says that you can't play hockey any more."

His reaction confused her. She expected disbelief or anger, but what she saw was fear. No, she must be mistaken. Fear wouldn't be his reaction. Unless... unless it had to do with his comment about not dealing well with pain.

She saw him straighten, pulling himself in, almost defiantly. He neither swore nor asked her if she was sure she'd read the news correctly. Then she added, "The doctor does mention surgery."

"The hell with surgery. It won't be enough." He dragged both hands though his hair, and when he turned around Celina thought he looked older. "Look, I could use a drink. Do you have anything stronger than beer?"

"I have a bottle of bourbon." He started for the kitchen. "In the cupboard next to the refrigerator. Slade?"

He turned and glanced back at her. Celina felt a lump swell in her throat. He looked absolutely terrified. She made herself not ask why, and doubted he was aware his eyes revealed so much. "Would you fix one for me, too?"

She reread the letter, then returned it to the envelope. His career was over. No fanfare. No farewells. No engraved gold trophies to line up on his mantel.

Just a letter he was too terrified to read. And if he was afraid to read it, no doubt he'd guessed its contents the moment he'd received it. The words were a mere formality.

She looked at the videocassettes and wondered if they were only the excuse to come over, but why her? Why not Nick? Or some of his friends?

He returned and handed her the drink. In his other hand he held an empty glass and the bottle.

"How do you feel about me getting drunk?" he asked. If his mood hasn't been so solemn, she would have laughed. Slade asking a woman for permission to get drunk seemed ludicrous.

"Do you get drunk often?" she asked, thinking about the stories she'd heard about players in professional sports.

"Rarely." He looked at her. "One of the times was after we broke up."

Startled that he would compare their breakup with the end of his hockey career, she thought of a hundred questions. But she didn't ask any of them.

He tipped the bottle over the glass and poured. Toasting her, he said, "Here's to the demise of Slade Garner."

Celina refused to drink. "Don't be ridiculous. You have your whole life ahead of you."

"To do what?" He tossed back the drink and shuddered.

"What do you want to do?"

"Play hockey. That's what I do, Celina. That's the only thing I know how to do."

"Then learn how to do something else."

"Yeah, right. Like that's as simple as going from an English teacher to the head of the department. Over-the-hill hockey players aren't exactly a hot item."

"But it is simple. From player to coach. Of course. I don't know why you didn't think of that."

"My sweet, concerned Celina, I did think of that. So did my agent and so have a few others."

Pleased, she smiled at him. "But that's terrific! Then you'll still be in the game, doing what you love."

He didn't smile back. "What I love is playing, dammit!" He slammed his glass on the table and walked over to the window. Celina watched him, then put down her own drink.

Crossing to stand behind him, she laid her palm on his back. She felt a steady tremble almost as though he was desperately trying to keep from giving into the feelings that tore through him. Wanting only to comfort him, to hold him, she slipped her hands around his waist. The rain continued, and neither moved.

Finally she whispered, "Stay and have dinner with me."

He turned then and drew her close, as though drawing something from her. Strength? Encouragement? Or maybe just simple understanding. "Yeah. I'd like that."

Alone a few minutes later, Slade listened to the sounds coming from the kitchen. Dishes clattering, cupboard doors opening and closing, water running. He caught the delicious smell of soup.

Outside the streetlights had come on, their yellow beams making the pavement a shiny, wet black. The envelope was back in his pocket, feeling as ugly and unwanted against his thigh as the words in the letter felt when he'd heard them. He'd intended to ask Nick to read the letter, suspecting that the medical report wasn't going to be good news. For reasons he didn't want to think about, he wanted to hear it from Celina.

He hadn't been afraid she would question his not reading the letter, or by some fluke guess that his reading ability was lousy. He'd been at this deception too long for that to be a concern. What he wanted was exactly what she'd done—she'd put her arms around him and held him together.

Nick would have blustered and cursed and blamed everyone from the Canadian player who'd put him in the hospital to the doctors who should be able to work miracles. "Those doctors charge enough money, don't they?" Nick would have bellowed. "Seems to me at those prices they could fix one bad knee." Nick cared, but for this news he needed something different. He'd needed Celina.

Slade put his hands into his pockets, his fingers nudging the letter. What in hell was he going to do? Coaching scared him, not because of what he'd have to do with the players, but because of the pencil-and-paper stuff he'd have to do off the ice. Set up plays. Read scout reports on other teams and how their strategy could be turned from an advantage to a disadvantage. There was no way he could bluff through that for any length of time.

His agent's other suggestion was so far off the wall Slade had asked him how much he'd had to drink.

He let out a long breath. Now what? Celina's words in the principal's office came back to him. There was life after hockey. But my God, he thought, what kind of life?

Chapter Four

Despite the leather boots and two pairs of heavy wool socks, Celina's feet were cold. It was Monday night and the Brentonville hockey rink was crowded with Slade Garner fans. She curled her gloved hands into the pockets of her blue-and-ivory-colored down jacket, asking herself what possessed her to be here? She should be angry with him, not adding to his fan club.

Lauren stood beside her, looking like an ad for a winter carnival in the pink fur-lined coat with a matching hood.

"I hear Slade paid for the ice time," Lauren said.

"I heard that, too," Celina replied, watching Slade. He deftly stole the puck from one of the defensemen, then stopped the play to show him how he'd done it. She wasn't surprised that he had paid for the ice time. He could certainly afford it, and when it came to hockey she doubted frugality was even a consideration.

Funny how she could be so sure of some things and not others. Like why he walked out on her Saturday night without a word. He'd neither called her, nor made any attempt to see her. She, however, had seen him. Once on Sunday morning when she'd gone to the drugstore to get the newspaper, she had spotted him studying aspirin bottles. Then again this afternoon, when she saw him talking to Nick and Glen Harvey.

A half dozen times over the past couple of days, she'd picked up the phone to call him but hadn't. Let it go, she told herself. Even coming to the arena tonight had been against her better judgment, and yet she'd come.

The question as to why he had walked out nagged at her. Not just at odd moments, but when she should have been getting deficiencies ready to be passed out to the students. Had she done something? Said something? She didn't think so, and in truth she had thought the opposite.

She sighed. Why is it a woman always assumes it's something she did? she wondered grimly. But she couldn't deny that she'd been disappointed when she'd come into the living room and found he had left. Taking into account his reaction to his ended hockey career, she decided perhaps he simply wanted to be alone. She could relate to that feeling from her own need for privacy following Brian's death.

Yet Slade had deliberately sought her out. Curious and puzzling, she concluded, also realizing his action added a new element to her feelings about him.

Her response in the living room had been different than in the past. Less sexual, more tender. Less the teenager, more the adult. Or perhaps she'd seen a side of him that she could relate to. Defeat. It was how she'd felt after Brian's funeral. For Slade, life without hockey was no doubt like a marriage that ended abruptly and finally.

She'd dealt with the defeat by throwing herself into teaching. Watching Slade with the kids now, defeat seemed to be the least of his concerns.

His movements on the ice were honed to perfection. It was called agility skating, and it combined every skill a player needed. From stopping quickly to changing pace to the breakaway that Slade had mastered. He flashed by her wearing no helmet, his dark hair rumpled and sweaty, his expression as intent and determined as if he were in a crucial NHL game. He stickhandled the puck with mesmerizing finesse and moved it down the ice, bringing the crowd roaring to its feet. Jeremy, holding his own and not about to lose an opportunity to go one-on-one with Slade, tried to steal the black disk.

As her gaze followed them, her eyes stopped on Eddie Hearn. Quickly she glanced at Jeremy to see if he was more conscious of his father than what he was doing on the ice. She hadn't forgotten what Slade had said when they'd watched the videos. Pressure from Eddie, or Jeremy's need to make his father proud of him, accounted for at least part of the teenager's boredom with schoolwork. Observing Jeremy now, Celina noted that all his attention was on Slade and on getting the puck away from him.

For another forty minutes, Celina and the crowd were dazzled and impressed not only by Slade's talent but by his handling of the kids. Fifteen players were on the ice, and Slade gave them all special attention. He criticized, yet it was a criticism liberally sprinkled with praise.

"You know," Lauren commented, "he acts as though no one was here but him and the kids."

Celina felt a fierce pride in Slade that brought a tightness to her throat. "It's refreshing, isn't it?"

"Too bad he's already employed by the NHL," Lauren said dryly.

"He'd make a great coach for the kids, wouldn't he?" Celina said, thinking of Nick's retirement.

Lauren sighed. "Dream on. When Slade retires, he'll be able to write his own ticket. Endorsements, coaching in the NHL, all the perks and advantages. He'd be crazy to settle for coaching high-school kids."

Celina was too busy thinking about the Slade she'd seen since his return to reply. His attitude tonight wasn't "I'm the star. Watch me." His comment, at her house on Saturday, about a memorial for Brian had been, "Don't put me on a pedestal. Brian deserves that place."

Her thoughts were jarred back to the game when Jeremy—in a defensive move to steal the puck—tripped Slade.

Celina gasped, forgetting her now numb and frozen feet. His bad knee was her first thought. Her hands clutched the chain-link guardrail, and her eyes grew wide with concern when she saw the gray color in his face as he got to his feet.

When he congratulated Jeremy on a skillful poke check, he glanced up for a few seconds and caught the worried look on her face. They spoke a private language.

"Your knee. You've hurt your knee."

"I'm okay. You look cold."

"I'm freezing."

He grinned, deliberately giving her an almost intimate look that lightened her mood and made her glad she had come to watch him play.

Finally the game ended and Slade and the kids trooped into the locker rooms. Celina started to make her way through the crowd. She intended to wait for Slade, but only to find out about his knee, she told herself.

Lauren touched her arm. "A bunch of us are going out for drinks. Come with us."

Celina shivered. "No thanks. I'm going home and climb under my electric blanket."

Dismissing her idea, Lauren said, "You can have a hot buttered rum. We're going to try to tie up the final details for the reunion. You haven't forgotten the reunion, have you?" It wasn't a looking-for-information question but Lauren's way of telling her Slade had come home for the reunion, and she wanted to make sure Celina planned to attend.

"Now, how could I forget the reunion with you reminding me every ten minutes?"

"Because knowing you, you'll find some excuse to not attend."

"Whatever gave you an idea like that?"

"That comment you made a month ago about living a boring life."

"It's hard to get excited about thirty-two years in Brentonville," she said dryly.

"Slade's back. He's worth getting excited about."

Celina frowned, letting a slight edge of irritation into her voice. "Would you say something like that if Brian were alive? Or if Slade were married?" Then at Lauren's surprised stare, she added, "Of course, you wouldn't. It's only because we went together fifteen years ago. Do you know how many things have changed in the world in fifteen years? Don't you think it might be reasonable to assume we've changed too?''

"Well, sure, we all change, but . . ." She paused, a sudden worried look in her eyes. "Hey, are you upset because I've teased you about Slade?''

"Just tired of it, Lauren. We're not kids any more."

Lauren thought for a moment. The crowd around them slowly dispersed, obviously deciding Slade was not going to appear. Finally she nodded. "Yeah, you're right. None of us is a kid anymore. I guess that's why we have reunions. Russ is motioning to me. Friends?"

Celina smiled. "Of course. Have fun."

Lauren and Russ and four other couples left. Celina still hadn't seen any sign of Slade. Nick came out of the locker room, gave her a measured look that Celina knew said in effect—see what the team is missing without Jeremy?

The arena slowly emptied. The resurfacing machine, which resembled a tank with wheels, chugged out onto the ice. Edmond, the rink supervisor, turned off most of the lights. Still no Slade. Had she missed him? She doubted that. But the bigger question she asked herself, with a deepening scowl, was why she was still here? To simply see him? To ask him about his knee? If her concern was only about his physical condition, she could go home and call him on the phone. Or she could have asked Nick. Or?

Celina faced one simple fact. She wanted reassurance that his walking out on Saturday night hadn't had anything to do with her.

Edmond approached her. "Gotta lock up, Mrs. Dennett."

"Edmond, has Slade left yet?"

"Nope."

She waited for him to say more, but he didn't. She rolled her eyes, and started for the locker rooms. "Never mind, I'll find him."

Edmond came to life. "You can't go in there. That's off-limits."

She smiled to ease his sudden paleness at her suggestion. His eyes darted in the direction of the No Admittance sign as though she were part of an enemy invasion.

"I promise not to faint, and I won't touch a thing," she reassured him.

"I don't know. Nick doesn't like women pokin' around the locker rooms. He says it's one of the last sacred places where a kid can, well—" He broke off, not quite looking at her. "Of course you being head of the English department, I suppose that makes it okay."

She doubted one had anything to do with the other. "I'll keep this just between us, and I won't tell a soul what I see in there."

What she saw were a few lights that had been left on, rows of steel lockers and puddles of water on the floor. Hardly sacred, she decided as she turned a corner. The lasting odors of sweat, wet socks and hockey shirts mingled with the more pleasant smell of soap and hot water.

She rounded the first row of lockers, walking slowly and feeling her heart speed up with anticipation.

"Celina, I'm in the office."

She jumped when his voice cut through the silence. The office was ahead of her, and the lights poured out into the darkness making her feel as if she had been caught where she didn't belong.

She could see only his head and shoulders. Nick's desk sat just inside the door, positioned, she had no doubt, so Nick could watch for any illegal antics in the hall.

Slade half sat and half lay on a couch that was too short for his long body, a muscled body, enhanced by a forest of dark chest hair. He wore only a pair of white cotton briefs.

Celina halted beside the desk, wishing for an uncomfortable moment that she'd taken Edmond's advice. Trying to tell herself that she'd seen bathing suits on men that were skimpier than his briefs didn't seem to work. Slade, to her vast relief, seemed unconcerned, unembarrassed, and didn't give her some lascivious grin.

From the safety of the doorway, she said, "I'm sorry. I didn't know you weren't dressed." Then her mind caught up with what she was seeing. She was about to ask why he wasn't, but the question was answered when she saw his swollen knee.

He winced and managed to get himself up and into a sitting position.

"Why did Nick leave you like this?"

"I told him to go. He had a poker game lined up. There's nothing he can do. It passes. I just have to wait it out."

"Slade, that's insane. I can see the pain in your eyes. Let me call a doctor."

"No!" he said sharply, then softened his voice. "I'll be fine. Look, I know this is a little unorthodox, but as long as you're here, could you help me with my jeans?''

Celina felt a funny shimmer run through her and quickly dismissed it. His socks, sneakers, a blue-and-green rugby shirt and his jeans lay across Nick's chair. She glanced at the faded denim, thinking of how the material felt against her when he'd lifted her onto his lap.

Another look at Slade told her he was serious. There was no attempt to flirt and toy with her, as though the awkwardness of his position transcended any sexual implications.

She slipped off her shoulder bag, laid it on the desk and put her jacket there also. His jeans were soft and smooth from many washings and wearings. The blue color was deeper in some places and almost absent in others. As she picked them up, she felt the weight in the pockets. Wallet, keys and change, she surmised. The belt was black leather and the buckle a rubbed-dull gold color. The third hole was worn.

She held the jeans in one hand and tried not to think how she could do this and maintain a cool objectivity.

Slade moved slightly, winced and raked his fingers through still-damp hair. "After I took a shower, my knee really began to throb. I knew if I left here while the crowd was out there, I'd have to sign autographs and smile a lot. My knee couldn't deal with it."

"I can see that." On the news recently, Celina had heard some sports stars complaining about always being hounded by the press and the public. Slade's complaint, however, was legitimate.

He glanced up at her. "I'm glad you stuck around."

She quickly dismissed the thought of trying to convince him she'd stayed for any other reason but to see him. Her presence in the locker rooms left her with little defense. "I was worried about you," she said succinctly, making sure her gaze was either on his knee or his face.

"Thanks for the concern." He tried to move his leg, bending it in the process, and swore. Celina saw the sweat break out on his forehead. "If you could just get the jeans over my knees, then I think I can manage."

She reached for his socks, deciding to put those on first. She lifted one foot and worked the white sock on, stopping when he winced. He nodded for her to go ahead. She did, and then repeated the motion with the second sock.

"You need some ice on that knee. Why didn't you stop playing when you were hurt?" She glanced up and when her gaze skimmed across the white briefs she paused for a second, out of curiosity. She felt her cheeks flush.

"Because the game wasn't over."

"You make it sound official and crucial."

"It was. To me. And to Jeremy and the rest of the kids."

"The kids are important to you, aren't they?"

"How they play? Yes. They're good players, but they don't play to their potential. That's a cop-out for the team." He studied her for a moment as though he'd seen something new, and he didn't know if he liked it.

"Why are you looking at me like that?"

"Forget it. It was a dumb comparison. Besides, Nick would accuse me of sandbagging the team. Could you hand me my shirt?"

She did, letting her puzzlement go, deciding it would probably lead to an argument.

He pulled his shirt over his head. The collar was up and the placket unbuttoned. He pushed the sleeves up over his elbows. "You were worried about me, weren't you? I saw it in your eyes."

Without thinking Celina adjusted his collar and brushed back his hair. "Of course, I was worried. I didn't want to see you get hurt."

"Embarrassing for the former star of Brentonville to collapse on the ice and not be able to get up, huh?"

Shaking the jeans, she sat on her haunches in front of him. She slid the denim up one leg, trying to ignore his warm flesh and the crinkly feel of hair. His thighs were tight with muscle from all the years on the ice. "I was thinking more about the man who can't play hockey any more making a public announcement about it."

It was a perfect opening for him to say something about Saturday night, she realized as she worked one pant leg over his foot. Celina glanced at him, but he was concentrating on keeping the leg from bending.

"You had to remind me. Easy moving over the knee."

She inched up the denim, wanting to keep any sudden movement to a minimum. It was slow going, as she repeated the same careful process on his other leg. Now all she had to do was get the jeans up to his hips.

"Lift up a little," she said, her fingers gripping the material and at the same time feeling the tension in his body.

Bracing one hand on the back of the couch and digging the other fist into the cushion, he raised his hips.

Celina let her eyes close for a moment. His effort took her thoughts into sensual possibilities that had nothing to do with relieving the pressure on his knee.

"Easy, baby," he murmured, when she struggled for a moment to make sure the open zipper didn't catch on anything.

She stilled, a vague memory of the last time he'd said those words at the edge of her thoughts, but eluding her. More fragments than words. She couldn't quite snatch them back, they were too blurred by time.

Slade brushed his hand along her neck just above her sweater. Then as if he had sensed her reaction, he murmured, "Somewhere between then and now, we grew up, didn't we?"

Celina stood. She felt trickles of moisture run down between her breasts. Being adult certainly hadn't robbed her of her reaction to him. Maturity could make those feelings even more dangerous, more far-reaching. Her face felt feverish and her hands burned.

With a heavy groan, and his own forehead breaking out anew in sweat, he managed to get the jeans up and zipped. He left the belt dangling. He sat back, taking short, quick breaths, then pushed himself forward once again.

He said, "If you give me a hand, I think I can stand up."

"Let's do the sneakers or you'll have to sit back down."

"What would I do without you?"

"Go back to Nick's in only your socks?"

"Like I said, what would I do without you?"

Celina glanced up at him, her hand on his ankle, the second sneaker only partially on. He stared back at her, and she lowered her head to break the eye contact.

She finished, leaving the laces untied. "I bet you walked over here, didn't you?" she asked.

"It's only a couple of blocks. Don't make it sound like I walked from Boston."

"In other words, don't feel sorry for you," she added, coming to her feet, almost glad for the sudden edge in his tone.

"No, I mean don't mother me."

"Is that what you think I'm doing?"

"I think that's what you're telling yourself you're doing. That way, you can help me without feeling guilty about it."

She backed up. She was standing and he was sitting, but she still felt at a disadvantage. If she picked up her coat and walked out, she'd only confirm what he'd said. She didn't feel guilty, but she wondered if he did. "Is that why you walked out on me Saturday night? Was giving you homemade soup mothering you?"

His look was steady, his voice low. "I would have been lousy company."

"You could have simply said you didn't want to stay. I would have understood."

His eyes blazed with a deep and sudden anger. "How in hell could you have understood? I didn't. You think I preferred getting drunk to being with you? Yeah, I got drunk. It was a stupid drunk, because nothing had changed when I sobered up. If I'd stayed to eat, I knew I would have wanted something more from you than soup and sympathy."

She met his eyes, knowing she should pretend ignorance and hope the conversation would go in a different direction. She didn't. "Sex? Is that what you wanted?"

"After what happened at the high school and at your house, that shouldn't surprise you. But, and there is a big but in here, charity sex doesn't turn me on."

Celina clenched her hands into fists. "Presuming, of course, that I go to bed with men I feel sorry for. And presuming that I feel sorry for you." She glared at him. "If—and I say if—I had chosen to sleep with you, it would have been because I wanted you, not because I thought it would be a cure for your ended hockey career."

He regarded her for a long, tense moment, then folded his arms across his chest as though he were afraid he might reach out and touch her. "I should have stayed."

"You should have. We might have found out we had a lot of things to talk about." She pressed her lips together to keep herself from saying anything more. The conversation had already taken on dangerous implications. And then there was the stark truth. For all her objections to any relationship with Slade, she wondered how hard she would have resisted if he had stayed, if he had wanted to sleep with her. That's what it would have been to him—charity sex. Her body, however, didn't respond in the same way her logic did. She felt a definite arousal that answered the question of whether or not she would have resisted.

She slipped her hands into the pockets of her wool slacks. Keeping her words even and her voice briskly cool, she said. "Now that we've settled that, let's talk about here and now. Unless you want to sleep on Nick's office couch tonight, then it appears to me you need my help." She paused and added, "My charity motives or lack of, notwithstanding."

He grinned. "Never one to back off from the tough stuff, are you? Nick is finding that out with your refusal to let Jeremy play."

She grinned back at him. "Surprised?"

"Pleasantly so," he murmured.

"I suggest we deal with getting you to Nick's. I'll drive you. And at the risk of being accused of mothering you, I suggest after we get there, we ice that knee and I'll see about calling a doctor."

"No doctor. Ice and aspirin will do it. There's some aspirin in my jacket pocket. I could use a couple."

She dug into the pocket of his bomber jacket. The aspirin was the extra-strength kind.

"Was this what you were looking for when I saw you on Sunday?"

"Yeah. Ragazzo said it was good stuff. Gotta admit it was like old times seeing him doing prescriptions. I would have thought he'd be retired by now. I'll never forget the time..."

Celina gritted her teeth. She hadn't forgotten "the time," either. And she certainly didn't want to revive that memory. "What about your doctor? Surely he must have recommended something."

His eyes were filled with that Slade Garner charm that had the power to warm the coldest heart. "You were embarrassed."

She narrowed her eyes. "You should have warned me, then I wouldn't have gone in with you."

"Celina, everyone in town knew we were going together."

"I doubt Mr. Ragazzo did, but he certainly did after you bought the condoms."

"I bought five other things. He barely noticed."

"Uh-huh. Well, I noticed and I wanted to die. If my parents had found out we were having sex, they would have been horrified. Sweet little Celina McKinley jeopardizing her college scholarship by getting pregnant would have killed them."

"Which, sweetheart, is why we were very careful." He swallowed the aspirin dry and shuddered. "I hope these do the trick."

Celina blinked. Slade had already changed the subject, but her own words repeated and repeated in her mind. What if she had gotten pregnant? What would they have done? Would they have gotten married? Abortion? She shuddered. She couldn't have done that. Not with Slade's baby. But there was her scholarship. And Slade's contract with the Sabers.

Because of their futures, Slade had always insisted on protection. Slade had, not her. At the time, she'd only been grateful she didn't have to get a prescription for the Pill. Now, with his remark, she wondered if deep down, conceiving Slade's child . . .

A child who today would be a teenager, a boy playing hockey, maybe a young girl with a crush on Jeremy Hearn. She probably wouldn't have married Brian. She might not have gone to college. Would Slade have married her out of duty? Would they have ended up hating each other? She thought of something Brian had said to her once. The past always affects the future like the roots of a tree affect the branches.

Suddenly she was grateful that the past consisted only of fading memories and was not tangled with anger and resentment and hate.

"Celina? Hey, you okay?"

She swallowed. "I—oh it's nothing. Just watching you take aspirin dry." She swallowed again to relieve her own parched throat. "I can't believe you don't have any pain pills."

"I don't like taking pills."

"I don't like taking them, either, but you're in pain. Look, do you have the prescription? I'll take it over and have Mr. Ragazzo fill it." Slade didn't argue with her. He got on his jacket and Celina shrugged into hers. She slipped her arm through his and with Nick's desk for support, Slade got to his feet. He draped his arm around her neck. He then balanced himself using a broken hockey stick as a cane. Celina put one arm around his waist and juggled her shoulder bag with the other.

Slowly they made their way out to the rink area. Two lights had been left on giving the empty arena a ghostly glow. Slade stopped, taking a deep breath.

"I'm parked right near the door," she said, hoping he wouldn't collapse. She doubted she'd be able to get him back on his feet. She caught his contemplative look.

In a soft whisper, he said, "If you listen you can hear the music."

He'd been less muscular then. She'd been thinner. "Yes, and if you watch the center of the ice you can see us skating."

He tightened his arm around her neck, pulling her against him. "We were so young, Celina. Crazy, and in love, and filled with each other. Standing here now, it seems like a million years ago. I wouldn't change it, but . . ." His voice trailed off with an uncertainty she understood.

From their kisses, both knew the hot sexual attraction hadn't died. Celina realized how easily they could pick up where they'd left off and ignore how their lives had changed in the past fifteen years.

They walked slowly toward the exit door, almost as if they were leaving the past behind.

The exit door slammed behind them as he gripped her tighter. Outside in the parking lot, she realized it was at about this spot that she'd almost hit him that first day. Then they'd been polite but awkward. Tonight they'd been friends.

Slowly they made their way to her car. The small compact wasn't made for a man with long legs who couldn't bend one knee at all and could barely bend the other. After four attempts to get Slade in the car, she stood up and glared at the car as if it were responsible.

"I'm going to call the rescue squad," she said, looking at him half in and half out of the car.

"Let's try one more time. Look, if you can drive with me as close to you as I can get, I can stretch my legs out and leave the door open. Don't look at me like that."

"This should be quite a picture."

"Yeah, well, I don't think it'll win any awards for comfort, but then Nick only lives a couple blocks away. You got anything in the trunk to tie the door steady? Like a rope or heavy twine?"

She had a quilt to take to the Laundromat and a stack of magazines she intended to leave at one of the nursing homes. She recalled having used a piece of twine to tie the trunk closed last December when she had bought her Christmas tree. But after a thorough search she hadn't found the string. She came back around to the passenger side to find Slade trying to get his sneakers off.

"What are you doing?"

"You can use the laces."

After they got the laces out, tied them together and threaded them from the door frame to the seat-belt hooks, the laces broke.

"Hell," he muttered in disgust.

"It's no wonder," Celina said. "They're all frayed." She glanced down at her boots. They were useless, but...

Slade stared at her as she drew the zippers down on her boots. "If you're planning on doing a strip, forget it. I hardly ever enjoy them in cold parking lots."

"No foot fetish, huh?" She leaned against the car while she pulled off her boots. When she looked at him, she almost smiled. He actually appeared shocked. She was a little surprised herself at her quick comeback, but she liked his reaction.

Lifting one unbooted foot up she wiggled her toes. "I'm wearing two pairs of socks. Tied together they should work."

"And in the meantime you'll have frostbite. Put your boots back on." But she didn't. "Celina, this is nuts. Don't take your socks off. Damn."

She ignored him and tried to ignore her now-bare feet inside the boots. She quickly anchored the door so that he could prop his foot against it and keep his leg straight. After making a second check to make sure the knots would hold, she came around to the driver's side.

"The console in your back can't be very comfortable."

"Don't even think about taking your coat off," he growled.

"I have a quilt in the trunk."

"I'll live. Turn the dome light off. I feel like a slab of exposed meat."

Bracing herself on the headrest, she switched off the light. Then eyeing the amount of room Slade had taken up, she shrugged out of her coat. Before he could protest, she said, "I'm just giving us more room."

"You'll freeze, just like your feet."

She slipped into the seat, what there was of it. Slade tried not to lean too hard against her, and when that didn't work, he tried to straighten. With all the maneuvering, his head kept brushing her arm, and when she moved, her breast.

"Put your head in my lap."

"No."

"Slade, this is silly. You can't concentrate on keeping your leg straight, if you keep trying to avoid touching me."

Again his head bumped her breast. He swore and slid lower. She grinned down at him when he'd finally settled his head on her thigh.

"Shut up," he snarled.

"I wish I had a camera."

"Thank God, you don't."

Without consciously thinking about it, she brushed his hair back from his forehead. "Are we all comfy?"

"Terrific," he muttered. Then before she could lift her hand away, his fingers gripped her wrist. "Your pulse is racing."

She wiggled her fingers. "It's all due to the thrill of having Slade Garner captured and at my mercy. Why, there isn't a woman in Brentonville who wouldn't freeze her feet for the opportunity to hold such a body against her."

Ignoring the sarcasm, he brought her hand down onto his chest where his jacket was unzipped. "Open your fingers."

"Slade, I was just teasing you."

"Open your fingers."

She did. Slowly as if she held some secret. He pressed her hand flat over his heart. "Feel that? It's called excitement and anticipation, and you know something else? It doesn't have anything to do with the past. It has to do with right now." He reached over and turned the key. "Let's get out of here, before we both freeze to death."

Chapter Five

At Nick's house, they slowly made their way across the yard and up onto the front porch. Slade dug a key out of his pocket and unlocked the front door. His knee throbbed, although he told himself it felt no worse than it had the morning after the brawl with the Canadian player. Tonight, when Jeremy tripped him, Slade knew he would have made the exact same move in similar circumstances. If they'd been in an official game, tripping to prevent a goal outweighed the risk of a two-minute penalty. Besides, the trick was to do it without getting caught.

Jeremy's move had surprised him only in that he hadn't seen it coming. Flawless, Slade concluded with a scowl, as he flipped on the inside hall light. He tried to recall exactly how Jeremy had gotten him in the vulnerable position. Admittedly, his own awareness of Celina had distracted him a few times, but at that precise moment all his attention had been on keeping the puck away from Jeremy. Or so he thought.

Nick had been right. The kid was good. Damned good. Celina must have seen that. She certainly must have heard the crowd's enthusiasm whenever Jeremy got the puck. However, convincing her to let Jeremy play based only on Jeremy's skill with a hockey stick wouldn't work. Celina would see it as sacrificing what, in her mind, was more important—passing grades in English.

While Slade agreed with her life-after-hockey theory, he knew it wouldn't go over big with Jeremy. Not at eighteen, when star status was a given and the future lay waiting like a treasure chest of possibilities.

Nor, he acknowledged honestly, was he blind to the larger truth—he saw himself in Jeremy. The star status, no. Slade knew that ego feeding never made him play better. Aware of that, he routinely avoided answering questions that had nothing to do with hockey, or being pressured into promotional stuff such as guest shots on TV and product endorsements. Another thought had crouched in his mind for years. The more public he was, the more chance some reporter or interviewer would find out he couldn't read. Self-protection, he knew, but his own personal ego protector, also. He might not like the applause, but he didn't relish taunts, laughter and rejection, either.

Yet the hockey side of Jeremy—his drive, his obsession with the game, his constant striving to get better—all that Slade understood. Hell, he was his own best example. At eighteen, given a choice between a contract with the NHL and Celina, Slade knew there had been no contest. If he'd chosen hockey over a girlfriend like Celina, then Jeremy choosing a passing grade in English over hockey was absurd.

Very cut-and-dried, he thought, until tonight when it occurred to him that if she buckled under Brentonville's pressure she'd be copping out. Maybe he wanted her to force Jeremy to do his schoolwork. Maybe he wished some teacher had forced him to learn to read. Or did he hold Celina to a higher standard because someplace inside him he knew she was right?

Terrific, he decided grimly. He'd come home for a reunion, to give Nick and the team some pointers, and wait on a doctor's report. And he ended up not only rethinking his priorities but damn close to getting too involved with Celina. And surprisingly his focus wasn't entirely in the one way he could have handled—sexually. No, he'd stepped into some vulnerable area that made his awareness deeper, more necessary than physical satisfaction.

Scowling, he tightened his arm around her, as they made their way across the cluttered living room to Nick's leather couch.

"Try not to think about it," she said softly.

He almost stumbled. Did she know? Could she read his mind the way she could read his body? "Think about what?" he asked warily.

"The pain in your knee."

"Oh, yeah. My knee."

"What did you think I meant?"

"Our disagreement over Jeremy playing," he said quickly.

She took a deep breath. "Jeremy isn't just a pawn in this. He does have some responsibility. He's the one who's drawing hockey plays in class, and he's the one not handing in his homework. And unless he gets a very high *B* in the test I gave today, he's going to get a deficiency.''

"I asked him tonight how he was doing in your class, and he said he aced the test.''

Celina gave him a speculative look.

"Hey, you might be surprised.''

"I hope I am, Slade. I really do.''

Slade got his jacket off and tossed it on a nearby chair before settling himself on the couch.

Celina watched him until he got his leg comfortable. "I'll be right back to get some ice for your knee. I'm going to get my socks.''

Slade knew he should say thanks and goodbye. With effort he could get the ice himself, and the aspirin had already made the pain tolerable. There was no reason for her to stay, except that he wanted her to. For a few moments he wanted to forget he could barely read, forget the years when she was sleeping with Brian, and he was either scoring on the ice or in some hotel room. And he wanted to forget that in a few weeks he would be gone.

"Forget the socks. I've got some you can wear.'' He nodded in the direction of a closed door. "In there. The gray duffel on the chair.'' He gingerly touched his knee.

She didn't move for a few seconds, and he wanted to smile. "You want me to get them for you?''

"No,'' she said too quickly, and then headed toward the kitchen. "I'll get the ice first.''

Slade sighed. "Get the socks, Celina. We won't need the ice, if you don't get your feet warmed up. You can just put them on my knee.''

She lifted her eyebrows before turning toward the bedroom. Slade put his head back and closed his eyes.

This change in his thoughts about Celina nagged at him. Where in hell was he going with her? And there was an additional complication. Not only had his reading managed to foul up his future, there was a very real possibility it could mess up Jeremy's. If Celina learned he couldn't read worth a damn, she would have a powerful argument for her side.

He sure didn't want his problem to cause ramifications that would domino down to every level. The hockey team. Nick. And Jeremy.

Slade shuddered. Would she use it, if she knew? Of course, she would—and frankly he wouldn't blame her. She was a stickler for education, and although he doubted she'd trot him out like a skewered piece of beef, she would seize the issue. If he needed any convincing of her determination to not walk away, all he had to do was think back over the past couple of hours.

She hadn't thought twice about helping him to get dressed, or bringing him back here to Nick's. Slade chuckled. Getting and wearing his socks, however, had been a debatable issue. He found himself intrigued by the contrast in her, or perhaps it was just his continual fascination with Celina.

Certainty about where his personal feelings were going scared him. Taking her to bed should be a matter of yes or no. Uncomplicated and uninvolved. Except this was Celina, and it was already complicated and involved.

She came out of the bedroom. Just watching her move toward him kicked in an instant desire and a fierce need to find out if she would be passionate and breathtaking as he suspected.

Celina unzipped her jacket and slipped it off. "You have enough socks in there to supply a men's store."

"I hate laundromats, so when I need clean ones I buy them. How are your feet?"

"Unthawing."

Her bulky red-and-white sweater topped a pair of black wool slacks. Gold hoops dangled at her ears, and her hair, windblown and almost loose from its pins, was too tempting.

Pulling the pins out, wrapping the whiskey brown silk around his fists and taking her mouth into his nudged at his thoughts. He concentrated on getting his leg repositioned.

She seemed a little uneasy, and he couldn't help but grin at her reaction to the living room. "Nick told me he doesn't mess with mops and dust. He has a theory about housework."

"Let me guess," Celina said. "He doesn't want to encroach on what he believes is woman's work."

"Exactly. Since he never married, he has a valid reason to avoid cleaning. It wasn't this bad when Brian and I were kids and we came over here for Mrs. Murphy's cookies. Nick's mom always tried to keep his magazine and sports collection confined in one corner."

"How does he find anything?"

"He has his own system. He tells me the reason he never got married is that a wife would throw out all his stuff."

Celina stepped over a stack of *Hockey Digest*s. "Probably because she'd like to think he cared more about her than about piles and piles of dusty magazines. I'll get the ice for your knee."

A few minutes later she was back with ice cubes in a plastic bag that was wrapped in a towel. Slade had swung around on the couch so that his leg was braced against the back cushions. Sitting down beside him, she centered the cold compress on his knee.

He unzipped one of her boots and slipped his hand into the opening. Working his fingers under the two pairs of socks, he thought of the red sling-back heels she'd worn, recalling he had told her how sexy they were. But wearing his socks turned him on. It seemed more intimate, rather than shallowly sexy. Such as if she wore his shirt to bed instead of some silk nightie.

"Your feet are still cold, aren't they?" he asked when she shivered.

"I thought they were getting warmer, but they're not."

"Why don't you take your boots off and let me warm them? Body heat is the best thing."

She didn't say no, but the shake of her head and the darkening color of her eyes said more than words. Slade removed his hand and raised the boot zipper. She stood up quickly as though suddenly released from an uncomfortable position. Slade shifted as a different pain unconnected to his knee pulled low in his gut.

Crossing the room, she studied the framed pictures of the Brentonville hockey teams from the first team in 1964 to the present.

"Third one from the bottom," he said indicating the team he and Brian had played on.

She studied it a moment, then said, "A lot of these guys thought they would play pro hockey, and yet you were the only one who did. That's quite an accomplishment." She glanced back at him. "And yet you're different. A maverick, according to one of the sports writers at the *Brentonville Daily News*."

"Nick mentioned it. That article appeared a few years ago. I'm surprised you remembered."

"I thought it was a good description of you. I still do. This whole playing down of the star status, the tight focus you have only on the game and, I suppose, dedication. You've never capitalized on your name or your ability."

"Are you asking me why? Or just making an observation."

"I wonder, because it's unusual. No full-court press. No staged arrival when you came home. Staying here with Nick, instead of at some luxury hotel."

He lifted one eyebrow. "A luxury hotel in Brentonville?"

"You know what I mean. The Brentonville Hotel is very nice."

"Yeah, if you don't mind thin walls and lukewarm showers. Anyway, I've had a bellyful of hotels, and if I'd stayed there I doubt you would have come back with me." She gave that a considering frown, but before she could disagree, he added, "I was referring to your credibility in the issue of school and sports, as well as the raised eyebrows over the moral issue. The core of Brentonville is still pretty straitlaced."

"I hate to admit this, but with the way Brentonville feels about you, I think the gossip would be more envious than judgmental."

"But the bottom line is there would be gossip, and you'll still be here after I leave." He deliberately made the terse comment. Self-preservation, he knew.

Was she pleased or disappointed? Her expression told him nothing.

He leaned forward and picked up an envelope from the coffee table. "I want you to take a look at something. Nick read it and gave me his opinion. I'd like to have yours."

Celina came over and sat down beside him. Slade resisted sliding his arms around her waist and pulling her back against him.

"This envelope wasn't in your pocket unopened," she said matter-of-factly as she removed the letter.

"Yeah, well, that one was bad news. This has some interesting possibilities."

The letterhead indicated a literary agency in New York. She quickly scanned it. Slade watched her face for reaction.

When she finally looked up at him, her eyes were wide. "You're going to write a book?"

"I'm going to talk. A collaborator is going to write the book." He watched her expression for a hint that she might think that was strange, but she didn't blink.

He relaxed. Izzy had told him that some people who did books worked with a collaborator. No one would suspect he couldn't read or write worth a damn. "Some publishers are interested, yes. Izzy Bozwell— he does all my contract work with the Sabers. Anyway, he and the head of this agency have known each other for years. Izzy first mentioned the book when we suspected my knee might finish me professionally. I thought he was crazy...." And in a lower voice, he added, "Maybe I still do."

"What did Nick say?" She moved a little closer, and Slade didn't scoot back to give her more room. He was full-length on the couch and she sat perched just beyond the cove of his thighs. He liked her this close to him, liked the strands of hair coming out of the pins to tumble onto her shoulders, liked looking at the straightness of her back, the slight flair of her hips. It occurred to him that kissing her at that moment would make his knee feel a lot better than the ice did. So why was he discussing a book, when he would rather kiss her?

"Nick's comment won't surprise you. He said he'd buy copies and give one to every player on the team."

"So Brentonville can turn out clones of Slade Garner?"

"God forbid, but probably." He was quiet a moment, considering if he should say what kind of book he wanted to write. So far the consensus of opinion was disbelief, as if he had presented an asinine idea like redesigning the hockey puck. Celina had turned so that she was facing him, and leaned a little closer.

Slade touched her waist, opening his hand and when she didn't pull away, he urged her back so that she nestled against him. "I know this sounds weird, but doing a book about how I hit a hockey puck doesn't turn me on. I know. I told you once hockey was the most important thing in my life—but the more I thought about that kind of book, the more trivial it seemed. As if I'm reduced to a robot with a stick, a puck and an ability to score goals. In other words, it could be done by any good hockey player."

"You want the book to be personally yours," she said, and he knew she understood.

"Something like that. I hesitate to say more meaningful, because as you pointed out, putting a puck in a net isn't exactly up there with history-making events."

"That's not what I said."

"But I'm saying it, and I guess with this knee ending my career I'm seeing what happens when your options are few. But as I've thought about the idea of a book, I've realized that a lot of people who write— I mean real writers—would give anything for an opportunity like this. Here it is handed to me not because I have any talent with words, but because I could hit a hockey puck. I've made a few awful blunders in my past, and I sure as hell would like to do it right this time. Izzy already said I was nuts. Nick agrees. Maybe it's a dumb idea, and maybe no one gives a damn that there's more to playing professional sports than a fat contract and being a star." He paused. Sometime during their conversation, she had settled her body full against him. His hand had moved to her hip, his fingers kneading. Softly, while he watched her eyes slide closed and then open, he said, "So since I'm asking for opinions, I thought I'd get yours."

She didn't answer, for a moment. Refolding the letter and sliding it into the envelope, she straightened enough to put it on the table. Slade, still holding her hip, urged her back before she got too far away.

Adjusting the ice pack on his knee, she said, "I think what you want to do, what you want to say is more important than the opinion of others. Neither way is wrong or right, only wrong or right by how you feel."

"So you're saying it would be a cop-out if I don't follow through on what I really want the book to be."

She gave him a slight smile. "Yes. As you said it would be a cop-out for the kids who play, but not up to their potential." She glanced at the envelope, as if it held some solution. "I suppose this answers your question of what you're going to do with your future."

"One book? Hardly. Besides, what these publishers have in mind and what I have in mind are two different approaches. I'll call the literary agent in the morning and run it by him. After he approaches the publishers with my idea, I might not even have to worry about one book."

She moved away and he let her go, sensing her restlessness. She walked over to the picture of him and Brian. "Do you know what Brian would say if he were here?"

"What?"

"He'd call you a maverick, like that sportswriter did. The easy way would be doing a 'how you hit a hockey puck' book. What you want to do is different because that's what you are—different. Lauren and I talked about that tonight, while we watched you and the kids. You acted as if you were just a guy who wanted to teach kids how to play the best hockey they could play."

"Why do I have the feeling I'm on the edge of sainthood? All those awful blunders I've made in my life qualify me more for the missed opportunity award."

"I think you're being too hard on yourself."

His short laugh wasn't humorous. "Have you ever got that backward. Too easy on myself is what messed things up."

She gave him a curious look. "Messed what up?"

Slade closed his eyes for a moment. How had he gotten started down this path? Not learning how to read had been the easiest route for him to follow, and now he was faced with the consequences, namely a very shaky future. To tell Celina, who was so focused on education . . . Damn.

He decided the other problem was simpler. "You. You were one of those missed opportunities."

She seemed to absorb that, and then tipping her head slightly, she said, "I'm almost scared to ask why."

Slade didn't like the truth. It reeked of jealousy, possessiveness and rejection. None of which he wanted or admired in himself, but they were there. Naked, raw and so real they taunted him. "Because you were mine, and you chose my best friend."

To his amazement, her immediate comeback wasn't anger, nor was it "And you chose hockey."

"I didn't choose Brian over you, Slade. You were gone. Part of the past, part of a teenage love affair. I did love Brian. I loved him very much."

At that moment he hated himself because he hated Brian. It clutched at him with a darkness and a fierceness that made him very glad he'd stayed away while they were married. For a long, tense moment they stared at each other.

She rubbed her palms down her slacks. "It wasn't on the rebound. You and I had gone our separate ways the end of that summer. . . . I knew there would never be anything more between us. Brian was here, and I didn't settle for him as if he were second best. I let myself fall in love with him. I didn't have any conflicts with him. I didn't have questions such as, is this sex or is this love? Will I ever be as important to him as hockey? I didn't have answers to those questions with you. With Brian I did."

She stared at the floor, as though trying to tie the present with the past.

Slade made himself ask the question, although he didn't want to hear the answer.

"Then you're saying we didn't love each other."

She nodded her head, agreeing so quickly he found himself angry. She straightened her shoulders. "We were kids. What do kids know about love? Besides, if I'd been really in love with you and you'd been in love with me, we would have stayed together. I certainly wouldn't have fallen in love and married Brian."

He had no answer for that, only regret.

Then suddenly changing the subject, she said, "I think I should go and get that prescription filled before the drugstore closes."

He didn't want her to leave, not yet. "Come over here and sit down. I'll warm your feet up."

She didn't move. "I don't think that's a good idea."

"It's the best one I've had all night. Come over here."

She scowled at him, still not moving. She glanced at her wristwatch. "It's getting late. Where's the prescription?"

He lifted his hip and pulled his wallet from his back pocket. Holding a folded piece of white paper, he said, "You're gonna have to come over here to get it."

She stalked over, grabbing her coat as she passed it. When she reached out for the prescription, he held it away.

"I don't want to play grab-and-feel with you, Slade. I could just walk out of here and leave you with your aspirin."

"Your choice."

Again, she reached for the paper. Again, he held it out of reach.

With a long-suffering sigh, she asked, "Why are you being difficult?"

"I want to kiss you before you leave."

For a scant second he was sure he caught agreement in her eyes. Now that what he'd wanted since he had seen her walk into the rink was out in the open, he intended to convince her she wanted exactly the same thing.

Her violet eyes darkened, and he knew if he didn't move instantly, she would walk out. Before she could back away, Slade pulled her down beside him, wrestled her coat away and tossed it on top of his. Then he shifted once more and cupped her hip to hold her down.

She scowled, glared darkly and absolutely refused to do anything with her hands except clamp them together in her lap. "I should have left you at the rink," she grumbled.

He pulled out one hairpin. "Then I would have had to kiss you there."

"You're so sure, aren't you?" She tried to push the falling curl back into place. It didn't cooperate.

He pulled out another pin, this time capturing a curl and winding it around his finger. He nudged his fingers into the sagging bun, drawing her closer, watching her lashes flutter. "Yeah, I'm damn sure we both want this...."

His mouth made no attempt to be polite, careful or seductive. He simply took. He pulled more pins heedless of where they fell. Gliding his fingers into her hair, he tangled them in the silk. He opened his mouth wider, coaxing her tongue around his, at the same time feeling intoxicated by the essence of her taste. She sagged down into him with the bonelessness of a marionette suddenly cut from its strings.

Slade ran his hand from her shoulder to her hip to her thigh fitting her against him, all the while keeping their mouths sealed. He was sure he could feel her breasts swell despite the sweater. He was hard. Instantly. To his own amazement, he held himself back from pressing into her. The kiss was blatant and wild, more than he expected, and handling her mouth was taking all his concentration.

He felt her go from surprise to denial to participation. She stretched into him, bending one leg, moving it higher, brushing him. Her attempt to be extra careful about not touching his knee just about blew away what little control he was hanging onto. He felt a racking pain that had everything to do with desire, and nothing to do with his swollen knee.

His hands moved under her sweater, roaming along her stomach, eager to touch her breasts, yet drawing out the anticipated feel of her as long as he could.

She moved, pulling her mouth away. He could tell from her eyes she knew exactly where her leg was and what was nestled so provocatively against it.

She lowered her lashes taking long deep breaths. "You must think . . ."

"Not think, know. I like you touching me. I like touching you. . . ."

She went very still, digging her fists into his chest. "This was more than a kiss."

"Better. Hot and truthful."

She tried to pull his hands out from under her sweater.

"Celina . . ."

"I really should get to the drugstore."

He wanted to shake her, to cut through her reservations. But forcing her would never work, even if he didn't recoil from the thought. She didn't move right away, and he wondered if she was waiting for him to argue with her.

He lay back on the couch, using all the resources of control he could muster to slide his hands away. Her hair was mussed, her eyes holding only traces of lingering passion, but he saw something else. Not a past desire, hot with its youthful vigor, but the mature passion of a woman.

Definitely more dangerous.

She stood and reached for her coat. Slipping it on, she ducked her head to center the zipper on its track. Sliding her hands into her pockets, she took a deep breath and lifted her head. She tried a shaky smile that failed.

"I'm glad about the book, Slade. I'm happy that you want it to be more than a shallow instruction manual on hockey."

"Thanks for your opinion. You helped me make up my mind."

Distance and coolness dropped between them like a sudden temperature change.

Her mouth, which he could still taste, was making it difficult for him to find any enthusiasm about books or opinions. Standing there, her shoulders back, her chin lifted, her eyes narrowed, he guessed this was the side of her Nick talked about. If it wasn't for the tinge of pink on her cheeks and slightly swollen lips, he might have wondered if he'd imagined the kiss.

He dug around the couch cushions and stuck his hand on one of her hairpins. "Damn," he muttered, finally locating the folded paper. Before he had a chance to hand it to her, she plucked it from his fingers. Then without another word, she walked from the living room and out of the house. Moments later he heard her drive away.

He slouched back down, cursing fluently. He rubbed his fist across his mouth. They'd been getting along fine. The rink, coming to Nick's, talking about the book. Only when they got into the area of touching and physical responses did all the red flags go up.

He slouched lower and folded his arms across his chest. He could still feel the imprint of her fists. Hell, he was reading too much into one kiss. Or was the real problem what he had gotten from the kiss? More deeply involved feelings that went way beyond sex?

At the Brentonville Pharmacy, after giving the prescription to Mr. Ragazzo, Celina walked over to the magazine counter. It was nearly closing time and the drugstore was empty of customers.

Although she picked up a magazine and flipped the pages, her mind was on what had happened with Slade. She felt as though she were playing hide-and-seek with her subconscious. No matter how many times she told herself that personal involvement with him would cause a multitude of problems, she seemed to end up in compromising situations.

She could have left Nick's right after she gave him the ice. Her feet would have survived without his socks.

Now, she wiggled her toes in the boots. The socks were a heavy knit cotton and they were too big, but they gave her feet a delicious warmth. A warmth that had spread through her with a pounding excitement when Slade had kissed her. But then why should that surprise her? The two other times they had kissed since he had come home hadn't exactly left her cold.

However, putting herself into situations that deliberately stimulated those feelings was either a subtle invitation or a case of stupidity.

She wasn't stupid. Helping Slade get dressed, driving him home, and even going in long enough to fix the ice compress were simply the actions of one friend helping another. Her mistake had been in lingering.

Okay, she would grudgingly admit she had stayed because she wanted to be with him. She had stayed because Slade excited her and he had honestly wanted her opinion on the book. Even though she had initially fought the kiss, in truth she had relished it. The man simply was unmatched when it came to making a kiss simulate all the passion of lovemaking.

She still had to take the prescription back. Or she could ask Mr. Ragazzo to deliver it, which definitely would show good sense. But then Slade would know she was afraid to come back, which, of course, was dumb. She was perfectly capable of doing a favor for him without getting involved. This time she would go in only long enough to hand him the medication and then leave.

"Celina, the prescription is ready." She started to pull out some bills, when he said, "I remember when you and Slade were just a couple kids going steady."

Celina held her smile, put the money on the counter and took the small sack. "Yes, well, that was a long time ago."

"You two were pretty serious. Always did wonder why you didn't marry him." He adjusted his glasses and glanced at the clock. "You better hurry along now. I gotta close."

Back in her car, she said aloud, "Because we both had different goals, Mr. Ragazzo. That's why we didn't get married." But she wondered if his comment about their being "pretty serious" was a gentleman's way of saying he had noticed that summer evening when Slade bought the condoms.

She rolled down the windows in the car and took deep breaths of the cold night air. Then she pulled her boots off and removed his socks. She put her own back on, ignoring their cold, damp stretched-out feel.

With her boots rezipped, she started the car. At the house she sighed with relief, when she saw that Nick was home.

The relief was immediately followed by a scowl as she climbed out of the car. Not one time had she thought about Nick. His walking in with her sprawled on the couch with Slade would have been embarrassing, but she could have survived that. However, the deeper implications made her shiver with a different kind of cold. Her credibility as the head of the English department fighting for education over sports would be destroyed. She would be reduced in Nick's eyes to just another female fan of Slade's.

She left his socks in the car. Zipping her coat to her neck, she tucked her hair into the collar. Damn you, Slade, you could have at least left me with two pins.

As she approached the house, she noticed that the front door was slightly ajar.

"You should have called me, kid," Nick said. "I would have come back and helped."

"And haul you out of that poker game? I made it okay."

Celina hesitated. She could just leave the medication inside the doorway and leave. Nick would find it when he locked up for the night.

"So where'd she go?" Nick asked.

"To the drugstore."

"About time you got that damn thing filled. Ouch! What is this? Hairpins? How did hairpins get in my—uh-oh. You two were doin' more than talkin', huh?"

She pushed the door open a little wider. She was eavesdropping, plain and simple, but her curiosity about how Slade would explain her hairpins couldn't be ignored.

His voice sounded hard and edgy. "Don't jump to any conclusions, Nick."

"Kid, the conclusions are stickin' in my butt. You did it. You charmed her and got her to change her mind. I knew it. Didn't I tell you that Garner charm is what attracts the ladies?"

Celina held her breath. She waited for him to deny it. She waited for him to say anything. And when he did, she wished she hadn't stayed to listen.

"I told you at the rink last week it wouldn't work."

She made herself count to ten. She told herself to walk in, hand him the pills and walk out. Or better yet, put them inside the house and leave. Then her dignity would be intact, and she would prove to herself she was completely unaffected by what she'd just overheard.

But she hurt, a deep hurt of betrayal. None of it meant anything to Slade. It was all a game. From their first meeting in the rink parking lot to all his talk about himself and Jeremy. From writing a meaningful sports book to his sweet words and hot kisses. Her temper, already seething at his deception or at her own

foolishness, she wasn't sure which, balked at a dignified retreat.

She stepped inside and closed the door, restraining
herself from slamming it. With precise steps, she
walked into the living room. Nick sat on one end of
the couch, a can of beer in his hand. Slade had his feet
propped up on the coffee table. The compress sat on
his knee. Her hairpins were lined up on his thigh as
though he were starting a collection.

He glanced up. "Hi. I see you got it."

"Hey, Celina, good of you to bring the kid home."

She put the small sack on the table, then lifted the
ice bag and opened it. "How's your knee?"

"Pretty good. Nick just added some more ice
cubes."

"How thoughtful."

Slade frowned. "You okay?"

She smiled—sweetly, she hoped—and then pulled
open his shirt placket. "Wonderful, Slade. I'm just
wonderful." She held the smile while she dumped the
ice inside his shirt.

Chapter Six

"You did what?" Lauren's gasp made her stop stirring her coffee.

"At the risk of sounding too gleeful, he deserved every ice cube." Celina speared a piece of turkey in her chef's salad.

It was a half-day session for the high school, and she and Lauren had gone out for a late lunch at Sally and Stan's. Known for its varied luncheon menu and efficient service, the popular restaurant did a brisk business during hockey season.

A smile worked across Lauren's mouth as she added another packet of sugar to her coffee. "I wish I could have seen it. Slade must have shot off that couch like a rocket."

The sconce lighting on the dark wall panels threw interesting reflections across the Roaring Twenties-styled dining room. The bar was to the left of their table. What possessed Celina to glance across the short distance, she wasn't sure. Laughter, a familiar voice, possibly only passing interest, but an alarming skitter ran down her spine the moment she saw him.

He was with another man whom she didn't recognize. He was older, heavyset, with a demeanor that made her think of loyalty toward Slade. They were seated on the bar chairs, so that Slade was in profile and somewhat shadowed, giving him a mysterious aura that she found maddeningly fascinating. She made herself focus on her disappointment and anger at him, not on his ability to beguile her senses. Separated by another table that was occupied by two chatty middle-aged women, Celina didn't think he'd seen her. Or had he noticed her and chosen to pretend he hadn't? Contemplating that possibility brought the unappealing sting of an obvious brush-off.

She watched him slowly drag one hand through his hair in a gesture of frustration. Celina clenched her own hand into a fist to block out what felt disturbingly like the sable thickness against her own fingers. She rubbed them on her napkin and took a bracing sip of tea.

"Well, did he?" Lauren asked.

She lifted her gaze and looked at Lauren over the rim of the mug. "What?"

"Slade. Did he leap off the couch?"

This is really not complicated, she told herself firmly, putting down her tea. Simply pretend you don't see him. Turn your back and keep your voice low.

"I haven't the slightest idea what he did," Celina said in a bored tone, giving her salad her undivided attention. She pushed aside the onions and reminded

herself to stop thinking about the way he'd touched
her or kissed her, or that he'd shared his hopes about
the book. That was what really bothered her. The
physical awareness was hard enough to handle, but
sharing hopes and ambitions and ideals as though they
had some bond of caring...

Spearing a cucumber with more force than the slice
deserved, she said, "I heard him swear as I left." She
had already told Lauren about taking Slade to Nick's.
She hadn't, however, told her about the kiss, or about
her own response to it.

The bartender brought Slade another beer and his
friend a second martini. She shifted in the chair, one
moment wishing she wasn't in the restaurant and the
next hoping he'd walk over, touch her on the shoulder and say, "I can explain everything."

Lauren continued, "And you're sure you didn't put
your own interpretation on what Nick said? Misun-
derstandings can cause more problems than arguments. Maybe he was just trying to feed Slade's ego.
Let's be real here. The women in town, and the girls,
too, would have jumped at the chance to help Slade
home. Nick, I'm sure, hasn't missed all the female
adulation. It's not out of the question that he would
assume the same thing about you."

Grasping for a plausible explanation, she considered that perhaps Slade, too, had put her into the fe-
male-fan category, but she didn't really believe that.
Even considering her anger at him, which made her
want to latch onto anything negative, she didn't honestly believe he had typecast her as such a shallow
person. Except for her going into the locker room, she
hadn't pursued Slade.

Stop trying to find an excuse for him, she told herself, reaching for the pepper. Now that she knew his real motive—to lay on the Garner charm—what he really thought about her, her principles, her concern for Jeremy, his comments about not copping out, the way he made her feel when he touched her, kissed her, shared his feelings and his fears about hockey and his future, didn't matter to her. It didn't. She scowled at the black spots on her salad. Damn! She hated pepper.

Sighing, she pushed aside the pieces in her salad that were now inedible. To Lauren she replied, "Nick is not happy with my decision about Jeremy, and frankly anything he tried to do so that I would allow Jeremy to play wouldn't surprise me. And if I had fled the house like some offended naïve girlfriend or fan, then I would have to admit to the possibility that I had misunderstood.

"However," she said, pausing to examine a piece of cheese, "it wasn't Nick's comment but Slade's answer, or I should say lack of answer, that annoyed me. If I hadn't heard him say, 'I told you it wouldn't work' I might buy misjudgment. But just the way he said it, it was evident that charming me was at the bottom of all this attention the last few days." Celina took a sip of tea, not quite looking at Lauren. Instead she turned her head slightly to the left.

He had leaned on the bar, his head lowered as he listened to something the man with him said. She'd always thought Slade in jeans could affect the direction of even the most bored woman's thoughts, but in uptown casual clothes, he was stunning. He was dressed in well-fitting gray slacks and a light blue ox-

ford shirt with two open buttons and the sleeves rolled
back so that they cuffed his forearms.

Celina watched him lift the glass of beer to his
mouth, remembering his hands in her hair, pulling out
pins, drawing her mouth deeper and deeper into his.

Hot and truthful, he'd called the kiss. Now just
thinking about his mouth brought on a wave of diz-
ziness. Hot, always. Every time she'd kissed Slade it
had been hot. Truthful, also, in that it stripped away
any pretense and simply dismissed whatever else was
happening between them. Perhaps his plan to charm
her, and her discovery of it, was a plus instead of a
minus. Wherever they'd been headed, what she had
heard at Nick's effectively stopped it.

She scowled at Lauren's speculative look.

"You see him, don't you?"

Lauren forked a piece of her ham-and-mushroom
quiche. "Actually I didn't until a moment ago when
you stared in that direction a little too long. Who's the
guy with him?"

"I don't know. They seem to be having a serious
conversation. Look, let's change the subject. You were
going to tell me what you're going to wear to the reunion."

"It's a blue-print silk with puffy sleeves." Lauren
leaned forward, eyeing the bar. "Do you think he's
seen you?"

So much for that topic, Celina thought ruefully.
"He hasn't looked this way. I'm pretending he isn't
there."

Lauren arched a finely shaped eyebrow. "Hmm, I
noticed, especially by the way you keep glancing over
at him."

Celina cleared her throat. "I'd really rather talk about the reunion. Or even more important, Harvey's pending decision about Jeremy playing."

Lauren's eyes gleamed. "But we're gonna talk about Slade's knack for charm."

Celina knew she had no one to blame but herself. By telling Lauren, she had declared her relationship and feelings about Slade an open topic for discussion. She wondered abruptly if this was her way of proving to herself that he meant nothing more to her than an old high-school crush. By slotting him in that rather silly category, she could tell herself that like any passing attraction, given a few days or weeks, she would recover.

She ignored the fact that before she married Brian, and since his death, no passing attraction she'd ever experienced had come close to the intensity she'd felt with Slade.

All right, she admitted, conceding the possibility that she might have been in love with him at seventeen. She'd given him not only her virginity but her heart and part of her soul.

However, that was a long time ago, and they had chosen to go their separate ways. His return had effectively churned up memories and a lot of restrained passion. But she knew that mature relationships weren't built on memories and passion. They were older, and agreement and common ground and simply liking each other as adults had to be the foundation. Yet, even acknowledging that they were laying some foundation, and disallowing the overheard conversation, she knew they were going nowhere.

He had said himself he wouldn't stay in Brentonville. His family was gone. Brian was gone. Though he enjoyed the kids, she was reasonably sure that a former hockey player with his stature wouldn't want to spend his future coaching teenage hockey players in a town that was small enough to fit in Providence about six times over.

And Celina knew that maturity, passion and hot, truthful kisses aside, Slade had not once given any indication he was going to hang around for her.

She turned her chair so she couldn't see him. However, that move didn't change the prickly awareness that seemed to have taken up permanent residence on the back of her neck.

"Are you still with me, Celina? You look as though you're deep in thought."

"Actually I was doing some reflecting." She smiled. Brightly, she hoped. "Yes, uh, we were discussing his charm...." She glanced back at him, remembering suddenly how, when they'd been sprawled on Nick's couch, her leg had intimately brushed him. Her thoughts arrowed into the possibility of doing that again—on a bed, naked, while they kissed and whispered and melted into each other. Damn the man! Damn her own response to him.

She took a breath, then spoke quickly. "Charming me wasn't a spur-of-the-moment decision, from the way he and Nick talked. It had been discussed and planned. Plus there's one other thing."

Lauren shook her head, and pierced the last piece of quiche. "I'd love to see your reaction if he walked over here and kissed the back of your neck," Lauren murmured. At Celina's frosty look, she raised her fork in a conciliatory gesture. "Okay. It's obvious you've analyzed this to death. What other thing?"

"I haven't heard one word from him. Say I did hear wrong, or I misunderstood, or I did jump to the wrong conclusion—"

Lauren interrupted, adding, "He would have called to clear it up. Or if he's seen you sitting here, he'd hustle over to at least eat a little crow."

"Exactly."

"Maybe he's waiting for you to approach him. You know, he thinks he deserves the apology?" At Celina's dismissing look, Lauren said, "Maybe he knows you're here. He might be waiting for you to make the first move. Male pride and ego. He probably thinks what you did to him is worse than what he did to you." Lauren paused thoughtfully. "From here, his knee doesn't look as if it's giving him any trouble. Do you think he faked that to get your sympathy?"

Celina, too, had noted he sat fairly comfortably on the bar stool, but she also noticed he once lowered his hand to rub his knee. "No. I read the letter he got from a medical complex in Boston, and I saw his knee after the game on Monday night." She took a sip of tea. "And speaking of Monday night—"

"Don't change the subject. Celina, look, in my opinion, I know you don't give two hoots for my opinion when it comes to Slade, and I haven't teased you about him, but I'm going to tell you what I really think."

"Lauren, really, I don't want to hear it."

"I know you don't, but bear with me. Please?"

Celina sighed, then nodded for her to continue.

"From that summer—and I know this sounds hokey—you and Slade were meant for each other. Brian was a nice guy and I know you loved him, but there are different kinds of love. You and Slade, I don't know, I suppose it's silly to call it destiny, but I think that's what it is. Sure, you need to get to know each other again, but I think you're aware that what you feel is deeper than just sex. And—'' Lauren paused giving her a direct stare ''—if he meant nothing to you, you wouldn't still be steamed.'' She nodded in the direction of the bar. ''You wouldn't be so aware of him. And you are. I can feel it coming off you in waves.''

Celina sat back in her chair, letting her fork clatter onto the plate. The frightening realization that she wanted to deny Lauren's words but couldn't suddenly overwhelmed her. Hadn't she spent almost every waking moment since she'd overheard Slade and Nick trying to deny that her feelings had already stretched beyond sexual attraction?

Her thoughts keyed into Lauren's words. Meant for each other. Different kinds of love. Destiny. Deeper than just sex. The next thing Lauren would be predicting was that Celina plus Slade equaled eternal bliss. And that, she knew, was ridiculous.

He'd been home for a week. He'd more than likely be leaving as soon as the hockey finals were over or Brentonville was eliminated. Eternal bliss, she thought with a rueful sadness, took not only time but trust. Trying to charm her to get what he wanted, and then not even making an attempt to apologize, didn't say much for the trust factor.

Stay angry, she told herself. That was the safest way. Her heart was already too vulnerable to him. She didn't want it broken. If she could pull this off with Lauren, who knew her so well, then possibly this would be the first step in making herself objective and dismissingly cool toward Slade.

Celina kept her voice precise and even. "Do you think I'm so desperate or maybe so enthralled with him that I'd overlook something so deceptive?" Celina frowned. "Damn right, I'm mad. Or call it plain old garden-variety disgust that he tried to use me, and I almost let him. It would have been one thing if he just wanted to get me into bed. Using devious means to seduce a woman is hardly a new approach, but this involves Jeremy. That makes his seduction technique calculating and unforgivable." She quickly lowered her head, her eyes stinging. She hurt, and what was worse was that she wanted desperately to find a reason to forgive him, a reason to believe he didn't mean what she heard.

Stabbing her fork into her salad, she said in a rough voice, "Please, let's change the subject."

"You're changing the subject, Slade." Izzy Bozwell relit his half-smoked cigar, puffed, and then with pinky extended, he picked up his martini.

Slade nursed his second beer. "I'm going to do this my way, Izzy. I've thought about it and discussed it with Nick and . . ." He started to say Celina but hesitated. On the subject of women, Izzy tended to deteriorate into crudeness. He wasn't about to subject even Celina's name to locker-room mentality.

Staring into the thin layer of foam on his beer, Slade said, "Never mind. I've made my decision."

Izzy sipped. "Not bad, but still too heavy on the vermouth."

"Cal barely passed the cork over the gin," Slade remarked, wondering how Izzy could drink martinis. They reminded him of bored women hustling drinks and attention in dark bars. Perhaps because he'd been the object of that attention more times than he wanted to remember, and he'd followed through by buying the drink for the woman and then picking up on the perks that followed.

"Hey, I'm not complaining here." Izzy ate the olive and continued their earlier discussion. "I'm tellin' you what I told you them. You were a helluva hockey player and that's what will sell the book, not your inner thoughts on why you played. Since I'm your friend, as well as your agent, I'm giving you the raw, unvarnished truth here, old buddy. You gotta think about money, since you're belly-up on the ice."

"Thanks for prettying it up with nice words," Slade said dryly.

"Nice words come from the ladies." Izzy puffed on the cigar, then rolled the ash in an ashtray. "Your little problem closes the door on some of the more obvious options. So—" he puffed again "—a book that profiles you as a star, the person who created a few shots that other players are still trying to master, and who made his own rules as well, is a godsend."

Slade didn't say anything. A star who made his own rules. Yeah, right. Rules to protect himself from being taunted and ridiculed, not because he was some hotshot who wanted to give the public lessons on how to create hockey moves. For about the tenth time since his return to Brentonville, he wished he could leap back to the fourth grade and start again.

He let Izzy talk, half listening, his mind again occupied with the table a few feet away. Seeing Celina, when he'd been consciously avoiding her since the incident at Nick's, only added to his problems.

He'd spotted her when they walked through the dining room to the bar. She'd been concentrating on

YOU COULD WIN THE
MILLION DOLLAR GRAND PRIZE
IN *Silhouette's* BIGGEST SWEEPSTAKES

THE BIG WIN

6 GAME TICKETS INSIDE!
ENTER TODAY!

IT'S FUN! IT'S FREE!
AND IT COULD MAKE YOU A
MILLIONAIRE

If you've ever played scratch-off lottery tickets, you should be familiar with how our games work. On each of the first four tickets (numbered 1 to 4 in the upper right) there are Pink Metallic Strips to scratch off.

Using a coin, do just that—carefully scratch the PINK strips to reveal how much each ticket could be worth if it is a winning ticket. Tickets could be worth from $10.00 to $1,000,000.00 in lifetime money.

Note, also, that each of your 4 tickets has a unique sweepstakes Lucky Number...and that's 4 chances for a **BIG WIN!**

FREE BOOKS!

At the same time you play your tickets for big prizes, you are invited to play ticket #5 for the chance to get one or more free book(s) from Silhouette. We give away free book(s) to introduce readers to the benefits of the Silhouette Reader Service™.

Accepting the free book(s) places you under no obligation to buy anything! You may keep your free book(s) and return the accompanying statement marked "cancel." But if we don't hear from you, then every month we'll deliver 6 of the newest Silhouette Special Edition® novels right to your door. You'll pay just the low members-only price of $2.74* each—a savings of 21¢ apiece off the cover price —plus 69¢ for delivery per shipment! You may cancel at any time.

Of course, you may play "THE BIG WIN" without requesting any free book(s) by scratching tickets #1 through #4 only. But remember, that first shipment of one or more books is FREE!

PLUS A FREE GIFT!

One more thing, when you accept the free book(s) on ticket #5 you are also entitled to play ticket #6, which is GOOD FOR A GREAT GIFT! Like the book(s), this gift is totally free and yours to keep as thanks for giving our Reader Service a try!

So scratch off the PINK STRIPS on all your BIG WIN tickets and send for everything today! You've got nothing to lose and everything to gain!

Here are your **BIG WIN** Game Tickets, worth from $10.00 to $1,000,000.00 each. Scratch off the PINK METALLIC STRIP on each of your Sweepstakes tickets to see what you could win and mail your entry right away. (SEE OFFICIAL RULES IN BACK OF BOOK FOR DETAILS!)

This could be your lucky day – GOOD LUCK!

TICKET 1
Scratch **PINK METALLIC STRIP** to reveal potential value of this ticket if it is a winning ticket. Return all game tickets intact.

LUCKY NUMBER

1Q 218575

TICKET 2
Scratch **PINK METALLIC STRIP** to reveal potential value of this ticket if it is a winning ticket. Return all game tickets intact.

LUCKY NUMBER

3A 215418

TICKET 3
Scratch **PINK METALLIC STRIP** to reveal potential value of this ticket if it is a winning ticket. Return all game tickets intact.

LUCKY NUMBER

9W 226769

TICKET 4
Scratch **PINK METALLIC STRIP** to reveal potential value of this ticket if it is a winning ticket. Return all game tickets intact.

LUCKY NUMBER

5V 217556

TICKET 5
We're giving away brand new books to selected individuals. Scratch **PINK METALLIC STRIP** for number of free books you will receive.

AUTHORIZATION CODE

130107-742

TICKET 6
We have an outstanding added gift for you if you are accepting our free books. Scratch **PINK METALLIC STRIP** to reveal gift.

AUTHORIZATION CODE

130107-742

YES! Enter my Lucky Numbers in THE BIG WIN Sweepstakes
and when winners are selected, tell me if I've won any prize. If PINK METALLIC STRIP is scratched off on ticket #5, I will also receive one or more FREE Silhouette Special Edition® novels along with the FREE GIFT on ticket #6, as explained on the opposite page.

(C-SIL-SE-03/91) 335 CIS ACG3

NAME _____

ADDRESS _____ APT. ____

CITY_____ PROVINCE _____ POSTAL CODE _____

Carefully detach and along dotted lines and mail today! Play all your BIG WIN tickets and get everything you're entitled to—including FREE BOOKS and a FREE GIFT!

Business Reply Mail

No Postage Stamp
Necessary if Mailed
in Canada

Postage will be paid by

SILHOUETTE READER SERVICE
THE BIG WIN SWEEPSTAKES

P.O. Box 609
Fort Erie, Ontario
L2A 9Z9

Canada Post
Postes Canada
125

a salad, and Slade didn't think she'd noticed him. He, however, noticed every detail.

The black-and-red plaid skirt, the fuzzy white sweater that outlined her breasts in a way that wasn't revealing or even particularly sexy. And yet he found himself more than mildly aware of the softness that he knew lay beneath. Her ability to draw him without any overt attempt to be seductive never failed to strike him as incredible.

He glanced to the side now, his gaze resting for a moment on her hair. She wasn't wearing it in the usual bun, but had caught it up in loose waves that sent him a message she doubted she intended to convey. Her hair beckoned his hand to muss and tangle it.

Slade silently swore and tightened his fingers around his glass of beer. He didn't need reminders of her. He wanted to dismiss her from his mind as easily as he had women in bars who sipped martinis and offered nights of intoxicating pleasure, with nothing heavy and involved. And yet every time he saw Celina, whether alone or in the most nonseductive situation... He scowled. That was part of the damn problem—finding any situation when he wasn't drawn to her. Unlike the women in his past, with Celina, heavy and involved were all he thought about. Those thoughts about permanence were the reason he'd deliberately made no attempt to get in touch with her.

The ice cubes, he had to admit after he'd cursed the air a hot blue, had been deserved. She'd obviously overheard the conversation with Nick. Slade knew if he was a decent guy, he would have called the next day, apologized and admitted that, indeed, what she heard was true. Nick had asked him to charm her. He had said it wouldn't work. But being a decent guy didn't have a helluva lot to do with anything.

The whole scene with Celina made him uneasy. Yeah, he wanted her. He wanted her bad. And what he had felt from her on Nick's couch convinced him she, too, wanted him. If good sex was his only intent, he would have been on the phone five minutes after his chest recovered from the ice cubes.

But he hadn't called. In fact, he'd gone out of his way to avoid her, deliberately letting her think the worst and making no attempt to explain. What he'd done was take the easy way out. Nothing new for you, right, Garner? You've been taking the easy way out for years.

The hellish thing was that involvement meant truth and trust and sharing, and doing that with Celina meant risking rejection. It all came back to the same thought he'd had outside the high school that first day.

The head of the Brentonville English department and a washed-up hockey player who could barely read would be a bad joke. And bad jokes, like wasting his time on a book about the fine art of hitting a hockey puck, he'd had up to his eyeballs.

The bartender took their lunch order. Slade ordered a roast-beef sandwich and fries. For his ulcer's sake, Izzy decided on an extra-large bowl of clam chowder, which he maintained balanced out the martinis.

Izzy tore open a package of crackers. "Daniel is willing to take a look at an outline of your idea, although he has his doubts."

"I gave him a verbal outline on the phone of what I wanted to do—explore some of the pressures from the parents the first time a kid puts on skates, the obsession with the game that can wreck your personal life, the too-easy money, the women, the drugs, the drink- ing and the loneliness. I thought I made that clear.''

"He wants it in writing. He has reservations, but he said he'd send it out to some publishers and see what their reactions are." He crumbled the crackers into his chowder.

"The last time I was in New York, they still had telephones," Slade said sarcastically.

"You gotta put it on paper, old buddy. Daniel ain't got time to call ten editors and hope they get it all straight. All they're gonna do, anyway, is tell him to send over an outline."

"Maybe we better just forget the whole thing."

"If it'd make you feel better, you'd have to do an outline for a fluff book, also."

"Well, then we gotta helluva problem, don't we?"

Izzy stirred the crackers in a folding motion. "Take it easy."

If ever there were times for regrets, Slade thought, this was one of them. Thinking back to the night when he'd almost registered for an adult reading class, he realized he should have swallowed his pride and done it. Izzy, no doubt, would have developed a second ul- cer, the press would have had a field day, and he would have taken some awful slurs from fans of opposing teams. But now it would have been behind him. He wouldn't be trying to figure out a way around it.

Slade took a bite out of his sandwich. Izzy speared him with one of his fierce you-gotta-do-this looks.

Slade chewed thoughtfully, swallowed and took a sip of beer. He turned only enough to see if she was still there.

Izzy tasted his chowder and blandly commented, "It doesn't have to be a long outline."

"I could say it doesn't have to be a book, either," Slade countered, sprinkling vinegar on his fries.

Izzy shuddered. "How can you ruin a good French fry with vinegar?"

He put the fry in his mouth. "A Rhode Island tradition. Wanna try one?"

Izzy took a long gulp of his drink. "I'll stick to catsup." Crumbling more crackers into his chowder, he said, "How do you know all the sports stars who write books can read?" At Slade's shrug, Izzy said, "I thought so. In fact, I know one who can't write his name, but his book is selling like gangbusters."

Slade sighed. He could write his name, though his scrawl was practically illegible. He took a long swallow of beer. "Don't bait me, Izzy. I'm not in the mood."

Izzy waved his spoon, apparently unconcerned about moods. "Slade, old buddy, listen carefully. You're thinking about this like I'm telling you that *you* gotta put the words on paper. That's what a writer does. You're not a writer, but not everyone who reads is a writer, either. That's why God created collaborators. A lot of celebrities who have great things to say but don't know diddly about putting it together in a book use collaborators. Biographies, kiss-and-tell books, how-to books, books on beating the drug scene or drying out from booze..."

"The collaborator for the book isn't the problem. The outline is."

"Then let him do the outline."

"I can't leave Brentonville now. Nick would blow his cork. Besides, I'd like to sit down with this guy and talk out the idea and where I can go with it. When I talked with Daniel, he said the collaborator is finishing up another project on a tight deadline, so coming here is out of the question." Slade paused. "Look, Izzy, maybe the whole idea is too complicated, and dumb, as well. For the time being I'm in pretty good shape for money."

"Pretty good shape is peanuts. What about ten years from now? The book would not only bring a fat advance, but royalties, a paperback deal. Maybe even a movie. You could do TV shows, appear at benefits. Hell, it would be a gold mine."

"Wait a minute. I can't even get an outline together, and you've already turned this into a circus. You know how I hate that stuff."

"Feelers, old buddy, just feelers. Relax, nothing is written in stone yet. I just wanted to find out what kind of reaction we'd have. Which brings us back to this offbeat idea of yours. Since money is the bottom line—"

"Money isn't the bottom line, dammit!"

As was Izzy's standard practice when he wanted his way, he simply took another tack. "You want kids to buy your book, don't you? Hell, no kid wants to read all that introspective stuff. And don't just toss off the money angle, not if you're planning to set up the scholarship in your friend's name."

The scholarship in Brian's name had been on his mind since the day at Celina's when he'd realized Brentonville had done nothing to honor Brian. He'd already started the ball rolling with Nick and the principal.

Taking a bite of his sandwich, Slade chewed slowly. "I got enough money to set up the scholarship right now."

"But this will give you more. Instead of just one kid, the fund could give scholarships to two or three, maybe more if the book is a blockbuster."

"What is this? Emotional blackmail?"

"Reality. You're worrying too much about this reading thing. Look, think about the bucks you'll make. For yourself and for the scholarship. I'll give you a couple days."

He speared Izzy with a direct look that despite the agent's steam roller tactics made Slade's position very clear. "If I do this book, it will be my book, understand? And I'm telling you now it will *not*—I repeat—it will *not* be a book about hitting a hockey puck."

Izzy blotted his mouth with a napkin, his face flushed. "Okay. Okay. It's your book. You do what you want, but you still need an outline for Daniel."

Slade wondered if Nick could write an outline. Or? No way. Dammit, no!

They finished their lunch. Slade saw Celina and Lauren get up from their table and walk over to speak to two other women. He decided to order a second cup of coffee.

"I thought you were ready," Izzy said.

Slade latched on to the most logical excuse. "I gotta go to the rink and help Nick. Beer on my breath isn't a good idea."

"Two beers, and you didn't finish the second one. Don't you think you're overdoing the clean-living bit?"

He heard Celina laugh. The sound rolled down his spine like a good massage.

Izzy lit a new cigar, glancing around the restaurant. "Hey, who's the broad in the white sweater?"

Slade didn't turn around. He frowned at the reference to Celina as a broad, but Izzy called all women broads, and to make a big deal out of it would only call more attention to his reaction. Besides, Slade thought, if he could put her into the "broad" category, it might be easier to forget about her. In a low, and he hoped disinterested voice, he said, "She's head of the English department at the high school."

Izzy gave her a more studied look. "Yeah? Jeez, when I went to school they all wore long, dark, shapeless dresses, had thick ankles and smelled like starch. You know her?"

Slade thought of the fresh scent of her uncluttered by heavy perfumes, the taste of her mouth, her enthusiasm about the book and the subtle shape of the white sweater over her breasts. "I know her."

"She part of this reunion you're going to?"

"We went to high school together, yeah."

"How come you didn't say hello to her, or at least nod in her direction?"

Slade glanced at Izzy. Was he just asking casual but obnoxious questions, or did he sense something? Turning, Slade lifted the mug of coffee. Stay loose, he told himself. Get too defensive and Izzy will zero in like a goalie trying to stop a flying puck. "I know a lot of people in here that I didn't say hello to."

"None that looked like her." Izzy leaned back against the bar, poked his cigar into the corner of his mouth. "Small-town but not bad," he said with the kind of observing tone Slade didn't like. "Breasts not bouncy enough for my taste, but good hips. She's got great legs."

"I'm warning you, Izzy," Slade growled.

Izzy rolled the cigar to the other side of his mouth. "Uh-oh. Did I hit a live wire?"

"Get off it, huh?"

"You making it with her, or still working on it?"

"Dammit, shut up!"

Cal, the bartender, stopped polishing a glass and glanced in their direction.

Izzy held up his hands and lumbered out of the bar chair. "Okay, I'm shuttin' up. Jeez, first you're off the wall about the book and now some broad— okay, okay... you didn't hear me say broad." He dropped a handful of bills beside his empty bowl. "I think the air around here is too purifying for you. You're turning into some straight-arrow weirdo. Next thing, you'll be tellin' me you're gonna live here, find a wife and hatch a few kids."

Shaking his head at the preposterous idea, he moved away. "I'll find the men's room while you're finishing your coffee."

Slade said nothing. He should have kept his back to her, but he wanted to see if she'd heard anything. At least that was what he told himself in that second before he swung around.

She, too, had turned, and this time their eyes locked. For a long breath-stopping moment they only stared.

Celina felt her heart skitter and slide, giving up all hope of a normal balance of rhythm.

Slade was glad Izzy had gone. He knew his reaction to her would not have escaped the most inattentive glance. To his own surprise, his mind focused on her and not on the sexual arousal hammering down his gut.

Ah, Celina, I can deal with the sex. But not with this...

She pressed her lips together, her eyes wide.

I'm afraid, Slade. I'm afraid of what's happening....

Slowly he let his eyes drift closed. *Go away, baby. Go away....* Then even more slowly he opened them. She was still there. Had time somehow been suspended? Had the entire world stepped back to allow this moment to fracture the fragile misunderstanding he wanted desperately to hold on to?

He formed the words silently. *Why did you have to be here?*

She matched him. *Why did you?*

"Hey, old buddy, you okay?"

Slade jumped, blinking. The noise around him resumed. Izzy was staring at him, as if he thought he'd been in a trance.

Slade lowered his head, shaking it. "Oh, God," he murmured in an almost prayerful plea, knowing and wanting to drift into ignorance. Yeah, he knew. Not from the twist in his gut, not from any anticipation of mind-blowing sex, but from the need clawing and dragging at his heart.

He wasn't going to be able to stay away from her.

Then, as if that revelation wasn't enough, Izzy added, "Hey, I got the solution. Your friend over there, she could do the outline. The head of the English department would be perfect. You wouldn't have to write anything. You could tell her what you told Daniel, flesh it out a little and she could do the writing. She could bang out an outline in a couple of days and we could get rolling on this deal." He gripped Slade's shoulder. "See? Aren't you glad we came in here and I spotted her?"

Chapter Seven

She could no longer deny that they would make love.

In her office at the high school, Celina stood staring out the single window. The hockey rink was to the left. Two teammates walked in that direction, hockey bags slung over their shoulders. About two miles to the west lay the Brentonville Country Club, where tonight their high-school reunion would be held.

She would see him, probably dance with him, and she had no doubt that after the raw truth in their eyes at Sally and Stan's a lot more would happen. Kisses that would lead to eager embraces...that would lead to more intimate touches...that would lead to love-making.

She felt almost coldly clairvoyant, knowing that no matter how she tried to deny it, it was going to happen.

What she didn't understand is how this had developed when she hadn't spoken to him since she dumped the ice cubes down his chest. How could she go from that—and she had no doubt now, it was justified—to the realization that she was probably going to end up in bed with him? Her pride should be screaming in protest. All her female instincts should recoil at being the object of a planned seduction.

"Damn him," she muttered, at the "on" cue stirring in her body, and she tried to forget what Lauren had said about destiny.

Perhaps, when it came to Slade, plain old pride and outrage weren't enough. Her emotions were too tied into her heart. Yet her pride balked at allowing herself to be swept away in some flash of passion, to offer no resistance and simply give in to... destiny.

Returning to her desk, she firmly brought her thoughts back to what should be foremost on her mind—that Eddie Hearn was obviously not coming to discuss Jeremy's deficiency in English. The aced test, that Jeremy had bragged to Slade about, barely managed to reach a *D* minus.

"Uh, Mrs. Dennett?"

Celina glanced up at the man who had halted in her office doorway, and for a few seconds she didn't recognize him. Then she smelled the faint odor of cigar smoke. He looked different than he had at Sally and Stan's. Here, under the bright overhead lighting, he reminded her of an old-time political handler who had spent too much of his life in smoke-filled back rooms trying to keep his candidate in line.

"Yes, I'm Mrs. Dennett."

"The name is Izzy Bozwell. I wonder if I could snatch a few minutes of your time?"

Celina recalled Slade had mentioned that Izzy did his contract work with the Sabers. He'd also been opposed to Slade's idea for his book. She felt an automatic defense of Slade slip into place, and told herself Slade hardly needed her to defend him.

She invited Izzy in, watching his discomposure with some amusement.

He crossed the room, a definite reluctance in his stride. Celina wasn't an expert at body language, but she saw that he moved with the cautiousness of a man who probably thought teachers still cracked knuckles with a ruler to maintain discipline. She doubted he encountered many situations where he wasn't the one to cause the discomposure.

Celina indicated a chair near her desk, and he gingerly sat down. "I'm not interrupting anything, am I?"

She straightened some papers and set them aside. "My appointment apparently forgot or has been delayed." Then to herself, she decided 'ignored' was a better explanation. Not surprising. Eddie Hearn kept appointments as well as Jeremy turned in homework, which was rarely.

Folding her hands, she met his eyes. They were a watery gray. "How can I help you?"

He began by telling her who he was and why he was in town. Celina nodded politely, waiting for the reason he had sought her out.

Deciding apparently that he could talk to her, he visibly relaxed by sitting back in the chair and making a steeple with his fingers. "Slade gets real uptight and ornery about people asking him questions or butting into his business." He shook his head slowly, as though Slade's attitude was a source of sleepless nights

and endless disagreements. "I like clients who con-
form, Mrs. Dennett. Clients who do as they're told
and let me do my job. Slade isn't like a lot of guys who
play professional sports. He hates the limelight, and
he wants to know what's going on off the ice. Guess
that's one of the reasons he wants to do a different
kind of book. Frankly I don't agree, but Slade already told me what I could do with my opinion."

Celina lowered her head, her smile coming easily,
her own feeling in agreement with Slade. His stubbornness about the book was probably what the conversation at the bar was all about. She admired him
when he first told her about his determination to address the multiple layers of playing hockey beyond
how to hit a hockey puck, and she still did. More so
because he was sticking to his idea and not allowing
himself to be pressured. "From what Slade said about
his proposal, I think it could be a very good book."

Bozwell eyed her closely. "Would you read it? I
mean you being a teacher and all, you probably read
a lot of literature and heavy stuff."

"Teachers do descend from the lofty academic
cloud on occasion," she said dryly. "Actually, I'm in
the middle of a historical romance." She watched his
eyebrows lift and then relax as though he was pleased
she wasn't too cerebral and didn't try to pretend she
was. "As far as the book Slade wants to do, yes, I
certainly would read it."

Izzy leaned forward. Obviously her enthusiasm
about Slade's idea was what he wanted to hear. "The
collaborator, who will do the writing and structuring
of the book, is tied up with another project. Slade's
agent in New York wants to get something together to
show some publishers."

While Bozwell talked, Celina's thoughts raced down the path of forgiving Slade for not calling her. She recognized that Slade may have been preoccupied with getting his idea nailed down with his New York agent. Hadn't he told her at Nick's that he intended to call the agent and talk about the approach he wanted to take with the book?

She was about to admit to herself that she had misjudged his silence, when Izzy said, "Would you be willing to help him do an outline? You being a teacher and all, I told Slade you could bang one off in no time."

Any thought of forgiveness came to an abrupt halt. "Slade knows you're here? Why didn't he come and ask me himself?"

"You know Slade when it comes to hockey," he said with an indulgent grin.

She frowned, finding nothing at all to smile about. Oh, yes, she knew Slade when it came to hockey. Was there ever a time when the man and the sport were separate? Not that she knew of.

Izzy assumed the role of a man in charge, a man doing what his client paid him for. "He's got these hockey play-offs on his mind. I'm trying to save him some time."

She glanced at her watch, her scowl deepening. "It's taken you less than five minutes, Mr. Bozwell. I would hardly call that intruding into his time with the team."

Izzy shrugged. "Look, I'll give it to you straight. Slade can be damn stubborn at times. And he gets screwball ideas like this one." He rolled his eyes. "All the players I represent thank me for the big contracts and spend the money. He does that, too, but he thinks."

"Well, of course, he thinks, Mr. Bozwell," she snapped, finding herself on Slade's side despite her fury. "Just because he plays hockey, doesn't mean he has a puck for a brain."

"Slade thinks too much, and one of these days all that thinking is gonna..."

"Is going to what?"

The composure slipped, and his skin turned slightly pasty. "Nothing. Just that he does too much thinking." He dragged his hands down his face and stood up. "I got to catch a plane in a couple hours. Tell him I came to you about the outline, if you want. He won't like it, but I'll be in Chicago so I won't have to listen to the music. You'd be doing Slade a big favor, if you agree to do it."

It occurred to her that she certainly didn't owe Slade even a tiny favor, after what she'd heard at Nick's. That, however, wasn't any of Izzy Bozwell's business. "I'll give it some thought, Mr. Bozwell."

Celina sat for a few minutes after Izzy had gone. In truth, she'd like to do the outline. But going to Slade and saying she would do it, without him even asking, wasn't what she intended to do. Naturally he would assume she had simply overlooked what she had heard at Nick's. Or worse, he might think she had forgiven him.

Why should she make this easy? If he wanted her to help him, he could damn well come and ask her himself.

She stood up, an idea coming to her. She'd been confused by his silence, and by his going out of his way not to offer any explanation. Perhaps it was time to stop steaming about it, and turn the tables. Instead of being angry with him, she could let him know she wasn't the least bit affected by what she'd heard. How would Slade like it if she gave him the cool treatment? She told herself this had nothing to do with her hurt pride. Or the deeper, fragmented thought she kept trying to ignore.

Dammit. She didn't want to fall in love with a man who had no such reciprocal ideas.

She had to track down Jeremy's father about his missed appointment with her. No doubt Eddie Hearn would be at the rink.

And so would Slade.

Later that afternoon, Celina stepped inside the cold arena as Slade was on his way out.

"Hi," he said, his fingers coming to a dead stop in the process of zipping up his leather jacket.

She made herself not think about how denim and leather and deep green eyes all combined to make her pulse race and her body react. She deliberately looked beyond him to Nick, who was out on the ice with the team. A few spectators were scattered around watching.

"Hi," she replied, hoping she sounded distant but cordial. She searched for Eddie Hearn.

He didn't continue walking but asked, "Were you looking for me?" Had there been a hopeful inflection in his voice?

"Uh, actually no," she said breezily as she glanced at him fully, her smile more polite than friendly. Silently she prayed he couldn't hear her pounding heart. "I'm looking for Eddie Hearn." Then she saw him at the far end of the rink. She tried to step around Slade. "Excuse me."

He reacted with a scowl. "What do you want Hearn for?"

"His son is failing my English class," she said, knowing he needed no reminder. She gave him her authoritative teacher look, which should have made him say, "Yes, ma'am" and step aside. Slade did neither.

He nodded in the direction of the exit. "You should be talking to him at the high school, not here."

"Mr. Hearn doesn't seem very inclined to see me there." She started to walk around him when he unzipped and shrugged out of his jacket. His eyes were a deep, deep green, and she told herself the color didn't fascinate her. "I thought you were leaving."

"I'll wait until you're finished."

She'd left her briefcase in her car, but she'd tucked Jeremy's deficiency notice into her coat pocket. Now, she curled her fingers around it. She shoved her other hand into the other pocket, telling herself it was because her fingers were cold. Touching his cheek would be entirely inappropriate.

"Really, Slade, that's hardly necessary," she said, making herself give him her full attention.

She wondered how such a range of emotions could fill his eyes. Annoyance, some anger, a little pain...fear? As though he wanted more from her than he could give back. No, she had to have misread fear. Desire was very evident, though. It seemed to run deep but with a tight rein. In one instant of clarity, she knew she wanted to feel the reins released.

Then the range of emotions was gone, replaced by a very clear and furious frown. "I'll wait while you talk to him, Celina."

"I don't need a bodyguard or a chaperon."

"I didn't say you did." He sighed, then took a deep breath as though pondering what to say next. Finally he lowered his voice to an almost intimate whisper. "Look, I know you're angry about what you heard at Nick's."

She knew he expected her to lash out at him. For a giddy moment, she wondered what he would do if she kissed him. She wanted to. She wanted to be the aggressor and catch him off guard, partly because he would be stunned, but mostly because assertiveness would give her the upper hand.

Kissing him here was not a smart idea, however, now that he'd finally brought up the subject of Nick's.

She tipped her head thoughtfully. "Actually, I did have a question."

"I know. I should have—" He broke off, a more than hopeful look in his eyes at her calmness. "You did? What's the question?"

"My hairpins."

For two seconds he simply looked at her. "What?"

She didn't have to be a mind reader to discern his confused and puzzled thoughts. Clearing her throat, she went on relentlessly. "Yes, hairpins. You know, the ones you took out of my hair?" She reached up, pulled out one and showed it to him. "Do you still have them?"

"Your hairpins." He growled the words, his face tight, as though the absurdity of her question blew away any chance of his explaining what he'd said at Nick's.

"Yes," she replied, determined to carry this through.

Slade glared at her. "We're standing here after what happened at Sally and Stan's and after what you overheard at Nick's—'' he took a step closer, his breathing rough, his eyes hard ''—and the only question you have is about a bunch of damned hairpins?''

No! she felt herself suddenly wanting to cry out. I have ten million other questions, and all the answers scare me. She blinked once, refusing to look away. In an even voice, she replied, ''I was just asking, Slade. There's no need to get testy.''

His hands gripped her shoulders, his eyes hot and sparking with green fire. ''Testy! Testy! For three days I've been hoping you didn't hate me, and now I find out the only thing you care about is a bunch of hairpins.''

He'd been hoping she didn't hate him? Then why hadn't he called? Why hadn't he come over to her table at Sally and Stan's? Why hadn't he come to ask about the outline? She felt as though she'd missed something. Celina wanted to tell him she could never hate him, that on the contrary, she was too close to falling in love with him.

With a steady hand, she raised her finger to her mouth. ''Shh, keep your voice down. Really, Slade. This is a public place.''

''I don't give two hoots in hell if it's Times Square on New Year's Eve,'' he shot back in a whisper, seething.

She tapped a finger on her lower lip thoughtfully. ''Hmm, I've never been there. I've seen the crowds on TV—''

He shook her a little. ''What in hell is wrong with you?''

Some distant voice said to stop here. Don't go any further, but her response slipped by the barrier, too quickly, too bluntly and too late. ''Will you stop swearing? You're beginning to sound like someone with a very limited vocabulary."

Abruptly he let her go. Celina blinked, still feeling the imprint of his fingers through her coat. He shrugged back into his jacket and stepped away from her as though she'd become a stranger he'd accidentally bumped.

"Hey, Eddie," he shouted over her head. "Jeremy's teacher wants to talk to you." Glancing down at her, he snarled in a rough voice, "I'll return your hairpins." Then he turned around and walked out of the rink.

Jeremy's deficiency slip lay in her hand. Yet, she couldn't take her eyes off the exit. She'd wanted to see him, she'd wanted to confront him, but somewhere between her original plan to get him to ask her to do the outline and Slade's terse comment, "I'll return your hairpins," she'd stumbled. Or rather her heart had stumbled, and instead of feeling gleeful she felt like crying.

She was late. A half hour late.

Slade had been at the reunion for exactly one hour and it already felt longer than the fifteen years it took for the event to arrive.

Hairpins. Until a few hours ago at the rink, he hadn't spoken to her once since she'd stalked out of Nick's, and all she had cared about was hairpins.

He scowled into his second whiskey on the rocks. The bar at the Brentonville Country Club was crowded, but he had managed to get a stool so he could watch the door. He knew his abrupt departure from the rink had confused her, but she'd had no idea how the words *very limited vocabulary* had torn through him. After his realization at the restaurant that he wouldn't be able to stay away from her, he needed all the mental reinforcement he could get.

Her comment had been an effective reminder, he thought grimly, of exactly why he didn't want to get involved with her; why he had not called or made an effort to see her; why letting her hate him for the wrong reason hurt less than if she rejected him for the truth. He wished his body would latch onto the same message.

He glanced at his watch.

She was probably looking for new hairpins, he decided as he took a swallow of whiskey.

So much for worrying about hurting her. So much for his attempt to keep them uninvolved. Dammit. Any other woman would have been furious. Celina should have given him a scathing look and told him to go to hell. Or brush him off. Or even been coldly polite.

"Slade?"

He didn't turn or glance up. "No, Lauren, I haven't seen her."

Lauren lifted both brows. "By the glower on your face you don't look as if you want to."

"Sorry, this has been a bad day."

Lauren studied the entrance, as if Celina would materialize. "I don't understand why she isn't here. I talked to her a little while ago and she didn't say she would be late."

Slade made himself not ask any questions. He sipped his drink.

Lauren said musingly, "Maybe you ought to go over to her house and see if she's okay."

Slade lowered his head and shook it wearily. "Lauren, quit trying to matchmake, okay? This isn't high-school stuff. Celina's a grown woman. Maybe she didn't want to come. Maybe she decided reunions are dumb and filled with faded memories, old songs and broken relationships."

Lauren sat down on a bar stool that had been vacated. Slade groaned, tossed down the remainder of his drink and stood.

All around were laughter, clinking ice cubes, the stuffy smell of cigarette smoke, perfume and school stories. Someone down the bar was talking about Brian Dennett. And that brought up Celina's name from someone else.

Suddenly Slade wished he was anywhere else. The rink. Back with the Sabers. Or in a hotel room with some faceless woman who only made him think about sex. To his annoyance, the woman on his mind wasn't faceless, it was Celina. He wasn't in a sterile hotel room but in her bed. And sex wasn't the only thing he wanted.

If you were smart, Garner, you'd pack your stuff and leave town. That way you won't do anything stupid. You won't put yourself in a vulnerable position.

He reached for his wallet.

"Wait a minute," Lauren said, grabbing his arm.

He put a bill under his glass and said, "Lauren, I know you mean well, but I don't want to talk about Celina."

"And she doesn't want to talk about you," she said releasing his arm. "You know, you two are trying entirely too hard to pretend there's nothing going on. In Sally and Stan's the tension was as thick as smoke."

"I didn't notice," he said dispassionately.

"Yeah, right. Just as she didn't notice you."

He paused for a moment. "Only long enough to send the daggers into my back."

"And well-deserved."

Slade plowed his fingers through his hair while expelling a long breath. "She told you, didn't she?"

Lauren lifted her hand to signal the bartender. "Hmm, while she destroyed her salad with pepper."

Slade frowned. Pepper on her salad? Celina hated pepper. She never put it on anything.

While Lauren's attention was on whether to have a wine spritzer or a screwdriver, Slade went back over that crazy conversation at the rink. Had that whole exchange about the hairpins been phony? Had she been as angry about what she heard at Nick's as the ice cubes down his shirt had indicated? She sure wouldn't have peppered a salad over missing hairpins.

Lauren settled on the spritzer. She grinned at Slade. "Russ is drinking martinis, so I'll probably have to drive home."

"What did she say about hairpins?" he asked once more glancing in the direction of the entrance. He'd bet a bundle she wasn't coming.

Lauren frowned. "Hairpins? Why nothing that I can think of. Should she have?"

Slade loosened his tie and started to leave.

"Where are you going?"

"To return some hairpins."

A half hour later, Celina heard her doorbell ring. She turned off her compact-disc player and went to see who it was. Her heart skipped a beat at the same moment she managed to scowl when she opened the door.

His tie was off, his shirt collar open. The jacket, hooked by his finger, hung over his shoulder. His stance was lazy and at the same time too assured. The shirt he wore was a soft mint color that made his green eyes darker; their intent, however, when they met hers was not soft. He regarded her not with a slow perusal, but with a possessive determination.

"Jeans and a sweatshirt are gonna look out of place at the club," he said as easily as if he were her date who had come too early to pick her up.

The jeans were old, slightly baggy. Her shapeless sweatshirt was a high-school leftover that advertised a popular rock group she had gone to see at the Providence Civic Center. Her hair wasn't down, but it wasn't stylishly up, either. She couldn't even call it carefully mussed. She had twisted and hastily pinned it in loose coils after her shower. She wore no make-up, no earrings and no perfume.

"I decided not to go," she said coolly. The decision had been made because she wasn't in the mood for reminiscing about the past, and she wanted to avoid seeing Slade. Especially after the realization in her office of where the night would take them.

Now she tried to match his self-assured look, although her stomach was jumping. She would not shut the door in his face. There was no reason to be rude. She would handle this with dignified objectivity, as she had the conversation about the hairpins. "What are you doing here?"

Slade thought she looked stunning. A little wild, very loose and deliciously unkempt. His body reacted, but not patiently.

Pushing the door open wider, he said, "Take a guess."

She didn't want to guess, nor did he wait to be invited in, but then she didn't try to keep him out.

She closed the door behind him, leaned against it and folded her arms. Her attire probably made her look as if she was about to clean the basement.

Inwardly she sighed with relief. If he had come ten minutes ago, he would have caught her in her robe. And catching her in her robe would have given him a blatant message—that she'd been deliberately late and was waiting for him to come looking for her, which wasn't true.

Plus, she decided, directing her thoughts into a less dangerous path, it was much easier to talk and diffuse any tension when she looked decidedly unseductive. Slade might be angry and determined, but she knew he wouldn't take any more than she allowed.

Don't give him any ground, she warned herself. She pushed a strand of hair off her cheek and deliberately misconstrued his comment. "You didn't have to return the hairpins tonight."

He tossed his jacket aside, moving toward her. "At the risk of a warrant being put out for my arrest—yes, I had to return them."

Why had she ever backed up against the door? She didn't feel deliciously trapped. She didn't! "That's a little extreme."

He stopped. He hadn't left her enough room to get by him without touching him. And she didn't want to even brush against his clothes. She made her arms stay loose, to stay down at her sides. Thank God the sweatshirt was roomy enough so that her lack of a bra didn't show.

Slade didn't touch her, but he didn't step back, either.

"Is it? As extreme as that asinine conversation we had at the rink?" he asked with a kind of sarcastic anger that she probably deserved. He reached into his pants pocket and pulled out her hairpins. "Do you want to count them?"

She rolled her eyes. "Oh, for heaven's sake." She scooped them out of his hand and dropped them on a nearby table, deciding to continue moving around him and into the living room. Ordering him out would be easier when he wasn't so close.

He pushed her back against the door.

"Slade!"

"I'm not finished."

He moved into her, his hands braced on the door, effectively caging her. She tried desperately to not look at him, to not acknowledge that the reins on his desire were now held with the barest of control, to not breathe in the slight smell of whiskey, to not give in to her body's need to touch him.

With as bland a tone as she could muster, she said, "Slade, if you think you can come here and seduce me because of that exchange at the restaurant..."

He never allowed his gaze to waver. "Seduce you. I think you've got it backward. You're the one seducing me. I have had one helluva time forgetting the way you felt at Nick's. The way your mouth tastes when you're turned on. The way your eyes turn to violet fire when you don't want to say no."

She closed her eyes for a moment, her lungs scrambling to find some air. And she had thought she could deny her willingness. She couldn't, no more than she could deny the sweep of sudden joy she felt at his words.

"You aren't exactly subtle," she finally said on a raspy breath.

"I want you to know exactly where I'm coming from and where we're going."

She met his gaze, knowing escape was unlikely, and she doubted she would choose it if it were offered.

"We're going to bed, aren't we?"

"You're damn right."

Celina struggled to get some control of the situation. How could they have gone from arguing about hairpins to admitting they would go to bed in the span of less than two minutes?

"We have things that need to be settled," she said desperately, unable to think of one thing except kissing him.

He slipped his hands around her neck. She could hear the steady tick of his watch. She reached up to grip his wrists, making one last feeble attempt to slow down the inevitable.

His thumbs brushed her jaw. "You want to know why I haven't called you, don't you?"

She tried to ignore the wonderful feel of him against her. "No."

"Why I haven't tried to explain what you heard?"

She let her eyes drift close. "No."

He whispered into the thumping silence, his thumbs strumming her lips. "Liar."

"Damn you," she murmured and wished she'd said nothing. His thumb touched her tongue, and as though drawn by some endless web, she coaxed it into her mouth for a second before he withdrew it.

She heard his intake of breath. In a husky voice, he murmured, "And what if I told you that right now, this moment, you don't care about anything but what we're about to do."

She wanted to tell him to stop talking, stop making her think and rationalize and face where they were going. "You think I deliberately didn't go to the reunion so you'd come looking for me, don't you?"

His thumbs were back on her jaw, tipping her face up as his mouth descended. "No, I don't think that. But I know you're damn glad I'm here and if I tried to leave you'd stop me."

Her eyes widened. "Of all the arrogant, insufferable, egotistical comments—"

But he captured her open mouth, not letting her finish, his kiss more powerful than any denial she could make. Fiery sensations burned through her with no mercy, and she had no desire to stop them. She opened her mouth under his, suddenly ravenous for the taste and feel of him. His hands slid to her hips, coaxing, then tipping her body into his.

She whimpered, sinking into the kiss while at the same time lifting her arms up and around his neck. His hands moved under her sweatshirt and closed over her breasts.

When he realized she wore no bra, his hands stopped as though he'd suddenly discovered the key to a hidden treasure.

He raised his head, his hands folded lightly over her breasts, his thumbs on her nipples, solid but not moving.

Their breaths swirled between them, rushed and impatient and unsteady. She was pressed against the door but not trapped. He was touching her but not pushing her. All her senses centered on his thumbs, so exquisite, so light against her nipples.

She brushed her mouth across his and whispered, "Don't go."

Chapter Eight

Their movements, from the front door to the bedroom, were awkward at best. Slade didn't want to let go of her. She couldn't get enough of his mouth.

He barely noticed the grace and feminine elegance of her bedroom—the brass-and-glass column-shaped bedside lamp that sprayed a triangle of light onto the ceiling, the soft blue-and-cream drapes or the delicate furnishings. He barely glanced into the wide floor-to-ceiling mirror that covered one wall and gave depth to the surroundings.

He did, however, notice the bed, and in a flash of cold reality, he saw her there with Brian. Sleeping only, he tried to tell himself, but acknowledging that a part of him wanted to deny that Celina and his best friend had been intimate.

She kissed him again, her arms tight around him with a touch of desperation, as if she sensed some change in him. Had they become that attuned to each other? Verbal honesty was one thing, but unspoken emotional glimpses rattled him.

"I want to please you...." she murmured, sliding her fingers under the collar of his shirt.

He cupped her bottom and lifted her into him. "Look at me." And when she raised feathery dark lashes, revealing violet eyes that were pools of honest desire, his heart swelled. "Ah, sweetheart, you couldn't not please me."

He eased her down onto the sleek blue-and-cream satin bedspread, allowing himself the pleasure of simply looking at her. Even with her mussed hair, lack of makeup and her baggy clothes, she turned him on with a speed that defied explanation. So much for sexy see-through teddies and seductive techniques, he thought, as a new shot of desire pumped low in his gut.

Her sweatshirt had risen up to expose a wide expanse of warm skin. He opened the button on her jeans and lowered the zipper. A pair of white satin lace panties banded her hips, provocatively shielding the softness he'd thought about in endless fantasies since he'd come home. With his finger, he traced the places where lace and warm skin met, then flattened his palm on the heart of the satin, feeling the nesting beauty beneath. He raised his eyes to meet hers. She tugged at her bottom lip, whispering his name, barely able to keep her hips still.

Feeling like a starving man at a sumptuous banquet, he wanted to devour her, yet savor every touch and taste and texture. His own body hummed with a passion that seared his control.

Seeing her sprawled there, looking innocent yet wild at the same time, made his senses twist. Being here with her, this close, this vulnerable, unlocked an emptiness inside him that transcended sensual appetite and satisfaction. With Celina he felt as if he'd discovered a raw, unexplored place that no woman had ever touched.

He traced the naked area between her jeans and her sweatshirt, and wondered fleetingly how she would look heavy with his child. He lifted his hand away as though the gesture would clear away the thought.

It had to be the feeling of being with a woman in a real honest-to-God feminine bedroom, and not some cold, sterile hotel room that made his mind fuzzy. And not just a woman, he reminded himself, as once again he brushed his fingers across her stomach. It was Celina, who just by her words ''Don't go'' made him long for stability and an ordinary life in Brentonville. Living in a house instead of out of a suitcase. Doing weekend chores instead of sleeping off too much drinking, or too much sex. Coaching the Brentonville high-school hockey team instead of worrying about his future. Making love to Celina every night instead of an eternity of nights without her. He closed his eyes for a moment, taking a deep breath. How could two words conjure up so many impossibilities?

''Slade?''

She hadn't moved, her arms flung up and relaxed, her hands open at either side of her head. Her violet eyes, the lashes fluttering once, twice, three times met his gaze with a mixture of uneasiness and confusion.

''Are you thinking about Brian? About him sleeping here with me?'' Her voice was husky and strangely soothing, as though she was trying to put him at ease, to let him know she understood his hesitation and acknowledged his reluctance.

He did wonder if he was looking for an excuse to stop things. Insane. No man in his right mind would say no now. She was here. She wanted him as much as he wanted her. Making love to her didn't have to be a mass of introspection, a tangle of complications.

He reached down, skimming his hands down her arms to grip her shoulders. Gently he lifted her forward so she sat on the edge of the bed facing him. Her legs nestled between his thighs. He tipped her chin up, felt the slightest of tremblings, and smoothed his thumb against her bottom lip.

Celina wet the tip of his thumb with her tongue as she slid her hands up the sides of his thighs. Despite a layer of clothing, her touch burned. Slade sucked in a long gulp of air. "I was thinking about how much I want you."

She wet her lips, swallowed and drew a shuddering breath, her hands still now. "No, you weren't," she whispered, her eyes begging him to be honest with her, to admit and face his feelings.

Again he brushed his thumbs across her damp lips. "A very perceptive lady."

Her fingers dug into his waist, as if she were holding him to her. "Are you sorry? Sorry you came over here? Sorry that we've come this far?"

He worked her fingers loose and brought her hands up so he could kiss her palms. He couldn't lie to her, not about this. "Some doubts, yes, but not sorry." Then he saw her guarded agreement. She too had doubts, and he found that pleased him enormously. He settled her hands on his chest. "And those are questions I should be asking you."

To his delight she didn't hesitate or reconsider. "I have doubts, yes, but I want you. I don't want to analyze where we're going tomorrow or next month or next year. I've been doing that since you came home. For tonight, I just want to be with you.'' Then, as though she had no intention of letting him change his mind, she tugged his shirt out of his pants.

Slade let her open the buttons, while he pulled the pins out of her hair. For tonight. That was all this would be. Just tonight. His fear that she would reject him if she knew he was only slightly literate could subside. Enjoy her. That was what he wanted. It was what she wanted.

With the last hairpin discarded, the loose waves spilled over his hands as he drew her closer. She shook her head, her hair tumbling back. She was a continual source of fascination to him. Prim and not quite sure of herself at times, and then there was this side of her—eager, wanting and a trace of wantonness in her expression. Yet her eyes made no pretense of playing seductive games.

"I'm glad we're here and not at the reunion.''

In her gaze he saw reflected his own desire. When her hands opened his belt, he sucked in his breath, deliberately misunderstanding her. "Doing this at the country club would raise some eyebrows.''

"Definitely.'' Light amusement skimmed her expression as she wiggled closer to him. "Are we talking too much? I mean, shouldn't we just be falling on top of each other?''

Slade grinned, wondering the same thing while a sharp awareness clung to the slow drawing out of these moments. The discovery of her, the unique quality of moving beyond the fulfillment of only their physical needs, intrigued him.

He stripped off his shirt, keeping his eyes on her. "I don't think there are any rules against talking."

She ran her hands up his chest to his shoulders, bringing herself to her feet. Then she knelt on the bed so their eyes were almost level. Slade steadied her hips, bringing their bodies into contact. He dipped slightly, adjusting his hardness into her softness. Both stilled, watching each other.

His eyes said, *"I want to be deep inside you."*

Her eyes answered, *"I want to hold you there forever."*

The unspoken words wound around them like silken strings. Their clothes added a friction to their contact that made him suddenly impatient to see her and let his body feast and draw nourishment from her.

She sucked in a deep breath, her words barely a whisper. "I...uh...never—" she gulped when Slade slipped his hands under her sweatshirt "—liked silent lovemaking... oh, Slade..."

His mouth covered hers, effectively stopping her conversation, but the kiss brought a shuddering moan. He angled his head, his tongue deep inside her, her mouth a well of hunger and texture and incredible sweetness. Nothing silent here, and he thought how he'd always preferred silence, sex and sleep. Yet here, his focus was entirely on her. What she wanted, yes. What pleased her, certainly. But beyond that raged his driving desire to know her. To simply be with her and know her.

When he drew her sweatshirt up and off, he felt awed. He went very still while he stared. Need pounded through him. Reverence left him shaking. Celina didn't shrink back or display any shyness, nor did she move except for the slight rise and fall of her chest as she breathed.

"Sweet God," he murmured, full of wonder at her breasts. Beautifully shaped and small, they swelled prettily as the pink buds pouted against the white softness. The firm flesh trembled just enough for him to know her shyness had returned.

"Let me look at you...." And he did. With his eyes he cherished, with his hands he touched, with his mouth he worshiped the fullness of each breast, the tightness of both nipples. Her breathing accelerated as she drew him down with her onto the bed.

"Don't stop. Please...."

"I couldn't..." With his hands holding her breasts he kissed her ribs. "Seeing you..." he glided his lips down her stomach "...being with you..." He smiled when she arched up as his mouth moved lower. "Ah, baby..."

Moving his hands, he slipped them under her bottom and lifted her hips. He kissed the lace, nuzzled the satin, and then pressed his mouth against her to allow his own heat to seep into her. Her hands pushed at her jeans, and he gripped her to hold her still.

"Not yet..." he whispered with a thick huskiness.

"I can't wait...oh, please..."

"Let me do this...shh... Let me..." He held her hands still until she quit wiggling, then once again lowered his head to kiss the damp silk panties. She moaned, tossing her head from side to side as her fingers tangled in his hair. He raised his head long enough to see her heat-flushed cheeks, her mouth parted enough to allow her tongue to wet her lips.

Their eyes met, and he saw her desire deepen with an intensity that made him slightly dizzy.

This time he tugged the band lower, his mouth following the descent. "Ah, Celina . . . yes . . ." he whispered when she whimpered. Then, "Sweet baby . . . yes . . ." She shuddered and just barely cried out. The pretty curls fanned like a sweet secret that couldn't wait to be discovered.

Celina cried his name, then a desperate, "Please, please . . ." when he kissed her deeply. The explosion rocked through her, nearly shattering Slade's own control. He didn't move. He now lay his cheek against her, feeling the tremors, basking in her satisfaction.

The room settled into a soft silence. Finally Slade rolled off her, impatient now, his own need roaring through his body. He swiftly tugged her jeans and panties down and off.

Seeing her fully naked stopped him. His own body, parched and taut with expectation, throbbed with a heavy thickness. Sucking in lungfuls of air, he grasped for the thin edge of control he needed until he was gloved in her softness.

She watched him, her breathing ragged, her voice hoarse. "That was incredible."

He stared at her mouth, his eyes lazy and hot. "I'm glad. I wanted it to be incredible for you."

She laid her hand against him, shyly and yet with an exquisite boldness. "I should have waited for you."

He pressed his fingers over hers, deepening her touch, his body immediately screaming for more. "Why? It will happen again."

"I've never . . ." She closed her eyes and he slipped his hand over the damp curls. She responded immediately.

"Tonight, for me, you will."

She couldn't speak for the sudden dryness of her tongue and the rawness of her throat. Yes, tonight, she would.

Watching his eyes deepen with arousal, she drew depths of satisfaction that she could have such an effect on him. Her thoughts then scrambled from satisfaction to searing pleasure when she saw him. Naked. Powerful. Gloriously beautiful.

The years of hockey had honed his body to taut leanness. She'd been aware of that the night in the locker room, but now she eagerly and slowly allowed her eyes the feast of coveting without shame, without embarrassment, with bold, unabashed desire. The muscled chest rich with swirls and coils of hair, the lean hips, the strong, hard thighs and his manhood...

He turned away for a moment, and she saw the flash of a foil packet. It occurred to her, for an instant, that he'd obviously planned this before he arrived, but at the same time she didn't care. When he came down beside her, and then pulled her beneath him, she knew why she didn't care.

Layers of fire fanned out into a burning fluid to rush and swell low in her womb. She pulled him to her as he braced himself and slid deep. Her legs came up around him with a naturalness that spoke of fifteen years spent together instead of fifteen years of abstinence.

"Why do you feel so good?" he murmured, the words sounding husky and thick with control. He made himself stay perfectly still wanting to absorb the velvet feel of her, needing to seal himself into her.

She moved her hands down his back, lifting her head to draw him into a kiss. "I want to feel so good to you that you can't get enough." She arched up against him, as his mouth came down in a fierce kiss. Slade groaned as he stepped up the rhythm, one part of him wanting to drag this out forever and the other part pounding for instant gratification.

Celina felt the release coming the second time. Wilder, hotter, tearing down her with a scorching sensuality that brought her hips high in an intoxicating effort to gather more and more.

Miraculously, Slade held himself back. He wanted to sink and smolder in her pleasure.

He lifted himself off her, but kept them intimately connected. Her head arched back, her mouth slightly open, the flush of gratification darkening her skin. Then her eyes opened. "Slade...please...I want you with me...."

Mutual release. No holding back. "Easy...shh, baby...I'm with you."

And for a shuddering moment he almost was. Maybe it was the violet fire in her eyes. The hauntingly virginal feel of her body enclosing him had nothing to do with the edge he teetered upon. But there in the bold truth of his soul, in a suspended second, some curtain lifted.

For a moment he felt drenching relief and then a crashing revelation when the realization closed over him.

He loved her.

Then as quickly at it came it was gone, and he couldn't hold back any longer. He squeezed his eyes closed, shuddering as she climaxed, then he gave himself up to the liquid fire of release that poured from him into her.

* * *

Hours later, barefoot, wearing just his suit pants, a glass of whiskey in his hand, Slade stood in front of the open drapes and stared out the window. It was after midnight. Her bedroom was dark except for the hazy light from a streetlamp.

They'd made love a second time, after which she had fallen asleep. He'd gotten up, gone to the bathroom and then into the kitchen to make himself a drink. He'd come back to the bedroom asking himself why he didn't get dressed, kiss her and leave.

Leaving was always less complicated than staying.

He knew that, but he was still here. For the past ten minutes he'd been trying to deny what was causing the deepening frown on his already worried face. With Celina everything seemed to be in constant overdrive. Raging hormones were for kids. At his age, his libido should be more mature.

He took a long swallow of whiskey, making himself not glance back at her, making himself ignore the ache of wanting to make love to her again. And then there was that other revelation.

He had to have imagined it. Or at the very least been too caught up in the exploding satisfaction of incredible lovemaking. It was the still, steady strength of it that gnawed at him. Dammit, no! He couldn't be in love with her.

Then a new thought came to him. Had he said it out loud? He put the glass down and raked both hands through his hair. No, he wouldn't have done that. He wasn't that far gone. Or was he? Not being able to remember was worse than knowing. If he had said *I love you,* then at least he could chalk the outburst up to the throes of passion that had gripped him, and dismiss it.

But not knowing...

He drained the glass, the whiskey doing nothing to dull or improve his mood.

"Slade?"

He grimaced at the husky way she spoke his name. "Yeah."

"Why are you clear over there?"

Swearing silently, he pulled the drapes closed and returned to the bed. He took off his pants and slipped in beside her. She scooted over, and as soon as he was settled she snuggled against him.

"Your feet are cold," she said with a shiver.

"That's a switch."

She pulled herself up, supporting herself on her arms. Her fingers touched his face, exploring. He took her wrist and pressed his mouth into her palm.

"We need to talk," he said, settling her back down against him.

"Sounds serious," she murmured, kissing his shoulder.

She was too relaxed, too content, indulgent almost. Had he said it out loud, and now she had some idea that they were on their way to love everlasting?

"About Jeremy," he said, before her mouth could get too intense.

She was about to kiss his ear. "Jeremy! I don't want to talk about Jeremy."

He didn't, either. He didn't want to talk at all. "When you hear what his old man told me, you will."

He glanced at her, hearing her sudden, uneven breathing, seeing her eyes widen as though she were trying to read between his words. Finally she said, "I talked to Eddie Hearn, remember? Apart from his excuse that he forgot his appointment with me, he was less irritating than usual. However, he said nothing I didn't know about Jeremy. Although I have to admit I did find his calm attitude a little unusual.''

''He had a good reason to be calm.'' Suddenly he wasn't sure he wanted to tell her this. In fact he wished he'd let her mouth continue its journey. He wanted her again, and he knew when she heard what he had to say, making love would be the last thing on her mind.

She sat up, the covers pooling around her hips, her breasts a soft white temptation in the darkness. The nipples winked at him, seducing him to taste, reminding him how tight and hot they felt on his tongue. When she touched her breast to push a strand of hair away, he almost lost it.

''What reason?''

What had they been talking—oh, yeah, Eddie Hearn. *Get with it, Garner. You made love to her twice. You shouldn't be hard and impatient.*

He sat up, trying to distract himself by bunching the pillow behind his back and keeping his hands to himself. Her hair was down, mussed, strands stuck to her cheek. She stared at him, waiting.

He cursed silently, then reached out and pulled her toward him, the need to taste and drink from her a sudden driving addiction. She struggled for a moment, but when he lifted her and settled her across his lap, she relaxed. She was warm, sweetly smelling of woman and lovemaking and the sharp renewal of desire.

''Are you trying to distract me?'' she asked, wiggling against him with a sudden intimacy.

''Yeah. And I can feel it working.'' He groaned. ''Easy...''

She pushed her hair back, shaking her head, then leaned forward, her mouth a breath away from his, and whispered, "What reason?"

"It could wait," he said, deliciously distracted, his interest in her throbbing hard and hot against her softness.

"So can what we're about to do," she said with a cool control that he wished he felt. She held too much power over him, especially when her bottom was planted on the most vulnerable part of his body.

After he told her the reason, they wouldn't be doing anything. He sighed, his hands cupping her hips to enjoy the wonderful weight of her for another few moments. "The word will be out by tomorrow. Hearn told me that Glen Harvey is going to overrule your decision and allow Jeremy to play."

Slade felt her body tighten like wire. Just as he expected. Damn. She stared at him for a full three seconds, then said, "How did he find out?"

"I don't know. All Hearn said was that it wasn't rumor or wishful thinking. More than likely that's why he was—how did you put it?—less irritating?"

"And that's why you wanted to stay at the rink while I talked to him? You thought he might tell me?"

"And take great pleasure in it. Celina, listen— hey, what are you doing?" She was reaching across him for the telephone.

Holding the phone, she punched out a series of numbers. "I'm going to find out why everyone in town knows except me."

"You're not calling Harvey? It's after midnight. Celina, for God's sake..." He lifted the phone from her hand and put it down. Taking her shoulders he made her look at him. That was a mistake. He could see the fury building like a coming storm.

"You didn't tell me," she said accusingly, pushing him away. "You knew at the rink. You knew when you came over here tonight, and all the time we were making love you knew."

"Dammit . . ."

"You seemed to have done a lot of things without telling me. Charming me into bed as you told Nick you could do, and now this. What else haven't you told me?"

Nothing much, he thought miserably. *Only that I think I love you. Only that I can barely read. Only that I couldn't take the rejection and the disappointment in your eyes.* His neck felt hot, and he was thankful for the darkness. The issue about Nick and charming her had suddenly become a gift. "I never told Nick anything like that."

"I heard you."

"You heard me say charming you wouldn't work. I told him that at the rink, when he asked me to convince you to let Jeremy play. Not one time has anything that happened between us been connected to Jeremy, Nick or my charm."

"Then why didn't you call me, or try to explain? You were deliberately silent. Even at Sally and Stan's, you could have done something."

"Because I didn't want us to end up where we ended up. Here in bed, making love and trying to figure out how in hell we're not gonna continue doing it."

"Well, this is quite a switch. Weren't you the one who said that first day that it didn't have to last forever? As I recall, the Garner charm has been in good form every time we've been together."

He scowled. "I didn't explain what you heard because..." Why had his not seeing her seemed so right,
and now... "I didn't want to hurt you, Celina."

"Then you did something wrong. I was hurt by your
silence. And now by you dropping this little tidbit.
Was this, too, to show me you didn't want to hurt me?
By waiting until after you got what you came for?"

"Stop making it sound so calculated. To be honest,
Hearn was the last thing on my mind. In fact, I didn't
even plan to tell you. I knew you'd get the word when
Harvey calls you tomorrow. The official announcement is planned for Monday."

"Then why did you get this sudden urge to tell me
now?"

Good question, he thought to himself. Some in-
stinct, male or otherwise, told him not to try to dodge
this. He wanted to settle her back on his lap and forget the whole damn conversation.

Her eyes narrowed. "You're not going to tell me,
are you?"

Yeah, dodging it would be worse. He made himself
watch her. "I told you so you'd get angry. So I'd have
a good reason to get up, get dressed and get out of
here. So I wouldn't do what I want to do, which is
make love to you until I can't walk." He swung his legs
off the bed, muttered an "Oh, hell," and reached for
his pants.

She didn't move, her eyes following his movements, not at all sure how she was supposed to feel.
Too many twists and turns, too many things he didn't
say and too many things she didn't want to hear.

Her sweatshirt was balled up at the end of the bed.
She pulled it on, telling herself to let him walk out. It
was bad enough that she'd done what she said she

wouldn't do—go to bed with him. Despite that sureness she'd experienced at the high school, she could have said no. She didn't have to whisper those "don't go" words to him. No, he might have come with the intention of taking her to bed, but she had wanted it the moment she opened the door and saw him.

He was almost dressed, and hunting for his shoes.

She worked her way off the bed, her sweatshirt barely covering her bottom. In the morning she'd sort out all her anger over Glen Harvey's decision. She'd call the principal and see if there was any chance of his changing his mind. Certainly he must realize what kind of message he was sending to every student who was involved in sports.

"Slade?" She wanted to ask him to kiss her again. She wanted to ask him to stay, but she didn't want to deal with him saying no.

"What?"

She turned on the bedside light. He blinked, his eyes dark, his frown deep.

"As long as we're covering things you haven't told me, there's something else. And frankly I was disappointed that you didn't come to me yourself. This seems to be my day for hearing things secondhand." She picked up the shoes he couldn't find and handed them to him.

Instead of taking them, to her amazement the color drained out of his face. He turned away quickly as if he was afraid to look at her. She heard him swear and reach for the glass of whiskey.

"I knew I should have left while you were asleep."

"That wouldn't have changed anything."

"Who told you?" he growled, making her think of a trapped animal ready to fight its rescuer.

She blinked, but with his back to her she had no way of reading any expression. Automatically she said, "Izzy Bozwell. He came to see me this afternoon."

The glass slipped from his hand and dropped to the oyster white carpet. Liquid splashed up the molding and onto the wallpaper. Celina gave it no more than a passing glance. Slade muttered a foul curse, followed by a lethal, "I'll kill the bastard."

She crossed the room and touched his hand. To her dumbfounded amazement, his skin felt icy. He swung around, his eyes filled with the fear she had seen when she read the letter from the medical complex.

"My God, you look terrified," she said before she could stop the words.

He gripped her shoulders, hauling her into his arms, his mouth against her neck, near her ear, whispering, hoarse with emotion. "Make love with me, Celina. Just once more."

She wrapped her arms around him as though he might collapse without her support. There was no arousal pressing into her stomach, only a kind of tight desperation—or was it distraction?

"Slade, what is it? All Izzy talked about was me doing an outline for your book. Why would that terrify you?"

He felt as though he had dissolved, his terror sagging down and away. "The outline," he muttered as though it was a synonym for salvation. He held her for a long moment, whispering, "I'm sorry. I thought..."

"You thought what?" She couldn't think of anything short of some hidden darkness that would have caused such a shock of reaction.

He heaved a long, relieved breath. "Nothing."

It was Celina's turn to be shocked. "Nothing! You don't expect me to believe the kind of reaction I just saw came from nothing?"

"I don't want to fight with you. Please."

"I don't want to fight with you, either, but be reasonable, Slade. You reacted as if you were hiding some dark secret. And don't tell me it's nothing."

He stepped away from her, shoving his feet into his shoes. She felt a frustrated fury.

"Slade, dammit, don't close me out."

But he did. Suddenly he was a stranger, not the man who so exquisitely had made love to her. His eyes were shuttered, his face closed of any warmth or expressive thought, his mouth grim.

As though she was no one he needed, he said in a low, neutral voice, "I'll ask Lauren to put the outline together for me."

Celina snapped, anger raging through her now, mixed with disillusion and confusion that he would prefer Lauren. "You certainly will not. Izzy asked me to do it. Lauren doesn't teach English, and she was always lousy at organizing thoughts into logical order. I'll do the outline."

As though he never heard her, he finished dressing. He stuffed his unbuttoned shirt into his pants. Celina shivered at his slow and obviously exhausted but precise motions.

When he passed by her, she whispered, "Please . . . stay and sleep with me."

In a hollow, emotionless voice, he said, "I can't, Celina."

He didn't explain. He didn't kiss her. He didn't even say goodbye.

Chapter Nine

Celina arrived late for the first game of the play-offs between Brentonville and Fairholm Academy. She wound her way through the thick standing-room-only crowd toward the bleachers. Lauren waved frantically as she approached. To Celina's relief, her friend had saved a seat on the sixth bench up and—bless her—beneath one of the gas heaters. Actually, Lauren's purse reserved the space, Celina realized when she saw the tiny spot.

After she had sat down next to a graffiti-littered wall, Lauren leaned over and said, "We're ahead by two goals. I came right over from chorale practice. What happened to you? I was beginning to think you might be so upset by Harvey's decision that you decided not to come."

"You mean sit home and pout?"

"Something. He did undermine your authority. If he'd done it to me I would have been not only embarrassed but furious."

"I wasn't thrilled, but I did know it was a possibility." However, to herself, she admitted Lauren was partially right. Months ago she would have been furious. It wasn't a lesser concern about education getting lost in the enthusiasm for hockey, but her own widening perspective. Due, she knew, to Slade.

Celina ran her fingers through her hair, telling herself she hadn't pinned it up in a bun because she didn't have time, not because the looseness reminded her of how Slade had tangled his hands in it when they'd made love.

"Anyway, I'm glad you made it." She grinned knowingly. "I was about send Russ over to Slade to tell him to go get you."

"Then I would have been furious—at you." She smiled, however. "Actually, I had a couple phone calls." She felt as if all she had done was answer the phone since Lauren had called late Saturday morning. After determining that Celina was all right, Lauren had concluded with an amused wryness that Slade and she must have had their own reunion.

When Celina met that remark with a cool silence, Lauren proceeded to relate every detail of the juicy gossip about one classmate who'd just divorced her fourth husband, as well as the tentative plans for their twentieth reunion. Celina listened closely enough to interject a few comments, but beyond that her mind was on Slade. And the terror she had seen. Terror he had denied.

"Who would call?" Lauren asked dryly. "Everyone in Brentonville is here." She offered Celina an open bag from the bakery. Celina reached in and pulled out an oatmeal-raisin cookie, immediately thinking of Slade's comment at her house the day they watched the videos. Oatmeal-raisin was his favorite.

Scowling, she bit into the crisp cookie. Somehow, in the complicated scope of what she now knew was their non-relationship, liking the same kind of cookie had the potential of being ridiculously significant.

"Look at that!" Lauren pointed to Jeremy, as he dodged one of Fairholm's left wingers. "Jeremy stole that puck like Slade taught him to do."

Slade, the teacher, a master at teaching hockey techniques to kids like Jeremy. For her, a gifted teacher who had taken her beyond the realm of just physical pleasure and into an emotional banquet.

Finishing the cookie and taking a second one, she leaned against the wall where someone had scrawled: Kathy and Neil were lovers—1984. Wistfully Celina thought of herself and Slade—lovers, too, at least for a few hours one March night.

Reminders everywhere. Jeremy, oatmeal-raisin cookies, even faded graffiti on a wall. She made no pretense of watching the action of the ice, but searched the Brentonville bench for Slade. Finding him was easy; her accelerated heartbeat confirmed that.

Wearing tight faded jeans and a black Sabers sweatshirt, he stood beside Nick. His arms were folded, legs apart and even from the distance across the width of the ice, Celina sensed his concentration. No change in body language when Brentonville scored, except a shift of his hips. No change at all when Fairholm scored. The rink lighting made his sable hair glisten, and his body was too sexily defined in the jeans. Celina wet her lips at the sudden melting shimmer that spread low in her stomach.

Thankful that Lauren was too caught up in the game now to pay any attention to her, she allowed herself to think back over the hours since Slade left her early Saturday morning.

Recalling it in hours instead of days made it seem not so long ago. Sixty-six hours to be exact, and yet her thoughts and feelings during those hours had shifted and rearranged themselves in a determined attempt to understand and to find some steady ground.

That same desperate search for steady ground had been her focus after Brian was killed and her life felt shattered and rootless.

At that time, she'd kept to herself, letting herself cry, letting herself heal. Then she'd gone back to teaching, and lived, or perhaps now that she searched back, existed was a better description. One day had spread into the next with a comfortable predictability. Then Slade came home.

Taking in all that had happened until they had made love—no, until after they'd made love—she would have welcomed comfortable predictability. Instead, in those few moments before he walked out, she witnessed his terror.

Micromoments, yes, but they had been seared permanently in her mind. Not what he had said or not said, not that he didn't stay, not even the painful mental withdrawal from her, just his terror.

For the past sixty-six hours his reaction, and her growing feelings for him had underpinned every thought she had, every decision and every action.

One such action she'd taken hadn't worked. She hadn't been able to change Glen Harvey's mind, though he did acknowledge that he privately agreed with her, but the pressure from the school committee plus his own belief that Jeremy could make up the work had prompted his decision.

Her own decision to not abandon Jeremy simply because she had been overruled came partially because as a teacher she could do no less, and because of something Slade had said about cop-outs. Buckling under pressure was a cop-out, but so was a dogged stand that did nothing more than keep her pride intact.

Shortly after the decision was made public, Celina approached Jeremy after school. She caught up with him when he was on his way to the rink to practice.

"You mean extra help 'cuz they're gonna let me play?" he asked, his face guarded, the question couched in suspicion.

"That's exactly what I mean."

"But I got practice and the games and, well, I don't know. I'm always sorta wired and restless when we gotta win, and..." His voice trailed off, and she knew that short of saying no, he couldn't think of a good enough excuse.

"We can work around all of those."

"Is this a trick?" he finally asked, and she was sure he wondered if she had the power to snatch back the principal's decision.

Celina sighed. She should have tried this position weeks ago. Slade had been right. Taking away hockey hadn't made him love English.

To Jeremy, she said, "It's called wanting you to graduate. You're setting a standard for exceptional hockey. When kids look up to you in the future, they'll see not only a hockey player to emulate, but a student

who didn't cop-out on graduation. What about after-
noons after school? I checked the schedule and you
don't have practice until five.''

He appeared somewhat stunned at this shift in her
approach, and still not totally convinced, but he nodded and agreed to her suggestion.

Dealing with Jeremy, however, seemed simplistic
compared to the intricacies of what she faced with
Slade. Watching him now, she knew she had to see
him despite his obvious desire not to see her. Although they had known each other in the most intimate of ways, she was beginning to see an unusual
pattern that shunned intimacy. The night she'd invited him for soup and he had walked out. The overheard conversation at Nick's that he hadn't tried to
explain. His ignoring her at the restaurant. And, the
most disturbing, the terror she had seen after they
made love.

The distance he kept creating between them wasn't
happenstance or governed by coincidence or outside
circumstances. It was deliberate.

Jeremy scored a goal. The Brentonville fans cheered
and whistled. Jeremy ate up the adulation, including
the traditional bear hugs from fellow teammates. But
Celina saw only Slade. She reached for a third cookie.
For some reason when she got too close he backed off.

She watched him prowl the length of the bench,
talking to the players, making changes on the ice, directing strategy. He was so knowledgeable and confident here, and yet with her he seemed torn between
wanting her and pushing her away.

We do have that in common, she told herself. She
too felt confident and knowledgeable when it came to
the classroom. But when it came to her feelings for

Slade... The wanting was rapidly overtaking her reluctance.

He signaled Jeremy's line off the ice and sent another one in. Would he show up to do the outline?
Considering that she hadn't heard from him, and
considering his pattern of backing off when she got
too close, she was doubtful.

Which meant, she concluded decisively, she would
have to approach him.

By Thursday morning, Slade's nerves were raw-
edged, and his temper trigger-ready. His general attitude, described by Nick in crude terms, could be
summed up as "miserable bastard."

In Nick's kitchen, Slade ignored the box of bakery
doughnuts Nick shoved across the table. Slade was
slumped in the chair, his face hard beneath the previous night's growth of beard. With his hair un-
combed, no shirt on, his jeans on and zipped but
unsnapped, he sipped his third cup of black coffee.

The morning newspaper blared with giddy head-
lines and a story that Nick had read out loud so many
times Slade had it memorized. Brentonville had won
three straight games and stood on the verge of going
into the finals unbeaten. There was an enthusiastic
column by the paper's sportswriter that praised Slade's
superior coaching strategy, and the hard-line encouragement that had invigorated Brentonville.

Despite the sweet fruit of probably victory, Slade
wore a frown that seemed to have drawn permanent
lines down his face. His eyes were cold and unmoved
by all the praise heaped upon him in the past few days.
From the moment he'd seen Celina walk into the rink

at the first play-off game, he felt like an addict in the throes of withdrawal.

He wanted her, and he didn't want to want her. He loved her, and he didn't want to love her. Despite the excitement of the game, he wanted to cross the distance of the rink, take her arm and find some private corner where he could kiss her and touch her and relieve his pain-racked body with the soft sweetness of making love with her.

And he wanted to run. Run from the newspaper's gushiness, run from who he was and the lies he had lived. Those moments in her bedroom when he thought she knew...

He put down his mug of coffee and pressed his fingers into his eyes. Terror. Never in his life had he felt such terror.

Nick threw his partially eaten doughnut into the trash, glaring at Slade, and finally cut the icy silence. "What in hell do you want from them? For God's sake, they've won three straight games."

Slade raised cold green eyes, his voice low and husky. "Yeah, because Jeremy is busting his butt, and from what I saw last night, being the star is turning him into a prima donna."

"The kid is terrific. They're winning because he's on the ice. Why shouldn't he bask in the limelight?"

"He can do his basking after the game. On the ice, he should have one thing on his mind. Team play and getting the puck by their goalie."

"So your solution is bench the kid for the first period in tomorrow night's game?"

"The kid isn't indispensable, Nick."

"We ain't gonna win without him. Just like when you played. We couldn't have won if you'd been on the bench. Besides, the final game of the semifinals is a lousy time to test the kid's character."

"A loss isn't going to keep them out of the finals. In fact, it will sharpen their skills for St. Luke."

"I don't like it. You know how tough St. Luke is. Pullin' Jeremy is a welcome mat for suicide."

Slade shrugged and got to his feet. Nick was right. To bench Jeremy would be suicide, but Slade didn't like what he was seeing in the teenager. The cockiness. The "I'm the greatest" attitude, and the snatches of locker-room talk he'd heard.

According to Jeremy, Celina was helping him after school. And instead of being grateful, the kid had gotten the idea he deserved extra help because he was a star. Typical of the prima-donna attitude.

He poured himself another mug of coffee. "You're the coach, Nick. I'm just in town to help. You make the decision."

"My decision is he plays."

"Fine."

"I want that championship for Brentonville."

"Fine."

Nick swore, and with more noise than necessary, he folded up the newspaper. "Look, I know somethin' has been eatin' at you for days. Those phone calls from that New York agent that you been ignoring, plus I hear you prowlin' around at night and goin' out..." Nick took a breath. "I'd bet my retirement Celina is what's buggin' you."

Slade glanced up at him, no denial in his expression. "You'd lose, my friend. Big-time."

Nick shook his head, muttering about women messing up men, as he shrugged into his jacket. "You comin' over to the rink?"

"Yeah, later."

Brooding and preoccupied, Slade rested his hip against the counter, and lifted his mug of hot coffee. If anything had impressed itself on his thoughts in the past miserable week, it was the simplicity of quick, uninvolved sex. Instead, he'd allowed himself to be caught by the sweetness of very involved lovemaking with a woman he'd stupidly fallen in love with.

"Nick told me you were in the kitchen."

Slade jumped, hot coffee spilling on his hand and splashing on his chest. "Hell," he muttered, followed by a quick indrawn-and-painful hiss. He just managed to put down the cup and grab a handful of napkins.

Celina dropped her purse and his socks, which she was returning, and quickly went to the sink. She wet a towel and squeezed it. "I'm sorry I startled you. Let me see."

"It's okay."

She was beside him, dressed in soft blue and smelling like spring flowers. Her suit jacket was unbuttoned to reveal a delicate, sheer white blouse. He stared for a hot moment, deciding he could definitely see the pretty shape of her breasts through the wispy layers. Pearls circled her neck, and he found himself remembering how many pulse beats in her throat it took before she moaned and arched her neck for his mouth.

She dabbed at the red spots on his hand and was headed for his chest when he grabbed her wrist.

This time she was startled.

Holding her hand a millimeter away from his chest, he growled, "What are you doing here?"

"I wanted to talk to you." She glanced in the direction of her purse. He could feel the thumping of her pulse. Just the slightest tinge of color swept across her cheeks. "I brought your socks. I forgot to give them to you the other night—"

"Celina..."

"I had them right there in the bedroom—"

"Celina..."

"But then you left so quickly—"

He gripped her shoulders, shaking her slightly. "Damn! I'm not going to explain what happened."

She started to say something, then her chin came up and her eyes narrowed. "I didn't ask, did I?"

Snappish and sexy and single-minded, he thought ruefully. He made himself count to ten, so he wouldn't crush his mouth to hers. "Don't give me that cool teacher reserve. I know I've hurt you."

"And disappointed me, too."

"This would have been a helluva lot easier, if you'd stayed away."

"Unlike you, who seems to like backing off when I get too close, I'm not like that."

"Yeah, I know. You're not like any woman I know."

"Is that a compliment or a criticism?"

"Observation. And don't confuse the issue. I hurt you. I hurt us. I wish I could change the way things are, but I can't."

"You mean you won't."

Slade sighed. "Won't. Can't. There's no difference. Look, this isn't getting us anywhere." He let go of her shoulders. "Let me go get shaved and cleaned up."

"No." She said it quickly, touching his chest as though to stop him. Slade stared at her hand, at its whiteness against the dark hair, at its softness against the muscle that suddenly felt mushy under her fingers. While her hand lay still they both stared at the contact, neither making any effort to break it. She said softly, truthfully, "I might lose my nerve and leave."

Slowly he lifted her hand away, making himself not raise it to his mouth and kiss her palm. "That was the idea," he muttered. Then at the determined set of her mouth, he nodded his head in defeat.

He walked back to the table more to put breathing distance between himself and the scent of her, than any need to sit down. He pulled out one chair for her, and then dropped into another one far enough away so he couldn't touch her.

She slipped into the chair, moved her purse to the side and wrapped her fingers around his folded socks as though they were her only connection to him.

Slade stared. A couple of lousy pairs of socks. Her hairpins. Both had become excuses to see each other. At least she'd had the guts to admit it. Slade softened his voice, the "miserable bastard" feeling that he'd been riding for days suddenly wasn't enough.

"Besides my uncanny ability to hurt you, what's on your mind?"

But one glance at her and he knew. Why had he been so terrified the other night seemed to streak across her expression, or was he just too damn conscious of the close call. She worked her fingers into the thick cotton of his socks.

"How about some coffee?" he asked, getting up, hoping to stop the conversation from going down that path. At the cupboard he took a mug down, then hesitated. "Or tea?"

She glanced up, her violet eyes filling him with a thousand impressions. "I'd love some tea."

Slade opened cabinet doors glad for an excuse to do something. Finally he located a jar of instant tea. Showing it to her, he asked, "Do you mind?"

"No, that's fine."

While the water boiled, she studied the threads in his socks. He studied the sheer silkiness of her blouse. When the kettle whistled, both came to attention. Slade picked up the jar of tea and turning so she couldn't see him, he frowned at the written directions on the back of the jar.

"Just one spoonful would probably do," she said making him swing around and face her.

His heart slammed in his chest, and he felt a cold clamminess down his neck. Quickly he turned his back. "One spoonful," he muttered dumping the tea into the mug and adding the water. He set the mug down in front of her and went back to his chair.

She took a sip. "Just right."

"Yeah, putting instant tea into a mug takes real talent," he said, and caught her smile.

"You have a few others."

So have you, he thought. A talent for stubbornness, for being beautiful and the talent for making me fall in love with you. Aloud, he murmured, "One of them being hurting you."

"But not wanting to."

He shifted in his chair, feeling more like a bastard because of her sharp perception. No, he didn't want to hurt her, and he silently damned himself for getting them so involved. He slumped lower and scowled.

She sipped her tea, sat straighter and tested another smile.

"The outline for your book." She lifted her lashes.

"What about it?" He knew how they felt against his mouth.

"You haven't changed your mind, have you?"

"About doing it? No. Celina—"

She interrupted him, her enthusiasm spilling into the conversation. "I read some sports books that have been done recently, to get a feel for what is involved. I think your idea is timely, and I want to help you put it together." At his glower, which he directed more at himself than at her, she added quickly, "This isn't about us or what happened. Just the outline. Slade, please. I want to do it. I really do."

"I'm not questioning that. I just don't think that us being together is a good idea."

"Did you and Jeremy get together and practice that look?" she asked with the barest of seriousness. "Don't be so suspicious and guarded. I won't cross-examine you about the other night, nor will I drag you off to the bedroom and make you do something you don't want to do."

His mouth twitched into the slightest of grins. "You had me worried there for a minute."

She grinned, too. "Yes, I know."

He brought himself to his feet, and felt her eyes follow him from his messy hair to the rough, unshaven cheeks, to his bare chest, which he had crushed against her breasts, to his jeans, unsnapped, riding low on his hips. With a startling fascination he watched her study him, wanting her to recall every detail of what the jeans hid.

He picked up the two pairs of socks and lifted them to his nose. "They smell like you," he murmured, and then as if suddenly realizing what he'd said, he added, "I'm out of clean socks, thanks."

"You're welcome. Now you won't have to go buy any."

"Huh? Oh, yeah..."

Quickly she added, "If you want to bring some laundry over to my house while we work on the outline, you can use my washer and dryer—"

"Your house?" At her house were privacy and a large bed, neither of which he was sure he could handle around her. "What's wrong with here or at the school?"

"I can't use the equipment at school for this, and I doubt Nick has a decent typewriter, never mind a computer."

"A computer?"

"You don't know anything about them? No, well, I can understand that. Brian never could get the hang of them, either. That's okay. I have a personal computer. We can put the material on a disk, and then if you want to add or delete, it makes it much easier." She glanced at her watch. "I'm late. I have to get to school."

She touched his wrist where the coffee splashed. "Why don't you come over about five? Think about your ideas and we'll begin to flesh them out."

He stared at her hand, his gaze traveling up her arm to her shoulder, to her neck, to the handfuls of hair that she hadn't confined in a bun. Asking her why leaped into his mind, but he scrapped the idea. "I thought you were helping Jeremy in the afternoon."

"I am, but he'll be gone by five. He told me yesterday that too much studying was rotting his mind."

Slade grinned. "I think I used the same excuse."

"Well, trust me. I have no intention of trying to rot your mind with the outline." She stood on tiptoes, pressing her hands into his chest, and in a natural gesture that came without pretense, without excuse, she brushed her mouth across his in a light kiss.

His hands gripped her shoulders, holding her there when she tried to pull away. She relaxed, tilted slightly into him, and he spread his legs to accommodate her. Against his body he could feel her compliance. Their noses barely touched. Their mouths were a whisper apart. Her fingers slid and nestled tightly into his chest hair.

Lightly he slipped his hands from her shoulders to her throat to glide into her hair. Holding her head, he moved his thumbs in a feathery caress along her jaw, to her chin, up to her lips. He coaxed her mouth open and skimmed his thumbs into the warm wetness. "You're gonna be late."

"Yes," she replied huskily, touching just the tip of her tongue to his thumbs.

"And there's no possibility I could talk you into playing hooky."

"No possibility."

"And all we're gonna do at your house is the outline."

"Absolutely."

Her eyes shimmered, the color a darkening violet, and Slade drew in a shuddering breath. Before he did what he wanted to, which was kiss her deeply and touch her intimately, he dropped a quick, hard kiss on her mouth. Then a softer one, followed by stepping away from her. It was all a smooth move on the surface, but a clamoring instant restlessness inside him.

Celina swung her purse onto her shoulder, and despite her slightly tangled hair, the lips that she rubbed and rerubbed, Slade thought Brentonville High was damn lucky to have such a classy woman heading up the English department.

She started for the door. "You aren't going to disappoint me, are you?"

Slade leaned back against the counter, arms folded, legs slightly apart. "You mean, am I gonna cop-out on you?"

"Yes."

He could hedge. He could give himself a solid out by saying that working together would end up in the bedroom. And they'd made that possibility twice as tough to resist since they'd already made love. From lovers to friends rarely worked.

Something was wrong here, he thought warily. His reason for staying away from her was because he couldn't read and he didn't want her to know. What happened? Not only had that not been his primary thought in the past few moments, but what they'd be doing—the outline—was a virtual time bomb.

Yeah, he'd be copping out if he didn't show up, but it would definitely be to his advantage to keep his distance. Who in hell was dumb enough to play with a time bomb?

But the bottom line was that he wanted to be with her because being away from her was killing him.

He wished he had the guts to say, "Sorry, baby, call me a cop-out, but I'm not interested." "I'll see you at five," he muttered instead.

She grinned.

He scowled. "I'm not coming prepared to do anything but the outline."

"Of course. That's all I'm interested in doing."

With that she said goodbye, and he made himself respond—although admittedly it was more of a growl than a goodbye. He stared at his socks, still neatly folded on the kitchen table. His socks that smelled like her. He listened to her heels tapping on the wooden floor. Finally the front door closed.

Damn. She knew exactly what kind of preparation he was talking about; she could have had at least some reaction. A blush. A mild protest. Even a teasing smile. But nothing.

He dumped her remaining tea into the sink, and then picked up his clean socks. It looked as if she'd managed the impossible. They'd gone from lovers to a friendly business relationship.

And he didn't like it. Not one damn bit.

Chapter Ten

Slade got through their first meeting on Thursday without touching her. That is, if he didn't count their hands brushing a few times in the kitchen later that evening when they decided to make sandwiches.

On Friday afternoon they got right to work. Slade sprawled on the couch and Celina sat in a nearby wing chair armed with a legal pad. The hours ticked by and the outline began to take shape.

Slade liked being with her, sharing with her, letting himself talk about hockey, not just as a player, but how the game had molded and changed him over the years.

"There's a lot of pressure on the ice. The speed of the game, and the physical one-on-one contact that leads to fights and all-out brawls. The losses that should have been wins. And yeah, the wins that should have been losses. It's like a continual high. Off the ice everyone needs something...."

"What about you? What did you do off the ice?"

"Not drugs."

"No. You would never do anything that would jeopardize your playing."

"You sound very sure."

"I know how much you love hockey."

As though the knowledge was both new and old, he thought, *Not as much as I love you.*

Glancing away from the promise in her eyes, he continued, "There's a lot of downtime. Time to think and wonder about the mistakes you made, the things you should have done and the things you shouldn't. It was weird, but after Brian's funeral I kept thinking about the way his parents had cried. The way you had looked so devastated. I felt like an outsider, as if I was a stranger at my best friend's funeral.

"Maybe it was my fast life-style compared to the coziness of Brentonville, but I felt a sort of emptiness. I had money, and women and success, but it was all a glossiness with no substance. Like being with someone and never looking beneath the surface. If they smile and act happy, we assume they are. When, in fact, they might have all sorts of secrets, or horrible things going on in their lives."

"And for you the horrible thing is your ended hockey career?"

He thought it was, but leaving Brentonville, leaving Celina struck him as pretty horrible. "To the average guy trying to make a buck, an ended hockey career is like put-your-feet-up-and-suck-off-the-success time. For me..."

"It's like the end of your life."

"Yeah. Like the end of my life."

He glanced over at her, surprised to see a glisten of tears. She quickly swiped them away.

He wanted to say something, but he didn't know what.

"Maybe we shouldn't use that. You know, maybe it's too sappy."

She raised her head, her eyes a little damp, but her smile came easily. "No, it's wonderful, because it's the way you feel. It should be in the book."

After they tied up a few more details, Slade had convinced himself that, yes, if he could see her swipe away tears and not take her into his arms, he could be with Celina and not touch her.

At least he thought so until half an hour later when the electricity went off, and they stumbled into each other. Celina had been on her way to the kitchen for some candles. Slade had been on his way to the living room with a fresh beer. He managed to save the beer from spilling, but in the balancing process he brushed his hand across her breast. Her thigh ended up pressed high and tight against his groin. The accidental touches froze both of them for too many maddeningly tense seconds that roared through his gut and hardened him instantly.

He swore. She murmured an apology.

He took a deep, shuddering breath. She let out a deep, shuddering breath.

He growled something about the electricity picking a lousy time to go off. She whispered something about there never being a good time for it to go off.

Finally she stepped away. Achingly he moved to the side.

She continued into the kitchen.

He leaned against the wall. His gut hammered and his hands shook. His mind, however, followed her into the kitchen, lifted her up onto the counter, drew her legs around his hips and kissed her senseless. He had not one shred of doubt that a single, deep, wet, hot kiss would kill any possibility of finishing the outline together.

He stayed where he was, rubbing the cold beer can across his forehead. A clammy sweat broke out across his back, and the burning sensation low in his belly screamed for relief. Lovers to friends, he decided with a grim frustration, had all the raging symptoms of classic stupidity.

He dragged in another desperate breath and made himself concentrate on what he intended to do. Finish the outline, get through the hockey finals, make sure the scholarship in Brian's name was in place and leave town.

He made himself wait until his voice could be trusted, then called out to her that he was going home.

Outside, the night air offered some relief at least for his lungs. He sucked in steadying gulps, fisted his hands and jammed them in his jacket pockets. His thoughts, massed in conflict, pride and pain, didn't spare him.

The word is coward, Garner.

The word is smart.

What about being in love with her?

I'll get over it. I did once before, didn't I? Out of sight, out of mind . . .

He slowed his steps, the words—I did once before—slipped around in his mind as if trying to find firm footing. Yeah, she'd been out of sight all those years since they were kids, but not once had she been completely absent from his mind. Terrific, he thought grimly as he approached Nick's house. Celina had become an emotional snarl he couldn't untangle.

Maybe she won't be shocked if you tell her you can't read. Maybe she won't reject you.

Maybe she will. Maybe she won't. *No! I can't tell her! Dammit, I can't!*

On Saturday she greeted him with a dazzling smile that outshone the brightness of the morning. Her hair tumbled with a dizzying lushness onto her shoulders, enhancing her red turtleneck sweater. Huge, gold hoop earrings swung from her ears, and for no logical reason his thoughts spun wild and hot. Snug jeans with a tiny braided loop attached to the center of the zipper flap had him too damn curious as to why it was there, followed instantly by the possibility that his finger could take its sweet time discovering why.

Dragging his eyes back up to that smile, Slade made no attempt to match it. He hadn't slept, which he blamed on her, on himself, on the ragged roll of his thoughts, on his knee that didn't ache, and on the particular spot where her knee had made contact. That spot now ached anew.

He felt irritable and edgy, and cursed himself for wanting to relieve his lousy disposition in the most basic way.

He mumbled a husky, "Good morning."

How it was possible he didn't know, but her smile got even brighter. "You didn't just walk out."

He stared at her unamused, his frown deepening, while his mind tried to play catch-up. Was this another hairpin conversation? God, he hoped not. Not today.

Swearing silently, he finally muttered a cautious, "What?"

"On Friday night you didn't walk out as you'd done other times when we got too close. You called to me and told me you were going home." Then with a naturalness that stunned him, she reached up and hugged him. Hugged him, for God's sake, as though he'd miraculously passed some test he didn't even know he'd taken.

"I don't what you're talking about," he growled, untangling her arms from around his neck before his resolve not to kiss her crumbled.

His abruptness had no effect, except to make her grin more dazzling. She swept her hands through her hair, sending the hoops swinging once more. "It's a beautiful morning, isn't it? Have you ever heard the soundtrack from *Oklahoma?* There's this great song titled, 'Oh, What a Beautiful Morning.'" She proceeded to recite the words while he simply stared at her. She acted as if his arrival was worthy of a brass band.

"Wonderful lyrics, aren't they? Be happy I didn't sing them to you." Then she lowered her voice, and he heard just a trace of embarrassment. "I never told anyone but Lauren the real truth. I'm the only one in Brentonville who tried out for the Sachuest Chorale and didn't make it. Miss Bewley suggested, and bluntly, I might add, that I confine my singing to a non-audience."

Slade seriously considered backing up to go around the block so he could try his arrival a second time.

Without more than a hasty breath, she continued. "It was a ghastly, humiliating experience, because I wanted so badly to join Sachuest."

Slade nodded automatically, pondering briefly on Miss Bewley's rejection, before Celina chattered on.

"Anyway, I've been up since six. I got all the outline notes organized and on the disk. I baked oatmeal-raisin cookies for you. Jeremy loves them. Come on in. He's here. I'm not getting any work out of him because of his nerves over the final games. Plus the rumors about an NHL scout coming to see him play." Then with a pat to his cheek she whispered, "I'm so glad you came back. Do you know this is the first time I haven't had to go after you? I was going to give you an extra half an hour and then I was coming to find you."

That did it. He'd had just about enough. She started into the house and he grabbed her, hauling her back and around to face him.

The sun was warm on his back, and touching her made him even warmer. To any passerby, they simply looked as if they were standing in the doorway talking.

Slade sorted through the thirteen million questions he wanted to ask her and narrowed them down to basics. He lowered his voice. "What do you mean go after me? And stop smiling like this is the best day of your life."

"But I have a lot to smile about. You're here. Oh, Slade, don't you know what this means?"

Wearily he said, "It means we had an appointment to work on the outline."

"No. You're not listening to me. Last night when we bumped in the dark. Remember what happened?"

He remembered it too well; her thigh pressed into him, his fingers nudging the softness of her breast.

And the long, sleepless night he'd spent trying to forget it.

Her eyes widened and for a moment she looked hurt. "You haven't forgotten, have you?"

Say yes, refresh my memory. Say no, how could I ever forget how good you feel?

He sighed. Why was he putting himself, and putting them, through this torture? The outline was almost finished. He didn't have to be at the rink until four. They could get rid of Jeremy, lock the door and... How many times could they make love before four?

"...and I know we touched, well, kind of intimately." Then with a dismissing shrug, she added, "But forget about that."

Forget about that? He blinked, trying to round up his rampant thoughts, which were already in her bedroom and slowly getting them out of their clothes.

She sailed on with a gleeful perkiness that made him want to shake her. He did grip her shoulders and nudge her into a corner inside the house by the front door, refusing to remember the previous time they'd stood here and where it had led to. Narrowing his eyes, he made his mind blank it out. "Hold it. Dammit, just shut up for a minute."

She did.

"And don't smile."

She didn't.

When she stood perfectly still, her head tipped to one side, her earrings the only thing on her that was moving, her hands clasped lightly in front of her, he told himself to not allow the tumbling waves of her hair, the violet of her eyes, the pretty sheen on her cheeks, the kissableness of her mouth, the swinging gold hoops, the shape of her breasts beneath the sweater, or that damn loop on her jeans to distract him. But they did. All of them. No, not them—her. She was the distraction.

That's enough, he told himself, dragging his thoughts back before they skidded into areas best left alone with Jeremy in the next room.

He was rapidly forgetting what she'd been talking about. He scowled, and she still didn't move.

"Let's back up," he said wearily, clenching the hand that wanted to cup her breast. "Why did my coming back here this morning make you look like Mary Sunshine? And what did you mean, come after me?"

She took a breath, shaking her hair back. "I realized something about you after we made love and you walked out. Wait, don't get all defensive. I'm not going to ask what terrified you." He didn't believe that for a moment, but before he had a chance to tell her so, she added, "At first I thought it was only a few incidents, but it goes clear back to when we were going steady in high school. There's a pattern, Slade."

"What pattern? What incidents? What are you talking about?"

She peeked around him in the direction of the living room. "I just have to give Jeremy some homework," she said, ignoring his questions. She started to slip around him, then stopped. "Don't you dare leave."

How did she know he'd already considered it? "And have you come after me?" he asked, feeling as if he were sparring with a truant officer.

She came up on her tiptoes and lightly kissed his mouth as she had done at Nick's on Thursday. He scowled and refused to touch her or grip her the way he had then.

She gave him another light kiss, a broad smile and a brief hug. His scowl got deeper.

She glided around him, and he watched her walk into the living room. He stayed by the door feeling a not-so-sudden urge to leave. He scrapped that idea. No doubt, she would indeed come after him. In a moment of clarification, he realized he'd spent most of life standing by a lot of doors ready to make quick exits. School doors. Bedroom doors. Life's doors.

Leaving was always less complicated than staying.

And no one had ever come after him.

No one had ever made him come back.

What kind of pattern? What incidents? His frown returned. How could she know so much about him when she didn't even know he couldn't read? He was the one with the missing piece, not her. She thought she had a pattern to some series of incidents, but the real reason why he always left, why he shunned the star-status garbage, why any commitment to her, even a wholly physical one, scared the hell out of him…was rejection. Always it came back to a deep, inborn fear of rejection.

He'd just about decided that to stay would be a complication he'd regret, when Jeremy appeared. He walked with a cool swagger, his eyes confident and cocky. The mouth full of cookies diffused Slade's immediate impression of a kid carried away with the star-status bull.

He shook his head, wondering what it would take to temper the teenager's pride with a little humility.

"I hope you left me some cookies. How's the extra help working out?"

He grinned, popping another cookie into his mouth. "She's got a thing about gettin' an education." Then in a brief glimpse that if Slade had blinked he would have missed, Jeremy dropped the cockiness. "Slade, is there really gonna be a scout at one of the games?"

"So I hear. You been talking to Nick, huh?"

"It's all over town. The guys are really psyched. He's comin' to see me play, isn't he?"

He was. Slade had gotten in touch with Zeke Pepper who scouted for the Sabers and told him about Jeremy. Zeke had jumped at the lead. Only one other time had Slade asked Zeke to scout a high-school player. That happened in Providence the night Slade had gone to sign up for the adult literacy class but then chickened out. After he left, he stopped at the local hockey rink to watch an A-league game. One kid, David Beck, captured his attention. Agile, fast and merciless, the right winger outskated every player on his team and the opposing team. That particular team was touted to be one of the best in New England.

Slade used the phone in the refreshment stand and called Zeke who was holed up in a Providence hotel room with scouting reports. Zeke arrived in time to watch the Beck kid score his third goal. On his eighteenth birthday, David Beck signed a five-figure contract and still skated in a Providence Sabers uniform.

When Slade called Zeke about Jeremy, the first question was, "Is he another Beck?"

"Would I call you if he wasn't?" Slade had asked.

Jeremy chewed and swallowed the last cookie. "You called him to come and scout me. I know you did. You won't be sorry, Slade. Man, I'm gonna blow the doors off St. Luke's."

"At the risk of blowing the doors off your cockiness, what about the St. Luke center? Zeke sure isn't gonna ignore him. The kid's already getting lots of serious interest from the Ivy League colleges."

"Then let him go play college hockey. I don't care about that." Yeah, right, kid. Because with your grades you couldn't get into any college, never mind Ivy League. Not unlike his own situation, Slade realized. If he hadn't blown the doors off the scouting report done when he played for Brentonville, where would he be today?

It was a question he'd never spent time thinking about, and a whole range of possibilities came to mind. Maybe married to Celina for about fifteen years. Maybe standing here on a March Saturday morning talking to his own son about playing pro hockey versus college hockey. Maybe staying in Brentonville to coach A league.

Yeah, sure. Maybe an illiterate jerk, trying to stretch a minimum-wage pay, swigging beer on Friday night and talking about what might have been.

Jeremy watched him, a fierce hope in his eyes, but also a desperate envy that went much deeper. "I'm gonna be like you and play in the NHL."

"I don't want to blow your bubble, Jeremy, but there's a slight difference between the NHL and Brentonville versus St. Luke." Slade's dry sarcasm sailed right by the teenager.

"You did it," Jeremy countered as if Slade being in the NHL was easy to attain. "Nick says I'm as good as you. You don't say much, but I know you think the same thing. The scout will, too. You'll see. I'll be playin' with the pros, and then my Dad will..." He lowered his head and shifted his books under his arm as his free hand quickly closed over the doorknob.

Leaving, Slade thought again suddenly, is always less complicated than staying.

"I gotta go," Jeremy mumbled, sounding as if he still had a mouthful of cookies.

Slade didn't move, didn't try to stop him, didn't ask him any questions. He hadn't missed the reference to Eddie Hearn. In fact, Slade knew from the moment he'd seen Jeremy on the videos, the teenager's need to please his Dad went as deep as his wanting to play for the NHL.

Pressure, Slade thought. Too damn much pressure.

Celina poured a mug of coffee for Slade, and carried it and a plate of oatmeal-raisin cookies into the living room. He was sprawled on the couch, his jacket off, staring at the makeshift desk she had set up in the corner.

After she'd transferred everything onto the disk, she'd made backup disks and then gotten rid of all the odd papers with notes she'd scribbled.

Slade had not written one word, claiming she'd never be able to read his scrawl. She'd seen his signature, and quickly agreed. The only decipherable letters were the *S* and the *G*.

They'd easily settled into his talking and her writing.

"I made fresh coffee," she said now, putting the mug down on the coffee table. He reached for a cookie. Before she thought about it, she perched on the edge of the couch beside him.

"Better than the bakery," he said after a moment of serious chewing.

"You better say that."

"Yes, ma'am." He grinned, and taking a second one, he settled back down on the couch, his gaze deep and thoughtful. "What do you think will happen to Jeremy?"

"You mean long-range? If he doesn't go to the NHL?"

"Yeah."

"His marks are too low for college. And he didn't take any SAT's. He might be able to get into a trade school, although his sole interest as long as I've known him has been hockey. And usually the kids who go to a trade school have taken shop, or have a knack for carpentry or mechanics. Jeremy always viewed school as a means to an end. To play hockey he had to be in school."

"Yeah, I had the same attitude." He finished the second cookie.

"And Jeremy probably knows that." She started to get up when he cupped her hip and held her in place.

"So what's the answer? Throw out the sports programs?"

"I don't know the answer. I'm not sure there is one, but as a teacher, I feel responsible for my students. I want them to have a broader scope to draw on than, such as in Jeremy's case, high-school hockey. The better the education, the more power an individual has over his own choices...." Her voice trailed off. "I'm beginning to sound as if I'm on a soapbox."

She raised her eyes and found him studying her. When he finally did speak, she had a sense of his thoughts being deeper than his words. "I've never told Jeremy to say the hell with school."

"But you have, Slade," she said, feeling her own passion about the subject suddenly renewed. "Oh, maybe not verbally over the PA system, but your actions and your attitude have given him that message."

"By helping Nick? By stressing team play? By skating with the kids? Come on, Celina."

"I don't want to argue with you."

"But you believe I have a blow-off-school attitude, don't you?"

"It isn't just you. To some degree it's true of everyone in Brentonville who protested and pressured Glen Harvey to change his mind. Nick, with his obsession for a winning season. Eddie Hearn, with his 'if you score a goal, Jeremy, you'll make me proud' attitude. Me, too. I'm giving Jeremy special help so he can graduate, yes, but I'm also going to hockey games." She paused, and too late she realized her hesitation only emphasized what concerned her. "I'm spending a lot of time with Slade Garner, who better than anyone else exemplifies what I've been fighting against."

Slade felt the cold stab of reality cut deeply through him. If she only knew how close she was to the real truth. "Thanks," he muttered.

"Well, you do," she said briskly, once again trying to move away.

Again, he held her next to him, wondering why he didn't either leave or drag her down and kiss her.

She tentatively relaxed, somewhat unsure if she'd aroused his suspicion or his pleasure. "As I was saying. You've done what every hockey player who has skated for Brentonville has wanted to do. Played for the NHL. Had a fantastic career. Done it all, had it all, seen it all. You come back here at the height of the school's hot hockey season, and instead of being an egotistical star, you pitch in and help Nick, as well as rent the rink so you can teach the kids. And if the rumor is true, you've even arranged for an NHL scout to come and watch a game.''

His annoyance deepened, giving way to a tight edginess while she talked.

Celina felt her heart accelerate and quickly added, ''All I'm trying to say is that you've set too good an example.''

But he wasn't listening. ''You forgot something,'' he said in a deadly calm voice.

''What?''

''In your done it all, had it all, seen it all theory, you can add that one of my most memorable moments since I came home was making love with the head of the English department.''

Hauling her down to sprawl across him, he kissed her. The frustration of the past few days, the longing of a lifetime, the love that swelled through him burst with the feel and taste of her mouth.

Celina didn't fight him, she didn't want to, and as he settled her on top of him, spearing his hands deep into her hair, holding her mouth sealed to his, she simply let herself unwind into an endless pleasure.

Turning so that they were lying side by side, he slid his hands to her breasts. ''Whose dumb idea was it that we shouldn't touch each other?'' he growled against her neck. With an efficiency that he didn't think he had, he opened her jeans and dragged them down over her hips.

''I think it was yours,'' she said, finding that his jeans weren't so cooperative. They rolled again, this time onto the floor. Slade held her with one arm and cushioned the drop with his other hand.

His mouth was on hers again as he struggled with the zipper on his jeans. He lifted himself away, swore and finally managed to get his jeans and hers down enough to release the heat that burned between them.

His eyes hot with desire, he watched her. "This was a lot smarter." He settled himself against her. Neither was mindful that they were still partially dressed, that they were on the floor when a nice, comfortable bed was only a room away.

She lifted her hips, and he slid deep inside her, groaning and then lying still for a moment.

"Slade . . ."

"How can you make this feel brand new?" He slowly moved, nuzzling her throat. He kissed her jaw, a breath away from her lips. Then he plunged into her, and her body arched against him. "And all mine . . . oh, God . . ."

Celina burned with the blazing pleasure, letting herself ride with the fire of truth. Here on the carpet of her living room, their positions awkward from partially shed clothes, the need for each other so strong, so intense that their bodies knew exactly how to respond, how to move, how to love.

She loved him. Her climax peaked with his, their rhythm perfectly timed, as the words seared themselves across her mind and her heart. She loved him.

Brentonville won the first game. Afterward, the crowd surrounded Jeremy when he came off the ice. As everyone had predicted, Jeremy had been the key player.

Later, while Celina stood by the exit door waiting for Slade, she watched Jeremy bask in the attention of four girls. Fresh from a shower and still beaming over his exceptional playing, Jeremy spotted his father. From where she stood a few feet away, Celina heard Eddie Hearn complaining that if the scout had been there his kid would already be destined for the NHL. Jeremy looked miserable.

Leaving the rink with his dad, the teenager walked as though he'd been a disaster on the ice instead of a hero. By the time Slade approached her a few minutes later, she was furious.

He dropped an arm around her neck, and a quick kiss on her mouth. "I hope that scowl isn't for me." When she shook her head, he guided her out to the parking lot. "Have a drink with me?"

"I was hoping you'd ask. I want to talk to you."

They walked the short distance to Sally and Stan's, and once inside the shadowed bar they worked their way through a crowd that shouted congratulations.

"Way to go, Slade."

"The Hearn kid is better than ever."

"Man, wait'll the scout sees him smoke up the ice. Old Eddie is already planning on a box seat to watch his kid play for the Sabers next season."

"Hey, you oughta think about coaching here. We could win every year."

"Yeah, one long endless hockey season. Summer games, winter games."

"Celina, honey, you better talk him into staying."

"Talk, hell. She can do better than talk."

With that remark, Slade came to a stop. Celina was more annoyed at the implication than angry, especially since she hadn't tried talking or seducing Slade into staying in Brentonville.

Whoever had made the last remark ducked into the crowd and the congratulations continued.

Slade gripped her arm, pulling her tight against him. They made their way toward the bar. "You're not upset."

"No. He could have been more explicit."

"Then he would have been very sorry."

She turned and smiled at him, thinking him delightfully old-fashioned, heroic and wonderful. "You would have killed him."

"No, but I would have made sure he never came to another hockey game."

So much for old-fashioned heroes, she concluded. "Locked out of the Brentonville hockey rink. A fate worse than death."

"In this town? You're damn right."

They grabbed two bar chairs just as they were vacated. Both ordered beers, keeping their heads close together so they could hear each other over the drumming noise.

"A table would have been better," she said, her mouth close to his ear.

"Besides there not being any empty ones, I would have been too tempted to do something not for public viewing."

She tipped her head to the side, immediately interested, and made no attempt to hide her desire. "What?"

Slade leaned closer, whispered an explicit term in her ear that should have shocked her, but instead made her bold. She in turn whispered something back to him.

Slade groaned. "God." Then with a sideways glance, he muttered, "I think I've corrupted you."

"Thoroughly," she quipped.

The bartender put their beers in front of them, along with a basket of pretzels. Celina reached for one.

Slade took a long swallow of his beer, then wiped the back of his hand across his mouth. "What did you want to talk to me about?"

She thought suddenly, *I want to talk about us, about making love, and saying sexy words, about being together forever, about how I've fallen in love with you and how I'm afraid to tell you.*

As intimate as they'd been, she still felt disconnected from him in nonphysical ways. It was as if they'd taken and given, but still lacked a basic trust.

She sipped her own beer, glad for the noise, for the crowd, glad they weren't alone.

"I wanted to ask you about Jeremy and this scout who's coming." Jeremy, at least, was a subject where neither minced words. Celina told him what she'd heard from Eddie and how Jeremy looked.

Slade leaned close to her. Their thighs made contact and neither seemed inclined to move away.

Slade said, "I deliberately didn't tell him when Zeke is coming. If he thinks he's under pressure now, how do you think he'd feel if he knew the scout was watching?"

"But he's miserable."

"I know."

"He never should have known about the scout."

"Celina, sweetheart," he said patiently, "every hockey player who's any good believes scouts come to championship games. Word gets around, and if I hadn't called Zeke he might have gotten wind of it, anyway. Jeremy has had a lot of publicity because of you."

She stiffened, finding the remark more bothersome than the earlier one about her seducing Slade. "In other words, I called more attention to him by not letting him play?"

"Yeah, it makes him seem more valuable to the team than he probably is. Plus the team thinks he's indispensable, and that adds more pressure."

Celina felt a sinking feeling in her stomach. In her attempts to make education more important than hockey, she'd done just the opposite. She'd placed Jeremy in a position where the team pressure, parental pressure and his own desire to play pro hockey had mushroomed from a disagreement about priorities into a frightening obsession the teenager couldn't escape.

"Besides," Slade said, reaching for a pretzel, "Zeke was at the game tonight."

Celina stared. "He was there? But Eddie Hearn said—"

"Sweetheart, scouts don't wear name badges. They blend. They don't want people like Hearn bending their ear, and they don't want to be asked a thousand questions that they can't answer. They come. They observe. They write a scouting report." He signaled the bartender.

Slade asked her, "Want another beer?"

She shook her head. Slade paid the bill and they made their way outside.

"When will Jeremy know something?" Despite her feelings about sports and education, she didn't want him to be disappointed.

"In a few weeks."

"In a few weeks what?"

"He'll know if the scouting report is favorable."

"That's all?"

"Impressing Zeke is crucial. Jeremy played well tonight, but since this is a three-out-of-five series, he's gonna have to play as well or better the next two games."

"Pressure."

Slade shrugged. "This is Sunday-school stuff compared to what's coming. He better get used to it, if he wants to play with the pros."

Chapter Eleven

Two hours before the face-off of the final game, Slade met privately with Nick and Glen Harvey in the principal's office. Slade had no sooner walked in than Glen Harvey excused himself.

"I'll just be gone a few minutes. Grace will get you some coffee," the principal said. With a mysterious twinkle behind his bifocals, he picked up a folder from his desk and left the office.

Grace Twitchell, who was still insistent a street should be named after Slade, brought the coffee, grinned beguilingly at Slade and backed out of the doorway.

Nick ignored the coffee and the chair where he usually sat for these meetings, preferring to pace the short length of the office. "Slade, we got a problem...."

Slade grimaced at the word problem, and barely listened. He stood by the window watching the press vans from the television stations in Providence pull into the parking lot. His retirement, according to Nick, had been the subject of sports columns for the past two mornings. There was a lot of speculation as to whether he would coach or move to the Sabers' front office.

Surprisingly, the arrival of the press didn't rattle him. Perhaps because he knew the fickleness of the media. In time, his retirement would become old news and slip into obscurity.

All week, the atmosphere in Brentonville had been electric with anticipation. Tonight would be the climax. A possible winning season for Nick. The surprise announcement of the scholarship in Brian's name.

Then after the celebrations, after Brentonville stored up all the images and highlights to be told and retold for a thousand nights to come, the town would settle into the satisfied afterglow of pride and accomplishment.

Slade felt raggedly aware that for him, the afterglow was more of an aftermath. No more distractions from what he had to face—the cold hard reality of life after hockey.

Doing the outline had been a stall of sorts, but he'd found both a satisfaction and the necessary conclusion as far as hockey was concerned. The outline was finished. Daniel had called to express his enthusiasm, and Slade felt good about the book that would come later.

For now, his secret was safe.

Always the goal, right, Garner? Keep the secret safe, no matter what. Use all your intelligence to hide....

Damn. To hide his shame, yes. To hide from rejection, yes. To hide from living. Grimly he realized keeping the secret had slowly paralyzed him, his future, his respect for himself when Jeremy and the other players looked up to him.

And his feelings about Celina.

He dragged a hand through his hair, a bleakness settling around him that had nothing to do with hockey or the outline, and everything to do with Celina.

He knew he loved her. He'd known that since the first time they'd made love. Grudgingly, because he couldn't escape, he no longer crept around the emotion as if love would trip him up. Yet loving her, wanting to be with her had trapped him just as his inability to read had. He knew that revealing one would lead to telling the other. Celina, I love you, and by the way there's something else—I can't read. Or maybe . . . Celina, I never learned how to read beyond the fourth grade, but I love you.

God, what was he doing? Even putting the secrets into words kicked at him with a gut-level intensity. Saying them to Celina—no way.

He also discovered new questions that had no answers. When would he quit feeling empty? When would the sadness go away? And what was this new terror that didn't have a name?

"Hey, Slade. Why am I havin' this one-way conversation with myself? You been starin' out that window like some depressed kid. Jeremy. Remember him? I asked if he'd found you?"

"No, I haven't seen him." Slade sank down into one of the chairs and stretched out his legs. His knee was bothering him slightly, which he directly attributed to that drop from the couch to the floor in Celina's living room. He rubbed his hand over the sensitive joint, his thoughts more on the intensity of their lovemaking than the slight discomfort. The lovemaking had been spontaneous, sweet, hot and fantastic but Celina had been more so.

He raised his eyes, to find Nick still pacing and glaring. Following a sigh, Slade murmured, "Okay, I'm listening. What's his problem?"

"His problem is our problem. The kid is real edgy. Just what I need. The championship at my fingertips, and what do I get? A strung-out kid. I told him all he had to do was go out there and do what he's been doin'. Is that tough? Is is too much to ask?"

"You're asking me? Why didn't you ask him?"

"Because he won't talk to me. He's done nothing but sulk. That scout ain't done us no favors by not lettin' us know who he is or if he's here." He eyed Slade, who responded with a shrug. "And don't tell me the kid is under pressure. I already got that lecture from Celina when he didn't show for English class."

She never quits, Slade thought, finding himself incredibly proud of her. His own leaving-is-always-easier-than-staying theory had hit a wall with her. Or perhaps she'd gone a step further. She didn't accept leaving as the final word.

To Nick, he said, "Don't tell me. She went looking for Jeremy."

"In spades. She came right into the locker rooms. The locker rooms, for God's sake. What happened to sacred and private? I mean what if the guys had been in there wearin' nothin' but their jock straps?"

Slade chuckled, recalling her finding him in only his briefs. "She wouldn't have gasped and blushed, if that's what you mean."

"Well, hell, she should!" Then with a sag of sudden defeat, he dropped into one of the chairs. Staring irately at his shoes for a few seconds, he added reluctantly, "I think I'm gettin' used to her. I didn't even tell her to get out."

Hiding his grin, Slade reached for a mug of coffee. "Really?"

"Really stupid, you mean. Why does she have to be so dedicated? Why doesn't she just do her job and go home? Why does she have to worry and fret and make waves?"

"Because she'd a good teacher, Nick. And you and I both know it."

"Yeah, I suppose. I don't like it, but you're right." Then with a scowl of annoyance, he added, "She still ain't got no business in the locker rooms."

Glen Harvey returned. "Sorry for the interruption." He went back to his desk chair and sat down. "Actually, I'm not sorry, since I have good news. Slade?"

Slade glanced up, the mug poised at his mouth, his gaze resting on the principal's beaming smile that threatened to split his face.

Without preliminaries, without any buildup, the principal said, "We want you to coach Brentonville High."

Slade didn't blink, and except for a slight change in his breathing, his reaction was only to put the mug back onto the tray.

The principal chuckled. "Surprised? You shouldn't be. There's been plenty of rumors flying around. I know you've probably had a lot of offers, but Nick said he thought you'd be interested. From what the school committee has seen in your handling of the team, they, and I, feel you are what Brentonville needs—an inspiring leader and teacher."

Slade raised an eyebrow at the word teacher. Irony was in good form, he thought ruefully.

"The players respect you and, well, I won't minimize that Slade Garner as the head coach for Brentonville High is going to make the rest of the league very nervous."

Slade made himself stay very still, the offer holding so much appeal he wanted to grab it before it was snatched away. His answer for life after hockey wasn't out in some distant beyond but lay here with the kids.

Maybe it always had. Hadn't the rink been the first place he'd come after he arrived home? Apart from being with Celina, weren't the kids his main focus? Wasn't seeing Jeremy scouted by Zeke as exciting as when he'd called Zeke to come and see David Beck play? As exciting as when he, himself, was scouted? And Nick, he'd be the ideal buffer to handle any of the reading and writing that needed to be done if he took the job.

"I'm honored," he said finally.

"Then you accept?"

Leaving is always easier than staying. But he wanted this. How damnably simple to say yes, if coaching were the only issue. Staying, however, meant his relationship with Celina would have to change. Staying equalled risk.

Glen Harvey said, "I know this is sudden, and we would rather you took some time to decide, rather than saying a hasty no."

"Thank you," he said, feeling as though he'd been given a last-minute reprieve.

"In the meantime," the principal said, "we have tonight to think about. Slade, I want you to know again how grateful the school is for the scholarship fund. Everything is in place for the announcement."

"One stipulation," Slade said. "I want to make very sure Celina, and only Celina, has the last word on who receives a scholarship. I don't want any overruling as was done with Jeremy."

The principal moved some papers around and then fiddled with his tie. He started to speak and stopped once to clear his throat. Finally he said, "No, no, of course not."

Nick had walked over to glance out the window. "I still think it should be your name on the scholarship, Slade. Brian never was that hot in hockey. Since it's a hockey scholarship, and you're puttin' up the bucks for it, it seems to me..."

Slade raised his eyes and gave Nick an appraising look.

Nick scowled. "I know what you've told me and I agree. But you're not exactly chopped liver around here."

Glen Harvey tapped on the desk with his pen. "Now, Nick, Slade is right. Brentonville should have done something for Brian a long time ago. This will be an ongoing memorial, and much more meaningful than a plaque." With both men now listening to him, the principal went on. "The ceremony is set to take place before the game. Celina is coming to the game, isn't she?"

Slade nodded.

"Nick and I, and the school committee members, discussed this, and we feel very strongly that you should be part of the announcement. Maybe escort Celina..."

"No."

"Come on, Slade," Nick added, "you don't just want to be the bankroll..."

"No, I said. No escorting, no announcements, no gushy praise. Brian was the hero, and I don't want this twisted into a Slade Garner appearance complete with banners, balloons and whatever else the Booster Club can make a buck from." He came up out of the chair and shrugged into his jacket. "Now if there's nothing else, I want to find Jeremy."

Instead he found Celina just as he was about to leave the school building. The double doors banged shut after she stormed inside. The hard sound was weak compared to her obvious fury.

He guessed her anger was about Jeremy, and he also knew he didn't blame her. "Nick told me he cut class," he said hoping to diffuse some of the fire by calmly getting right to the point.

Her hair was down and flying wildly. Her eyes snapped with irritation. "For three days he's cut class."

Slade wanted to run his hands through her hair, kiss her, hold her. He wanted to say he loved her. He shoved his hands into his pockets. "Look, tonight is the last game. He'll be okay after all the hype wears off."

"Will he?" she snapped, with enough rage and sarcasm to make him flinch.

He wanted to believe this was a simple school-versus-sports issue, but he knew better. Her frustration and her anger came from caring what happened to Jeremy.

"Sweetheart—"

"What about the scout?" she demanded ignoring his attempt to calm her down. "Whatever the report says, Jeremy will be so preoccupied with whether the NHL wants or doesn't want him, I'll be lucky to see him in the hall. Dammit, Slade, this is all your fault."

Was it? he wondered fleetingly. "Celina, I haven't got time to argue now."

"No, of course you don't. Hockey and the rink are more important. They've always been the only thing important to you. And you've managed to make them indispensable to Jeremy. He's a clone of you, that's all. Pushing every other possibility out of his life so he can be a damn hockey player. Well, I hope he becomes a big star like you, because as of this marking period, his graduation is in serious jeopardy."

With that she stepped around him and continued down the hall. Slade leaned against the big double doors and swore.

At the rink, Slade walked right into a TV reporter. The guy was so flustered that Slade had simply appeared without anyone having to smoke him out, he couldn't find his notebook.

For Slade, it was a new experience. The guy's fumbling nervousness made him seem human, very different from the rapid-fire quizzers and nosy press people who usually surrounded him. He answered a few quick questions about the coming game, and gave him a vague "I'm not sure about the future" to the personal ones.

He then excused himself and made his way, searching the arena for Jeremy.

The refreshment stand had opened; the scent of freshly brewed coffee drifted into the air. He passed the Booster Club booth, where Bill Knight was already doing a brisk business in buttons, key rings and T-shirts.

Slade finally spotted Jeremy in a section of the bleachers that was rarely used because it had been positioned behind two poles. Jeremy sat alone on the top bench, the darkness of the rink shadowing him. Burnout or fear, Slade concluded as he made his way to the bleachers. He knew the feeling. He'd sat on that same top bench before a lot of games and worried himself into a mass of insecurities. What if he got hurt? What if he couldn't play? If anyone learned he couldn't read he'd be off the team. And if he was off the team, the NHL scout wouldn't see him play.

Like a rolling snowball, his fear just got bigger, denser, and terrifyingly close.

Slade sat down beside Jeremy. "Nick said you were looking for me. You okay?"

"Yeah," he muttered, sounding as depressed as his torn jeans and his wrinkled shirt looked. He tossed a hockey puck back and forth from one hand to the other.

"You all set for tonight?"

"Yeah."

"How'd you do on the English test?"

He shrugged.

"Does that mean you flunked it or aced it?"

Again, he shrugged, squeezing the hard puck between his hands.

Slade leaned back and folded his arms across his chest. "You blew off class, didn't you?"

He glared. "She been cryin' to you?"

"Let me put it this way. She isn't happy with either of us. Since you cut class, I assume you did a no-show at her house this afternoon."

"So what? I hate English. I hate school. All I want to do is play hockey and—"

Slade heard himself, at seventeen, saying the same words. "And what? Be a star and make your dad proud?"

"There ain't nothin' else besides playin' hockey that I wanna do. You gotta know how that feels."

He knew, but the price could be higher than satisfaction. "Are you sure it's because hockey is the only thing you wanna do, or is it the only thing you can do?"

"It's the only thing I wanna do."

"And what if you can't?" Despite Jeremy's strange expression, Slade didn't soften his words. "What if you're not good enough? Or what if you are, but you get hurt so you can't play? Your career is done and there's nothing else you know how to do."

"That won't happen."

"Come on. Get real. You know damn well it can happen."

"You're just tryin' to scare me."

"Right out of your cockiness. I'm trying to make you see what I didn't."

Disbelief ringed his reaction. "Ah, jeez, don't give me that. You can write your own ticket when you're done playin'."

"If it were only that simple."

Jeremy stared off into the distance, his face looking grimmer by the minute. "It's real simple for me, though, ain't it? That's why the scout didn't come, huh? I'm not good enough. It was all a trick, wasn't it? A setup by her to make me do school work."

Insecurity. Slade knew it well. "You know Celina wouldn't set you up."

"What about that first day? You ain't gonna tell me you just happened to walk into the study hall? And rentin' the ice? I saw her there. I saw the way she watched you when I tripped you, like maybe you were hurt so bad you'd quit playin' and then her plans would be blown away."

"Hold it. Celina is determined to get you educated, but she isn't devious. She doesn't have a plan, as you put it. And believe me, you tripping me wasn't any plan, either."

Jeremy rubbed the hockey puck down his thigh and back up again. "Then how come when Harvey said I could play, she got all sweet about it? She should have been mad."

Slade recalled her still warm from their lovemaking, reaching across him for the phone to call Harvey. He also remembered how good she felt, and how he'd wanted to make love again. And that they hadn't. "Trust me, she was *not* mad."

Jeremy swore. "She acted like nothin' happened. Telling me she wanted me to graduate, givin' me extra help. Saturday, she even asked me about the scout and tried to make it sound like she was worried I'd be under too much pressure. Then you showed up with all that junky talk about the scout comin' to watch the St. Luke center. It was all talk, yeah, nothin' but talk."

Slade let him continue, let him air out all his anger and his defeat. When he finally unloaded everything, Slade leaned forward so that they sat shoulder to shoulder.

In an even voice, he said, "You're not only wrong about Celina, but you owe her an apology." When Jeremy started to say something, Slade shook his head. "You had your say, now you're gonna listen."

Jeremy slumped back and dropped the puck. With his eyes hooded, he folded his arms across his chest.

Slade slowly and carefully explained that Celina's motives had always been centered on Jeremy getting an education. The fact that she'd offered to help, instead of complaining, after Harvey had overruled her showed her acceptance of a decision, even if she didn't like it. Then Celina's earlier words repeated themselves, weighing on him, dragging at him with their truth. *He's nothing but a clone of you . . . pushing out every other possibility in life but to be a damn good hockey player.*

"You oughta be glad to have a teacher who cares about you, cares that you learn." Slade took a deep breath, murmuring, "I didn't. Or at least I didn't take advantage of the ones who did care."

"Big deal. I know enough. I don't need—"

"It's a helluva big deal and you don't know enough to get yourself out of high school with a diploma. What are you gonna do if you can't play hockey? I'm thirty-three years old and a has-been. Retired with a bad knee. I've got nothing to fall back on."

The teenager's eyes widened and then narrowed. "You're Slade Garner. You can do anything."

"Except read."

Slade closed his eyes, his mind reeling, screaming, clawing for some way to change, explain or deny what he'd said. Cursing, he wanted to run from the layers of deception and shame and frustration. Suddenly he was back at that adult literacy class, back clinging to hockey because there was no other lifeline, back holding a diploma he couldn't read, back falling in love with a woman who deserved an up-front hero like Brian, not Slade Garner who couldn't even read the letter that ended his hockey career.

He felt a driving pain in his chest, the two words screaming and beating at him. He stared down at the arena below. Fans moved about, getting coffee, buying souvenirs, finding seats. A few players skated out onto the ice. A radio blasted scratchy rock music. Nick walked over to the bench to check equipment. All normal. Nothing unexpected. Nothing out of the ordinary.

Maybe he just thought he said the words, like that night with Celina when he realized he loved her. Hadn't he been afraid then that he'd said the words aloud? But he hadn't, or had he? His mind raced for solid answers, not emotions and feelings.

When he looked at the teenager, Jeremy stared back, his eyes wide with—wonder? Slade scowled. Wonder? No, he had to be seeing things.

Then came Jeremy's awed whisper, which sounded more inspired than curious. "Jeez, you can't read? No foolin'?"

Denial was useless. "Yeah, no fooling."

"Wow."

Slade frowned. Not only wonder, not only inspired, but respect. Where was the shock? The questions? The pity?

"Wow," he repeated, nodding his head up and down as though savoring something he'd known all along. "See, you just proved you don't need all that school stuff to be a success." Jeremy stood, a smile on his face, an eagerness in his words. "Gotta get dressed for the game. See ya."

Slade didn't move. Jeremy clattered down the bleacher seats, headed for the locker rooms. See ya. See ya, for God's sake. He'd just told this kid something he'd never voluntarily revealed to anyone but Nick and Izzy, and what had Jeremy done? Twisted it into a plus that not only impressed the kid, but no doubt sealed forever any chance Celina would have of arguing graduation as a necessity for success.

The new terror he'd wrestled with in Glen Harvey's office, the new terror he couldn't name—now he could.

Celina would not only blame him, but she'd hate him.

Leaving was always less complicated than staying. Never had that been so true as right now.

Celina couldn't find a seat, which was just as well since she wasn't in any mood to be a fan. The short argument with Slade earlier had simply capped off a bad day with a painful reminder. He would be leaving, and part of her wouldn't survive. So what was she going to do about it? Risk her heart and tell him she loved him, then watch him walk away? She remembered what he'd said—hockey was his life. He'd never suggested or even hinted during the times they'd been together that he had any intention of staying in Brentonville, or of allowing their relationship to continue.

Yes, she thought, continue. The beginning had been gradual and tentative, as if both were afraid the only thing they had in common were memories. But they'd shared and grown and changed and . . .

She'd fallen in love.

Tell him, an inner voice cried. You didn't hesitate to voice objections about Jeremy playing hockey. You didn't hesitate about getting sexually involved, or at least not for too long. You didn't hesitate about going to him about the outline.

And then there was that pattern she'd discovered. She'd intended to explain that to him, but they'd made love and then they'd worked to finish the outline. With the finals, she knew he'd been busy. They hadn't had time to do much more than share a few kisses or, as they'd done today, argue.

Coming to a stop, she was surprised to see the entire school committee filing over to a makeshift platform. She wondered briefly if the school committee's full presence was a commentary on the high value placed on Jeremy and the Brentonville hockey team.

Maybe she should resign, she thought, considering the frustration and failure with Jeremy. Maybe she was ineffective, or at the very least too out of the mainstream in Brentonville's priorities.

She glanced over at the Brentonville bench, expecting to see Slade deep in conversation with the players. He wasn't. He wasn't even there. Strange. Hadn't he told her he had to get to the rink?

Where was he?

Glen Harvey stopped by her side. "Glad you're here, Celina." She frowned at his beaming smile and the patronizing pat he made on her shoulder. "Everything will work out all right. I know you've had a time of it with Jeremy."

"He's not the flu, Glen. The attitude of you and the school committee—"

"Now, now, nothing so serious tonight. You're going to be so pleased. I know it. When Slade, oh, well, never mind. I'm sure he'll tell you all about it later."

"What are you talking about. And where is Slade?"

He beamed another smile at her and hurried off.

She watched him leave, skirting his way through the crowd and over to where the school committee stood.

What was Slade going to tell her later? Where was he?

Again she scanned the arena. A riser had been put in place at one end of the rink. Mats led across the slippery surface. Glen Harvey and the school committee made their way gingerly out to the platform. Microphones were tested, and the crowd quieted. After the national anthem, Glen Harvey came to the mike.

"This is an announcement that gives me great pleasure to make. Celina Dennett? Celina, if you could come up here, please. Nick, if you'd give her a hand onto the ice." Harvey leaned closer to the microphone. "For those of you who are St. Luke fans, Celina Dennett is the head of the English department. She has been a vigorous supporter for education at the highest level."

Celina made her way slowly to the riser, puzzled as to what had been planned. She stepped over to the microphone after a nudge from Nick. The lights made it difficult for her to see outside the ice area. She felt conspicuous and she desperately wanted to see Slade.

Where was he? She turned to whisper the question to Nick, when Glen Harvey said the word scholarship.

"It will be known as the Brian Dennett Memorial Scholarship. The fully paid college scholarship will be awarded annually to the hockey player who has met the highest standard of academic achievement in the classroom and shown exceptional skill on the ice. The final decision on who is to receive the scholarship will rest with Brian's widow, Celina Dennett." Glen Harvey turned then. "Celina, it is long past the time when Brentonville should have honored Brian."

Stunned into speechlessness, Celina blinked back the raw tears that threatened to spill. She tried to swallow and found that difficult. Finally in a husky, halting voice, she said, "This is a wonderful honor for Brian, and for the students who will receive the scholarship." Her eyes blurred with new tears, and everything else she wanted to say sounded sappy and gushy. "Thank you," she finally added.

After a few more words from Glen and a "good luck" for both teams, the lights were turned down. Celina made her way back off the ice with Nick holding her elbow. She felt shaken but happy. She wanted to talk to Slade.

"Nick, where's Slade?"

"I saw him go out. He'll probably be back in a few minutes."

Before she had a chance to question why he'd left, three reporters surrounded them.

"Is it true?" one of them asked Nick shoving a tape recorder into his face.

"Hey, watch it. Is what true?"

"Is it true Slade Garner can't read?"

Chapter Twelve

Take a win anyway it comes, and say thanks, was the collective comment by the fans of Brentonville.

The final game, which grew into a crowd-roaring frenzy, wouldn't go down in hockey history for its nail-biting tension or its polished skill. Brentonville made some potential game-blowing mistakes that should have cost it the championship, but St. Luke never found its stride, and the more the players stumbled, the less chance they had of loading on the pressure. The final score gave the win to Brentonville by two goals.

The trophy was presented to the team, and afterward when Jeremy was on his way to the locker rooms, Zeke Pepper introduced himself.

"You're the scout?" Jeremy's mouth gaped with astonishment. He stared at the worn blue cords, the jacket with sagging pockets, the perceptive eyes that never confused dazzle with instinctive talent. "Ah, jeez, you been here for every game, and—" he swallowed hard "—I told Slade the scout talk was a bunch of—"

Zeke grinned. "Like I tell Slade, the best part of this job after watching a kid play is the kid's reaction." He waited until Jeremy raised his head and looked at him. "You're good, Jeremy."

Jeremy gulped. "Yeah? You mean like good enough to play—" Again, he couldn't say the words.

"I mean good enough for me to give a thumbs-up scouting report to the front office."

"Ah, jeez..." He sighed deeply, and swiped the back of his hand across his eyes, blinking and wiping away the embarrassing wetness. "Wait till the guys and Nick hear. And my Dad." He glanced around. "I gotta find Slade." He started to rush into the crowd and then changed his mind and continued toward the locker room, then stopped and turned to Zeke. He shoved out his hand. "Thanks, uh, Mr. Pepper. Thanks a lot."

In the thick crowd of fans and friends that surrounded him with congratulations and questions about his future, Nick grinned broadly, his chest seemingly expanded three inches with pride. "It's like I been sayin'. Retirin' with a winner is better than fadin' into coachin' history with a loser."

The press scrambled, concluding instantly from the haunted white expression on Celina before the game that Slade Garner not being able to read wasn't a wild rumor. Firing questions, jamming tape recorders and microphones under the nose of anyone who knew Slade, they realized they'd lucked into a reporter's dream—a bizarre and national twist on an otherwise local story. But getting confirmation from Slade himself eluded them.

The three-member school committee called an emergency meeting by the refreshment stand.

"Incredible. Do you think it's true?"

"He hasn't come forward to deny it. In fact, the Hearn boy said he told him."

"But he's so successful, and funding a scholarship of that magnitude and not even in his own name...it's not what I would have expected from a hockey star who can't read."

"If we withdraw the coaching offer, he'll get plenty of others."

"Of course we can't withdraw it. How would that look? Brentonville has won. We all know Slade is partially responsible."

"But he can't read."

"But he can coach. The question is are we hiring him to read books on how to play hockey, or are we hiring a professional hockey player to teach them how to play?"

"Yet the question remains. If this was anyone but Slade, would we hire him?"

"Hypothetical. It is Slade, and he's more than proven himself these last weeks."

"I think we're rationalizing."

"Like we did with Jeremy when we pushed Glen to overrule Celina?"

The three members each thought about that for a few moments.

Finally one commented. "Perhaps that was a mistake. Maybe we should discuss Slade with Celina. The two of them seem to be close. I wonder if she knew. And where is she? For that matter where is Slade?"

* * *

Celina knocked once, and then pushed the front door open, unsure of what she was going to say or how to express it. In teaching, she was rarely at a loss for words. In dealing with Slade, in knowing Slade—no, that was the problem. She didn't know Slade. Somehow, through her own ignorance or blindness, she'd never suspected he couldn't read.

And she, a high-school English teacher; no, more than that, the head of the English department, she of all people should have known.

He lay sprawled on Nick's couch in the shadowed living room. She stood in the doorway, shivering slightly, her mind struggling with self-accusation, her heart searching for some sign of affection from him. A clammy moisture spread beneath her clothes. Her throat felt raw from the tears she was determined not to cry. Shock, denial, anger at Slade for closing her out battled with the disturbing conclusion that given her views on how sports was destroying education, she didn't blame him.

He didn't move, and as her eyes adjusted to the darkness, she saw him differently from before. Sprawled, but not with the lazy comfort she had seen so many times while they worked on the outline. He seemed empty and tired...defeated. She, too, felt drained, and empathized with him.

His ankles were crossed and his boots were off. He wore socks that they'd washed and dried at her house. Faded jeans, so familiar, yet so special because of her memory of helping him dress the night he'd hurt his knee. The Sabers sweatshirt, covering his muscled chest where she'd rested her head after they'd made love. His mouth that could kiss her both wildly and sweetly, a mouth that spoke the words for his book, words that came from deep within him. She knew so many intimate things, except . . .

He lay with one arm flung behind him, his wrist resting on his forehead. His very stillness screamed withdrawal, while at the same time she had a sense that her coming here wasn't unexpected, nor did it displease him.

Don't be foolish, she told herself. If he were pleased he'd be on his feet greeting her, drawing her into his arms, telling her he could explain why he'd never told her, why instead, he'd told Jeremy.

No, explaining wasn't Slade's pattern. He'd withdrawn when he had no answers. Hadn't he done it before? At her house? Here at Nick's? Just as he'd walked out of the rink tonight before the press and the crowd could confront him? Keeping his lack of literacy locked inside him set the pattern; fed, she now knew, by his terror.

She reached for the light switch.

"Leave it off," he said in a low, raspy voice.

Startled, she jumped back, feeling her pulse race faster, and her adrenaline pour and pump. She let her hand slip down her side.

Outside, the sounds in the night hailed the hockey victory. Brentonville celebrated with honking horns, an occasional siren and overworked speakers in car stereos.

Inside Nick's cluttered house, she measured her words in the dark silence, whispering cautiously, "Why didn't I know?"

She sensed from him not an invitation to come on in and talk this out but a total weariness that seemed to say he dreaded the question. She knew if she could see his eyes they would be guarded.

The locked fear that she'd seen at her house when she'd read the letter from the medical complex, the terror she'd seen when he heard Izzy had come to see her, both were clear, now, but no less frightening.

The couch creaked with his slight movement. "I didn't want you to know," he replied simply, then with a thread of hope in his voice, he added, "I don't suppose you'd just drop this and go away."

Celina didn't dwell on his comment or the implication that, even now, he didn't want to talk about it. She'd effectively trapped him by coming here, and yet if he truly wanted nothing to do with her, he wouldn't have come back to Nick's. He would have taken a cab to the airport and left the state. But he hadn't. He'd stayed, and from that decision, she drew a scant measure of encouragement. Despite his coolness and probable rejection, she couldn't leave him now without knowing why.

Coming a few steps closer to him, her arms aching to hold him, she made herself simply unbutton her coat. "If I leave, I will only make it easy for you."

He groaned. Then impatiently he dragged his arm across his eyes. "Easy. . ." He drew the word out as if the meaning were lost to him. "Nothing with you has ever been easy. I'd like to get out of this conversation with at least my pride intact."

She paused at the end of the couch, her fingers loosening the last button. "Is that why you're hiding here in the dark?"

"A lousy choice, since you found me."

"But I'm not just anyone, Slade."

"God, I wish you were," he muttered in a tired voice.

Celina paused for an unsure second. No, she had to see this through. For herself and for Slade. Determined, she slipped out of her coat and laid it on a nearby chair.

Instead of perching on the edge of the couch and crowding him, she sat on the coffee table facing him.

She laced her hands together to stop them from shaking, to prevent herself from touching him, to focus her mind on how stupidly blind she had been, yes, but more on how dreadfully isolated Slade must have felt all these years.

Tentatively he asked, "Did Jeremy tell you?"

"No. Some reporters asked me after the scholarship presentation. It was a wonderful way to honor Brian's name, Slade. I know that you're responsible—"

"Stop, right there," he said cutting her off with a wave of his hand. "Lay off the praise and thanks. I've had enough of that to last me three lifetimes."

She grabbed his wrist, feeling the race of his pulse, but determined that he would listen to her. "That's just too bad, Slade Garner, because I'm going to thank you. I know you hate the fanfare, but did you ever consider that the praise might be the public's way of saying thank you? For your skill on the ice, for the way you taught and handled the kids, and for your generosity in Brian's name? All those deserve praise and thanks because they're real, they're what you are. They're not attention seekers. Maybe the reason you hate the limelight is because you've always been afraid someone would discover—"

He interrupted her, his voice less abrasive, but still judgmental of himself. "Let's call it what it is. I can barely read, and I can't write. I got lousy grades, slept through classes that I didn't skip, and by making myself a hotshot on the ice I got through high school." He pulled his wrist out of her grip, and again his arm shielded his eyes. "I have a diploma I can't even read."

She had to touch him, if no more than a light caress on his arm, but something. Her fingers slipped over his forearm. "Maybe the fault isn't entirely yours. Maybe part of the blame lies with your teachers."

He lowered his arm, not pushing her hand away, but she saw his fury. "Stop making excuses for me. Is it still some teacher's fault fifteen years later? Hell, no. It became my fault when I walked away from a chance to learn to read because of pride and ego." He told her about almost signing up for the adult literacy class but getting cold feet. "Can Jeremy get away with blaming you for not pushing him harder?"

She lowered her head. If Jeremy failed to graduate she'd always wonder if she could have done more. More time, more attention, more effort. "Jeremy's not you."

"Yeah. He can read."

"But he's also lazy. I told you that the first day when I showed you his test. My God, you couldn't read it, could you? That's why you were so distant about the poor marks."

"And I couldn't read the letter about my knee. My whole career ended, and I couldn't even read the damn letter. I didn't want to do the outline, and I didn't want to—" He stopped himself, his breath hissing out, the next words barely audible. "That was my biggest mistake."

"What was?"

He stared at her, and even with the darkness shadowing his expression, she knew he felt he'd said too much.

After long seconds of waiting for him to answer her, she said, "You were never a man who made too many mistakes. You've always been focused and clear about what you want. Your hockey career. The book. You knew exactly what you wanted to do in your book. Even that day in the study hall when I showed you Jeremy's test, you could have determined then that we wouldn't see each other. And certainly after that kiss we both felt reluctant to let things go any further."

He swung his legs around and sat up. "Except I wanted you. Sexually, yes, but more than that I wanted to be with you. I wanted to know you." He let his head fall back onto the couch, his body suddenly loose and boneless. Then, as if he couldn't leave the issue alone, he said, "Do you want to know Jeremy's reaction?" Without waiting for her to answer, he raised his head, his voice filled with disgust. "He said wow. Wow, for God's sake! The kid acted like I'd won some prize or deserved some medal."

"Jeremy worships you, Slade."

"Yeah, so you've been telling me all along. Clone of Slade Garner."

She winced, as she recalled their most recent argument. Suddenly she realized that in every conversation, every disagreement and every argument they'd had about Jeremy, she'd used Slade as a negative. For Jeremy to emulate Slade, in her eyes, had not only been wrong, but she had blamed Slade. She had, in effect, used Slade as a standard to be rejected.

Realization rushed at her. Oh, God...no...

In a shallow, whispery voice, she ventured the next question. "Why did you tell him?"

His sigh was heavy and deep. "Because he had me up there as some praiseworthy example of success. No, that's not the only reason. Kids need heroes, and if my being his hero had depended only on my skill on the ice, then fine, but somehow it got mixed up with becoming a star. He took on a cockiness, and an 'I'm better than anyone else' attitude."

"And you wanted to let him know you're human and make mistakes."

"Yeah, and I saw myself in him. I didn't set out with any intention of telling him or anyone, but when he said I could do anything because of who I was...the words just slipped out."

Celina tried to avoid the question that scraped insistently at her thoughts. In truth, it had been the one she wanted to ask him the moment she'd walked in the door. Perhaps, she realized with her own growing wariness, his answer was what scared her.

She stood and walked over to the light switch. Whether he swore, ignored her or rejected her, she had to know. Not wanting to miss one nuance of truth in his expression, she flipped on the light switch. The sudden brightness exploded around the room.

Slade blinked, swore and came to his feet.

Before she lost her nerve, she threw the question at him. "Why didn't you tell me, Slade?"

He went very still, and he didn't say any of the things she expected. He didn't turn away. He didn't lower his gaze.

Hesitantly but clearly he said, "Because I love you."

Celina felt her legs wobble. "You love me?"

He grinned a little, a kind of relief whooshing out of him. "Yeah."

She made herself not rush at him. She longed to throw herself into his arms. She ached to tell him she loved him, too. She wanted to forget that every time he could have told her his secret and he hadn't he had added another layer of mistrust.

She recalled their passion, the insights he shared for his book, his support of her about Jeremy despite his wanting him to play. All of those were certainly evidence of trust, and yet he hadn't trusted her enough....

Meeting his eyes, she felt an inordinate sadness as she said, "If you really loved me you would have told me. You told Jeremy. No, I don't think it just slipped out. You've kept the secret too long and too well to get careless."

He scowled, walking toward her. "And why do you think it was easier to tell Jeremy than to tell you?"

She braced herself as he loomed closer. "I don't know."

"Well, I do." He cupped her neck, his thumbs tipping her chin up. Studying her mouth, her eyes, he said softly, "I knew it the moment I realized what I'd done. The worst reaction Jeremy could have had was rejecting me. Of finding out I had clay feet and wasn't the great star he thought I was. And you know what? That didn't matter a whole hell of a lot because the alternative, telling you..." He paused, his eyes intent, searching. Then his hands gripped her wrists as though to hold her, to not let her get away. "Telling you, Celina, and having you reject me did matter."

"Oh, Slade..." Celina wet her lips, and when he released her wrists, she didn't back away. Instead, she slid her arms around him, wanting somehow to block out what she now knew. Her negative attitude toward Jeremy looking up to Slade screamed rejection louder than any words. She laid her head against his chest, listening to his heart beat out the words: *Having you reject me did matter.*

Slade tipped up her chin, his eyes softer now. "Sweetheart, it's always mattered, but when I came home and I saw you that day at the rink, saw you in your red coat with your tea and that awful bun..." He framed her face, looking deeply into her eyes. "You know what I thought of?"

She took a crumb of comfort from his words. His fear began before they'd ever spoken about Jeremy. She wanted now only to kiss him, to draw him to her in the most accepting of ways. "What did you think of?"

"My fourth-grade teacher who thought learning to read was more important than hockey. Do you know how long it's been since I thought about Miss Agnes Potter? I told myself it was the bun, but seeing you made me see myself as the kid who bluffed and charmed his way through school, and I didn't like what I saw. And if I didn't like what I saw, how in hell could I expect you to accept me that way?"

"But you not being able to read had nothing to do with whether I would accept or reject you. I wasn't your teacher, Slade...." Then with an annoyance at herself, she added, "But I acted like one, didn't I? Criticizing, pointing out your faults. Using you as some poor standard—"

"Shh, no, sweetheart. The head of the English department and a washed-up hockey player who can't read aren't exactly an ideal match."

Her voice trembled as she spoke, the real truth clear now. "But being in love isn't making sure education or careers match. Being in love is being sure our hearts match."

He stared at her, his expression changing from despair to hope. He asked the question with just the slightest hesitation. "And do they match?"

"I love you," she whispered, drawing his mouth down to hers and tightening her arms.

His lips hovered a breath away. "Say it again."

"I love you. I love you. I want you. I want to be with you forever."

He kissed her then, his mouth hungry, his hands cupping her bottom and lifting her into him. He tasted her kiss, drank from her mouth and savored her words in his heart like the sweetness of life.

He led her over to the couch, pulling her down beside him and settling her between his legs. Holding her for a few long silent minutes, he felt his heart soar with joy. He kissed her again, then whispered, "Before we get too serious here..."

She touched his cheeks, loving the slight whisker scratch. "Hmm, Nick might come home."

"He'll be out celebrating. No, this is about us."

She drew back, her eyes wide. "You don't want to be with me forever?"

He feathered his hand across her hair. "Longer than forever."

"You don't want to get married? I know we haven't talked about that, but—"

He hugged her and Celina fell in love again. "I want to marry you. What did you think? That I wanted to just move in and sleep with you?"

"Is it the house? Is it because it was mine and Brian's, and you . . ."

He sighed, drawing her mouth to his in a fierce kiss. "It's not the house, although I'd like us to have something that is ours."

Celina felt dizzy. "Then you're going to stay in Brentonville?"

"Both of us, sweetheart, not just me. Yes, if that's what you want. I was offered Nick's job, and I'd like to take it, if the school committee hasn't changed their minds now that they know I can't read."

"They won't. They'd be crazy to pass up your teaching." She touched her forefinger to his mouth to stop any protest he might make at her word choice. "Teaching is what I meant, Slade. You're giving to others what you know. That's what a teacher does. I've known that since I saw you the night you rented the ice. And the school committee saw it, too."

He tightened his arms, and lightly kissed her temple. "That brings me to the question."

Her mind scrambled in an effort to find what they hadn't talked about. "You're scaring me, Slade."

"It scares me to ask it."

She swallowed.

He kissed her once more for courage. "Will you teach me how to read?"

For only an instant she wondered why the question was so difficult, then seeing the softness, the love in his eyes, she knew. For him, it was the final commitment, the one question he'd never been able to ask anyone.

She took a deep breath. "I would have been hurt if you hadn't asked me."

With the last emotional barrier gone, he slipped his hands beneath her sweater, gliding his fingers over her breasts. "Ah, Celina, I love you. I don't ever want to hurt you again."

"No more hurting, no more secrets. Only loving each other and being together," she whispered, kissing him deeply and knowing this kind of love lasted forever.

*   *   *   *   *

SILHOUETTE·INTIMATE·MOMENTS®

NORA ROBERTS
Night Shadow

People all over the city of Urbana were asking, Who was that masked man?

Assistant district attorney Deborah O'Roarke was the first to learn his secret identity . . . and her life would never be the same.

The stories of the lives and loves of the O'Roarke sisters began in January 1991 with NIGHT SHIFT, Silhouette Intimate Moments #365. And if you want to know more about Deborah and the man behind the mask, look for NIGHT SHADOW, Silhouette Intimate Moments #373.

 *Silhouette Books*®

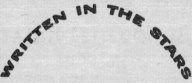

**Star-crossed lovers?
Or a match made in heaven?**

Why are some heroes strong and
silent... and others charming
and cheerful? The answer is
WRITTEN IN THE STARS!

Coming each month in 1991,
Silhouette Romance presents
you with a special love story
written by one of your favorite
authors—highlighting the hero's
astrological sign! From January's
sensible Capricorn to December's
disarming Sagittarius, you'll
meet a dozen dazzling and
distinct heroes.

Twelve heavenly heroes... twelve
wonderful Silhouette Romances
destined to delight you. Look for
one WRITTEN IN THE STARS
title every month throughout
1991—only from Silhouette
Romance.

STAR

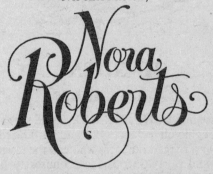
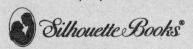

Silhouette Romance®

HARDEN
Diana Palmer

In her bestselling LONG, TALL TEXANS series, Diana
Palmer brought you to Jacobsville and introduced you to
the rough and rugged ranchers who call the town home.
Now, hot and dusty Jacobsville promises to get even
hotter when hard-hearted, woman-hating rancher
Harden Tremayne has to reckon with the lovely Miranda
Warren.

The LONG, TALL TEXANS series continues! Don't
miss HARDEN by Diana Palmer in March . . . only from
Silhouette Romance.

LTT-1

SILHOUETTE'S "BIG WIN" SWEEPSTAKES RULES & REGULATIONS

NO PURCHASE NECESSARY TO ENTER OR RECEIVE A PRIZE

1. To enter the Sweepstakes and join the Reader Service, scratch off the metallic strips on all your BIG WIN tickets #1-#6. This will reveal the potential values for each Sweepstakes entry number, the number of free book(s) you will receive and your free bonus gift as part of our Reader Service. If you do not wish to take advantage of our Reader Service but wish to enter the Sweepstakes only, scratch off the metallic strips on your BIG WIN tickets #1-#4. Return your entire sheet of tickets intact. Incomplete and/or inaccurate entries are ineligible for that section or sections of prizes. Torstar Corp. and its affiliates are not responsible for mutilated or unreadable entries or inadvertent printing errors. Mechanically reproduced entries are null and void.

2. Whether you take advantage of this offer or not, on or about April 30, 1992, at the offices of Marden-Kane Inc., Lake Success, NY, your Sweepstakes numbers will be compared against the list of winning numbers generated at random by the computer. However, prizes will only be awarded to individuals who have entered the Sweepstakes. In the event that all prizes are not claimed, a random drawing will be held from all qualified entries received from March 30, 1990 to March 31, 1992, to award all unclaimed prizes. All cash prizes (Grand to Sixth), will be mailed to the winners and are payable by check in U.S. funds. Seventh prize will be shipped to winners via third-class mail. These prizes are in addition to any free, surprise or mystery gifts that might be offered. Versions of this Sweepstakes with different prizes of approximate equal value may appear at retail outlets or in other mailings by Torstar Corp. and its affiliates.

3. The following prizes are awarded in this sweepstakes: ★ Grand Prize (1) $1,000,000; First Prize (1) $25,000; Second Prize (1) $10,000; Third Prize (5) $5,000; Fourth Prize (10) $1,000; Fifth Prize (100) $250; Sixth Prize (2,500) $10; ★★ Seventh Prize (6,000) $12.95 ARV.

   ★ This presentation offers a Grand Prize of a $1,000,000 annuity. Winner will receive $33,333.33 a year for 30 years without interest totalling $1,000,000.

   ★★ Seventh Prize: A fully illustrated hardcover book published by Torstar Corp. Approximate Retail Value of the book is $12.95.

   Entrants may cancel the Reader Service at anytime without cost or obligation to buy (see details in center insert card).

4. This Sweepstakes is being conducted under the supervision of an independent judging organization. By entering this Sweepstakes, each entrant accepts and agrees to be bound by these rules and the decisions of the judges, which shall be final and binding. Odds of winning in the random drawing are dependent upon the total number of entries received. Taxes, if any, are the sole responsibility of the winners. Prizes are nontransferable. All entries must be received at the address printed on the reply card and must be postmarked no later than 12:00 MIDNIGHT on March 31, 1992. The drawing for all unclaimed Sweepstakes prizes will take place on May 30, 1992, at 12:00 NOON, at the offices of Marden-Kane, Inc., Lake Success, New York.

5. This offer is open to residents of the U.S., the United Kingdom, France and Canada, 18 years or older, except employees and their immediate family members of Torstar Corp., its affiliates, subsidiaries, and all the other agencies, entities and persons connected with the use, marketing or conduct of this Sweepstakes. All Federal, State, Provincial and local laws apply. Void wherever prohibited or restricted by law. Any litigation within the Province of Quebec respecting the conduct and awarding of a prize in this publicity contest must be submitted to the Régie des Loteries et Courses du Québec.

6. Winners will be notified by mail and may be required to execute an affidavit of eligibility and release, which must be returned within 14 days after notification or an alternate winner will be selected. Canadian winners will be required to correctly answer an arithmetical skill-testing question administered by mail, which must be returned within a limited time. Winners consent to the use of their names, photographs and/or likenesses for advertising and publicity in conjunction with this and similar promotions without additional compensation. For a list of our major prize winners, send a stamped, self-addressed ENVELOPE to: WINNERS LIST, c/o Marden-Kane Inc., P.O. Box 701, SAYREVILLE, NJ 08871. Requests for Winners Lists will be fulfilled after the May 30, 1992 drawing date.

If Sweepstakes entry form is missing, please print your name and address on a 3" ×5" piece of plain paper and send to:

In the U.S.	In Canada
Silhouette's "BIG WIN" Sweepstakes	Silhouette's "BIG WIN" Sweepstakes
3010 Walden Ave.	P.O. Box 609
P.O. Box 1867	Fort Erie, Ontario
Buffalo, NY 14269-1867	L2A 5X3

Offer limited to one per household.

Silhouette Special Edition

This April,
Silhouette *Special Edition* is pleased to present

ONCE IN A LIFETIME
by Ginna Gray

the long-awaited companion volume to her bestselling duo

Fools Rush In (#416)
Where Angels Fear (#468)

Ever since spitfire Erin Blaine and her angelic twin sister Elise stirred up double trouble and entangled their long-suffering brother David in some sticky hide-and-seek scenarios, readers clamored to hear more about dashing, debonair David himself.

Now that time has come, as straitlaced Abigail Stewart manages to invade the secrecy shrouding sardonic David Blaine's bachelor boat—and creates the kind of salty, saucy, swashbuckling romantic adventure that comes along only once in a lifetime!

**Even if you missed the earlier novels,
you won't want to miss**

ONCE IN A LIFETIME #661

Available this April, only in Silhouette *Special Edition*.   OL-1